"García's tremendous empathy for her characters is the magnetic force of her fiction, and her lifeblood theme is the scarring legacy of oppression and brutality, particularly the horrors and absurdities of the Castro regime. In her most honed and lashing novel to date, she goes directly to the source. . . . An ingeniously plotted, boisterous, and brilliantly castigating tale."

—*Booklist*

"García's writing is laced with candor and wit as she portrays the lives of two men united by the past."

—*Publishers Weekly*

"Mordantly funny and insightful . . . *King of Cuba* has its roots in long-simmering political strife, but it is finally a novel about the human condition, about aging and loss and undying love for a country that once was paradise, at least in memory."

—*Tampa Bay Times*

"[A] wry new novel, *King of Cuba* . . . tell[s] the story of two macho, aging men in alternating voices. These two narratives, interspersed with a chorus of other Cuban voices, combine to define an exhausted country and the bonds between its people."

—*BookPage*

"Cristina García . . . merges the exhaustive research of historical fiction with the suspense of a thriller. Think of *King of Cuba* as a beach read with great depth, the ideal vacation book for anyone interested in the history and culture of that embargoed island to the south. Whatever your view of this country's ongoing embargo with Cuba, whatever your opinion or hopes . . . García's book will pique your interest in all things Cuban."

—*The Chapel Hill Herald-Sun*

THE LADY MATADOR'S HOTEL

"The novel has the energy of an obsessive tango. Or, indeed, a bullfight."

—*The New York Times Book Review*

"Exotic, lush, and sensual."

—*O, The Oprah Magazine*

DREAMING IN CUBAN

"Dazzling . . . A work that possesses both the intimacy of a Chekhov story and the hallucinatory magic of a novel by Gabriel García Márquez."

—Michiko Kakutani, *The New York Times*

"Remarkable . . . A rich and haunting narrative . . . An intricate weaving of dramatic events with the supernatural and the cosmic . . . Evocative and lush."

—Jackie Jones, *San Francisco Chronicle*

THE AGÜERO SISTERS

"A beautifully rounded work of art, as warm and wry and sensuous as the island she so clearly loves."

—*Time*

"A vibrant tale of a repressed Manhattan cosmetics saleswoman and her sexy, Havana-based sister that blends family, culture, and García's shapely prose into a rich, velvety world one is loath to leave."

—*Elle*

ALSO BY CRISTINA GARCÍA

Novels

The Lady Matador's Hotel
A Handbook to Luck
Monkey Hunting
The Agüero Sisters
Dreaming in Cuban

Anthologies

*Bordering Fires: The Vintage Book of Contemporary
Mexican and Chicano/a Literature*
*¡Cubanísimo!: The Vintage Book of Contemporary
Cuban Literature*

Books for Young Readers

Dreams of Significant Girls
I Wanna Be Your Shoebox
The Dog Who Loved the Moon

Poetry

The Lesser Tragedy of Death

KING OF CUBA

A NOVEL

DISCARD

Cristina García

Scribner

New York London Toronto Sydney New Delhi

SCRIBNER

A Division of Simon & Schuster, Inc.
1230 Avenue of the Americas
New York, NY 10020

First Scribner trade paperback edition October 2013

SCRIBNER and design are registered trademarks of The Gale Group, Inc., used under license by Simon & Schuster, Inc., the publisher of this work.

For information about special discounts for bulk purchases, please contact Simon & Schuster Special Sales at 1-866-506-1949 or business@simonandschuster.com.

The Simon & Schuster Speakers Bureau can bring authors to your live event. For more information or to book an event, contact the Simon & Schuster Speakers Bureau at 1-866-248-3049 or visit our website at www.simonspeakers.com.

Book design by Ellen R. Sasahara

Manufactured in the United States of America

10 9 8 7 6 5 4 3 2 1

Library of Congress Control Number: 2012037553

ISBN 978-1-4767-1024-2
ISBN 978-1-4767-2566-6 (pbk)
ISBN 978-1-4767-1453-0 (ebook)

To Pilar, always, and to Linda Howe,
beloved traveling companions

What sorrow is greater to us
than returning from misery to the sweet time?

  —*Robert Lowell*

Truth is that
which history scorns

  —*Octavio Paz*

KING OF CUBA

JULY 26–28

TROPICAL FORECAST: Mostly sunny throughout Cuba with scattered thundershowers. Hot days ahead with temperatures up to 35 degrees Celsius. Global warming begins here, compays. ¿Qué? You were expecting another Ice Age? The winds are blowing in from the Atlantic at 30 kilometers per hour. The sea will be turbulent on the northeast littoral. Save those inner tubes for another night . . .

1.

By the Sea

Havana

El Comandante gazed out the window at the stale light of another tropical morning, at the long curve of crumbling seaside buildings. Spindly, sun-sick palms splintered the skies with their spiky fronds. The sea was a rumpled bed of blues. The usual lovebirds tangled on the malecón, verging on public fornication. He'd passed laws against such displays but it hadn't deterred the couples. The seawall remained theirs, as it had for generations of lovers before them. It was bad enough that Cuba had a reputation as the brothel of the Caribbean—in a desperate bid for foreign currency, he'd once pronounced his country's prostitutes the healthiest and best educated on the planet—but this was hardly a laudable distinction.

The tyrant was accustomed to being exceptional, and so he didn't expect that rules governing ordinary human mortality should apply to him. Nothing in his life had followed anyone else's rules, so why must he go the way of every mediocre nobody on the planet? Dying, he'd decided, was a fate for lesser men. He didn't believe in death, at least not for him. From the corner of his eye, he checked the expression on the nurse's face as she cleaned him up. Not a trace of derision or disgust. He'd read her dossier. Twelve years in the secret service, here and abroad. A regular Mata Hari. Certainly she'd had to execute more disagreeable tasks than this.

El Comandante struggled to open the window nearest him. "Carajo, somebody help me with this goddamn thing!" he thundered, prompting the assistant his wife had dubbed El Huele Huele, the ass sniffer, to scurry in and prop it open with a wedge of plywood. Turbulent southeast winds blew straight for his enemies in Miami. The distaste of their collective name—gusanos—was an old poison on his tongue. Those worms were a wiped-out class here, their legacy extinct, and he'd made sure it would stay that way. He elbowed aside a goose-down pillow. He'd left his mark on history with ink, and action, and blood. Not even the most bitter, pathetic exile shopkeeper could deny him that. The tyrant shifted onto his left hip, aiming his scrawny buttocks at the Straits of Florida, and released a sputtering, malodorous stream of flatus.

"Take that, you fat-livered idiots," he muttered, slumping against his padded headboard. Satisfied, he smoothed the top sheet over his withered knees, then coughed until he felt his ribs would snap.

Another minion appeared with a pitcher of water, his pills, and the day's newspapers stacked high on a portable desk. El Comandante reached for his bifocals. He didn't trust anyone's editing of world events. Nobody saw opportunity, the plots and betrayals bubbling below the surface of politics-as-usual, like he did. His grandchildren had taught him how to navigate the Internet, but its distractions were pernicious: pornography websites and chat rooms on penile implants that wasted precious hours of what remained of his life. These days sex seemed to him a muscle memory in the loins—a waxy heat that had telegraphed pleasure to the very root of his spine, rendering him pure animal. Those sensations had vanished in the end, and only the many lives he'd engendered remained, trapping him in nooses of competing demands until he regretted that celibacy hadn't come sooner.

There was no mention of him in the foreign press, though it was the official anniversary of the Revolution. Instead other world leaders populated the front pages like so many party crashers. Hijos de puta. His government's rag had published a ten-page spread of him that included the same old photographs, recycled interviews, and a picture of his brother Fernando that was a quarter inch larger around than his. Somebody would pay dearly for that mistake. In recent years, El Comandante was usually featured, when he was featured at all, with his junior bad-boy counterpart in Venezuela, now deceased, a megalomaniac toward whom it had been difficult to keep a civil public face. If it hadn't been for his vast reserves of oil—sugar and oil, the island would grind to a halt without either—their alliance would've ended like the infamous party at Guatao.

Dry toast and oatmeal again. What he wouldn't give right now for a porterhouse steak and three fried eggs, over easy, followed by a double scotch. Fuck it if his insides turned to lead. It was only a matter of time before his dentures were on display at the Museum of the Revolution, which, it so happened, was preparing another cradle-to-near-grave retrospective on his life. El Comandante examined his hands, which bulged from his wrists like oven mitts. The doctors had no explanation for the swelling, which seemed to come and go with the tides. He pulled out a pocket mirror and checked his eyes. They looked pouchy and tinged with gray. Sleep was a luxury he couldn't afford. In any given twenty-four hours, somebody, somewhere, was plotting to kill him. By staying awake,

the tyrant believed he could detect plots like radar, monitor conversations, sotto voce vituperations, allegiances forged with a curse
and a handshake.

Over the years he'd thwarted every dirty trick and assassination attempt in the book. The most ludicrous failures gave him the
most pleasure to recount: the exploding Cohiba cigars, the arsenic-
laced milk shakes, the foot powder meant to make his beard fall
out. There was that memorable CIA agent, too, who'd masquer-
aded as a journalist—the comely Elizabeth Bond, a lesbian, had
volunteered for the assignment, certain she could resist her target's
charms (she couldn't). Another low point: the sixteen-foot Nile
crocodile trained by its exile handlers to attack his femoral artery.
The reptile, unleashed at a black-tie affair in Cairo, dispatched the
French ambassador instead.

The price of power—ceaseless vigilance—was high, but El
Comandante was willing to pay it. Who was it who said if you
lived long enough, you'd see your reputation maligned three times?
That, in his estimation, was a modest number. Soon enough he
planned to set the record straight, to put an end to the creeping
amnesia regarding the glories of his revolution. He'd ordered Fernando to develop a program that would reenact the regime's most
illustrious days: the attack on the Moncada barracks; the "History
Will Absolve Me" speech during the despot's 1953 trial for treason;
the landing of the *Granma* on the shores of Oriente; the triumph
at the Bay of Pigs. El Comandante hoped that these commemo-
rations would draw hordes of tourists—politically sophisticated
ones, not the cheap rum and whore chasers currently invading the
island. Hard currency in hand, they, too, would help cement his
legacy.

The inaugural program, a restaging of the sixty-eight-hour Bay
of Pigs invasion, had been scheduled for April but was postponed
due to logistical problems until his birthday next month. The tyrant

had warned that heads would roll should there be further delays. His ambassadors had extended invitations to dignitaries worldwide and, after extensive auditions, he'd personally selected a dashing militiaman to play the younger him. The soldier had no acting experience but boasted impeccable Communist Party credentials and promised to grow a suitably scraggly beard for the role.

El Comandante flung aside *La Prensa*. A staunch ally in the Buenos Aires workers' movement had been killed during a strike. It was a much-battered cliché to say that when a man approached the portal of death, even as die-hard an atheist as he would quaver at the prospect of eternal nothingness and beg, at the last humiliating moment, for a priest and the promise of salvation. But to El Líder, God remained an elaborate fiction, at least the God of his Latin-spouting Jesuit teachers. If, as they'd maintained, every man was made in His image, why not simply go a step further and become Him? After all, the tyrant hadn't merely survived, he'd lived—flauntingly, outrageously—in the shadow of an imperial power bent on his destruction for the better part of adjoining centuries. If that didn't qualify him for deification, nothing could.

He rejected agnosticism, too, though an agnostic was probably the most sensible thing to be if you were a gambling man. These days when he tried to imagine God, something he did more often of late, he pictured Him as a massive, pulsing neural network of simultaneity and multidimensional consciousness. Come to think of it, this image was pretty identical to his own job. Such sacrilegious thinking pleased the tyrant. Years ago he'd incensed the island's archbishop by arguing that the Church, given its propensity for propaganda, dogmatism, and absolute authority, could be construed as the perfect Socialist state; a good Catholic as the perfect, unquestioning Socialist man. Even death was a form of socialism, leveling the noble and the ignoble, the king and the humble shoveler of shit to the same classless fate.

In the end, who was to say what mattered—illusion, or reality? After more than a half century of revolutionary reality, not a single soul on the island could've survived without illusion. Revolution required illusion. The two went hand in glove, like a plate of rice and beans. His revolution had attempted to wrest dreams of a better future from the ever gristly, unyielding present—and without the luxury of an afterlife either. At the very least, it'd provided every citizen with this: the opportunity to participate in the greatest narrative in modern times. In the end, Cuba could support just one utopia—his. Why? Because nobody on the island had bigger cojones than he did. Nadie. Except perhaps, at one time, his father.

The tyrant recalled his first vision, at age four, of Papá's prodigious pinga, steaming like a locomotive after a hot bath and flanked by grapefruit-size balls (or so they'd seemed to him) that hung confidently, hirsutely, where his thick thighs flared. That same evening, as his mother bathed the little despot-to-be, taking care to wash the pink bud of his manhood and dust it with enough talcum powder to make it look like a lump of sugared dough, he worked up the courage to ask: "Mami, will all of me grow?" His puzzled mother had helped him into his calzoncillos before it occurred to her what he was asking. "Ay, mijito, your pinga will be the greatest in the land, in all the Americas, perhaps in all the world!" The boy was cautiously pleased. "Okay, the greatest. But will it also be the biggest?"

His mother grinned, eyes shining, and brought her lips so close to his that he inhaled the garlic from that night's ajiaco stew. "Don't you doubt that for a second." The pint-size tyrant's chest filled with pride, and he strutted off to bed with big dreams, the biggest of all. He imagined his pinguita growing and growing until it floated high in the skies, a massive flesh-toned dirigible draped with parachute huevones and a proud snout that served as the control room for the whole impressive operation and that nobody—not even the Yankees, with their warships and gun batteries—would ever dare shoot down. "Good night, mi amor." His mother kissed him on the forehead and gave him an encouraging pat. "Sleep with the angels." "Good night, Mami." And with that, the pint-size tyrant rolled over and fell deeply, happily asleep.

~⌒~

Café

As if my nerves weren't already shot, now the coffeemakers are exploding all over the island. The government is distributing this half-assed café mezclado made with chickpeas. Chickpeas! The mixture clogs up the coffeemakers, heats up too fast, and—¡PÁCATA! Already two people have died, a viejita in Pinar del Río lost her hyperthyroid eye, and I don't know how many others have been seriously injured by this latest descaro. Not to mention the holes and purple blotches on everyone's ceilings. I, for one, prefer the blotches to my old, peeling paint.

I swear this must be part of a larger conspiracy to keep us down. How can we protest or organize against the state when we fear for our lives making coffee? This is terrorism at its worst! Hummus terrorism! Mira, I'm going to put the flame on low then head out to the garden and wait. If it blows, at least I won't go with it.

—*Aracely Mondragón, caffeine addict*

~⌒~

Miami

Goyo Herrera wasn't afraid to die, but he was tired of waiting for death. Waiting for the body to shut down, organ by organ, accruing its critical mass of toxins and blockages. There were places in

Switzerland, he'd heard, that would facilitate the dying; expensive, antiseptic places in the Alps where tubercular patients once waited like so many hothouse orchids. Already, he might've died on any number of occasions in the fifty-plus years since he'd left Cuba: the time he got hit by a taxi on Lexington Avenue, his right leg crushed and shortened by an inch; or the night he was held up outside his Manhattan diner, pistol-whipped and left for dead. There was that kidney stone, too, that nearly killed him in 1978. But if Goyo had learned anything in his eighty-six years, it was that pain alone didn't kill a man.

Besides, he wanted that son of a bitch in Havana to die first.

Years ago he and El Comandante had been acquaintances, Goyo told anyone who would listen. But the truth was a lesser and more complicated reality. The two had barely known each other at the university, where Goyo was a quiet chemistry major and *he* was a loudmouthed law student perpetually hungry for the limelight. Goyo had spent many waking hours and a good number of sleeping ones regretting the lost opportunity of shooting the bastard. In those days it wasn't uncommon for even a quiet chemistry major to carry a gun, and Goyo was a crack shot, having practiced since boyhood on tin cans and chickens.

Ay, he would gladly give up everything he owned—his ocean-front condo on Key Biscayne, his collapsing brownstone off Second Avenue, every last cent of his considerable fortune, even the weekly rendezvous with the shapely bank teller Vilma Espín, who was a magician of hand-mouth coordination and kept him in fighting form since his wife of fifty-nine years had died unexpectedly last New Year's Eve—for the privilege of killing his nemesis. He'd wear chains on his ankles, chisel stones for his remaining days, even become a goddamn Democrat for the gratification of personally expediting the tyrant's journey back to the Devil, with whom he'd obviously made a pact.

It wasn't for politics alone that Goyo would've murdered that swaggering cock but for his mistreatment of the woman Goyo had loved above all others: Adelina Ponti, a pianist whose interpretations of Schubert's early piano sonatas had won his heart. That good-for-nothing had disgraced Adelina, left her with a child, a boy she named after her errant lover, who never recognized el niño as his own. For two years, Goyo anonymously sent Adelina money to help support her son, until the day he learned that she'd hanged herself from a chandelier in her parents' sunny music room, her bare feet grazing the keys of their Steinway baby grand. A plaster bust of Franz Schubert stood watch on a nearby shelf.

Goyo's reasons for wanting to kill the tyrant multiplied prodigiously after the Revolution—his father's suicide, his younger brother Marcos's death in the Bay of Pigs—and his hatred deepened with the ensuing decades of Communist corruption and lies. There was no one in the world he loathed more, no one for whom he stoked a more bottomless fury, no one else he unwaveringly blamed for invading, oppressing, and misshaping his life than that fearmongering, fatigues-wearing, egotistical brute who continued to call the shots from his deathbed overlooking the sea.

His fixation with ending the tyrant's life had begun to consume Goyo day and night. The thought that he could die a hero tantalized him, probably more than it should. His heroism would've been greater had he undertaken the mission as a young man, but even grizzled and arthritic as he was, he might yet achieve mythic status. HERE LIES A CUBAN HERO. Goyo imagined these words chiseled on his headstone, the wreaths and tributes, the eulogies and Martí-inspired poetry read in his honor. Luisa might even grow jealous of the pretty women who'd sigh as they surrendered a rose on his tomb, praying that a man of his stature might someday sweep them off their feet.

He reached for his inhaler and took a bitter breath. Goyo's

lungs had weakened since his bout of pneumonia last winter on an emergency visit to New York. His Turkish tenants had set fire to his brownstone while grilling lamb shish kebabs, nearly asphyxiating the other occupants. The building had become one unceasing headache. Goyo would've sold it in a heartbeat, but the real estate taxes alone would amount to millions and leave him next to nothing. He was trapped, and no amount of wistful gazing at the sea would change that sorry fact.

A regatta was under way in Biscayne Bay, and Goyo raised his binoculars to get a better look. It was the same parade of self-important fools he'd battled at the yacht club before submitting his resignation and telling them all, in no uncertain terms, to go to hell. This hadn't done much for his social life. But it wasn't the solitude of endless tropical days that bothered Goyo. After years of crushing work in New York and a frenetic retirement with the ever-restless Luisa, old age held for him an appealing laxness, a mellowing and decadence of the flesh, the freedom to nap—something he did despite the crises afflicting him daily—like the feral cats that used to roam his childhood village in Honduras.

Smarter people than he had philosophized about confronting the deaf immensity of death. He wasn't particularly original in his thinking. But he found it ironic that true languor—precursor to the eternal one, of course—hadn't invaded his bones until after his wife had succumbed to a brain aneurysm. Luisa had been aggressively social and socially climbing, especially in Miami, but too mistrustful to have any real friends. Goyo had loved her profoundly at first, then more shallowly, until the feeling devolved into obligatory affection and lapsed into ordinary tolerance. Love had flared at the beginning, but then who the hell knew what happened? Decades of tired entanglements later, he still didn't know.

Goyo felt unending shame when he thought about his wife, partly due to the guilt she'd induced in him over his affairs with their diner's siren waitresses; for gambling away a million dollars in the stock market pursuing a "bulletproof" strategy advocated by his hotshot ex-broker, now incarcerated; for not defending her against the barrage of insults by his mother early in their marriage. The shame, however, was most piercing, most unendurable, when Goyo revisited what he considered his principal failing: surrendering his children to his wife's violence and unreasonableness.

His son, Goyito, now pushing sixty, lived on disability in the Florida panhandle, his brain irremediably fried by cocaine and further addled by the medications he took by the fistful to prevent him from killing himself. Alina, six years younger, was troubled in her own peculiar ways. Ever since she'd come to live with him— ostensibly to help him recover from precipitous widowerhood— Goyo had suspected her motives. His daughter had no visible means of support, had taken up long-distance swimming (he could spot her now, porpoise-like, making her way along the horizon), and when she wasn't swimming, snapped her fancy cameras in his face.

The other day Alina had the nerve to ask him to pose nude for her. Goyo was the first to admit that he didn't have much in the way of artistic inclinations, but pose nude for his daughter? This was perversity, plain and simple. He'd heard from one of the garage attendants that Alina had asked the same of other retirees in his condominium, embarrassing Goyo to no end. He had half a mind to kick her out for this alone. Within the hour, if she hadn't drowned or been eaten by sharks, Alina would walk through the front door tracking in rivulets of sand and disturbing him with the strange configurations of seaweed plastered to her manly shoulders.

Goyo wondered whether El Comandante suffered such troubles with his own children, a veritable tribe at this point, if the reports he'd read in *El Nuevo Herald* were even half true. Some years ago, one of the tyrant's illegitimate daughters had written a tell-all memoir about growing up on the island, neglected and suffering from bulimia, an all-but-unheard-of disease among her hungry fellow citizens. The book had made her a celebrity in Miami for one short-lived season.

Unlike his compatriots, Goyo wasn't a blind believer in exile gossip. He'd spent too many years in Manhattan honing his cynicism and reading the *New York Post*. Goyo took pride in his ability to distinguish fact from fiction, the honorable from the crooked, the deal from the scam. Yet this skill seemed increasingly irrelevant at his stage of life. It was all a fiction, he decided, a pliable narrative one could shape, photographs one could freeze at selected junctures, then engage in speculation and pointless deductions. Wasn't that what El Comandante had done? Bent history to his will? Cunningly divided and spliced it into a seamless whole?

The sea was calm, mocking the agitation Goyo felt inside. He was weary of the excuses he'd made for sitting on the sidelines of life, the never-ending rationalizations that choked him like a fetid mangrove swamp. What would he say to El Comandante if they ever met again? Or would they immediately resort to insults and blows? What would they have in common anymore besides arthritis and diverticulitis? Like the tyrant, Goyo had spent his early childhood in the countryside, had two brothers and a Spanish father—Galician, too—who took years to formalize relations with the mother of his children. In short, they were both bastards.

Goyo's mother wasn't Cuban by birth but Guatemalan. After she'd borne three sons by her itinerant Spanish lover, the young family moved to coastal Honduras, the headquarters of Arturo Herrera's burgeoning shipping business. Goyo lived on a beach where he once watched the sea recede for a mile before a tidal wave destroyed their town. Undeterred, Arturo relocated his family to Cuba and finally married Goyo's mother, who was seized thereafter with a sporadic religiosity incited by her gratitude for her good fortune. By then Papá had become very wealthy and Goyo's days on the beach were supplanted by a stint at a Jesuit boarding school in Canada, where he learned Latin, played baseball and the clarinet, and fell in love with chemistry. To this day, the delightful symmetry of the carbon cluster C_{60} moved Goyo to tears. He'd also closely followed the efforts of chemists to make the polyhedral hydrocarbon dodecahedrane ($C_{20}H_{20}$), a challenge they finally achieved in 1980.

Goyo pricked his finger to read his blood sugar, which was a little high but nothing to panic over. He reached for his pills but forgot which tablets were for what and washed down a random handful with a glass of diluted orange juice. His ailments had accrued faster than he could keep straight, upsetting the color-coding medications system his wife had devised. In descending order of importance, Goyo suffered from heart disease (he'd had a triple bypass four years ago), crippling arthritis in his lower spine and both knees (he walked at a thirty-degree angle to the floor), borderline diabetes, irritable bowel syndrome, and intermittent impotence. Perhaps the impotence should've topped the list. It certainly would have in his prime, when he could screw a dozen times in a day and still roar for more.

The flotilla had rounded the southern edge of Key Biscayne, returning to the yacht club's docks. In his boating heyday Goyo and his wife had motored around the Bahamas and other parts of the Caribbean for weeks at a time, usually in winter, when the weather was best. Once he came dangerously close to trespassing Cuba's boundary waters. He'd been fishing for marlin, and the efforts of those magnificent fish—each one battled ferociously for its life—had dared him to try. Goyo got as close as twelve miles off the northeast coast of the island, close enough to imagine the scent of ripening sugarcane, to recall the prance of his best Arabian horse, Velóz, on their weekly inspections of the ranch. The days when he was still a master of real things: land, horses, cattle. Twelve miles. A scant twelve miles from his past. Only Luisa's hysterical threats ("Are you out of your mind? They'll chop you up for shark bait!") made him turn around.

Sometimes Goyo liked to fantasize that he could see, telescopically, back to his homeland; zoom in on his archenemy. What living hell could he concoct for that despot? For inflicting a plague of grief on millions of his countrymen? Goyo's first order of business would probably be to tape the bastard's mouth shut. Next he'd turn off his flat-screen televisions and deprive him of watching the news. (It was said that El Líder compulsively channel-surfed for even a passing mention of himself.) Last, cattle prod in hand, Goyo would force the son of a bitch to listen to a taped litany of every victim, living and dead, whom he had wronged. Goyo could keep this up for eternity, since it would undoubtedly take that long.

His daughter often accused Goyo of staying alive for one purpose only: to celebrate the news of the tyrant's death. He couldn't deny it. Goyo subscribed to an exile website—Hijodeputa.com— that charted, hourly, the Maximum Leader's body temperature (it was 99.6 degrees the last time Goyo checked, at 7:00 a.m., the apparent result of a minor ear infection). Inside operatives, the website assured its followers, had infiltrated the National Palace, hovered by the dictator's bedside, worked as cooks and gardeners in his multiple homes. But if the bastard actually had died as many times as had been prematurely proclaimed, he would've lived more lives than Hemingway's polydactyl cats.

The truth was this: El Comandante had fossilized into a monstrous constant, into time itself.

Frank País's Shoes

I guard the room at the Museum of the Revolution that contains
the shoes that Frank País wore on the day he was executed. I
stare at those shoes a lot, eight hours a day most days, and I've
grown—what is the word?—not fond of, exactly, but identified
with those shoes, heavy and large for a man neither heavy nor
large, and whose life was snuffed out—*paf!*—like a breath
extinguishing flame. There are other items in my room at the
museum. You might recall, if you've been here, the torture
instruments used by Batista's henchmen to pull out prisoners'
nails. Other contraptions for this and that. But to me, the only
things that matter are Frank País's shoes. Oh, I've dreamt about
those shoes, and the baby-faced man who wore them—
a legitimate hero of the Revolution. Who talks about him
anymore? Like his shoes, the memory of Frank País has faded,
and I am left wondering what it would be like to try them on,
to fill the shoes, as it were, of this great, forgotten man. Let me
confess: I am in love with Frank País, this dead man, this once-
vibrant hero, who I imagine would've been a tiger in bed. You
know, I like my men dominant, bien machos. Take me, tell me
what to do, a slap or two, and I'm happy to serve. My husband
is too weak for me, too gentle. Sometimes, I think, if only he
could wear Frank País's shoes for one night, to bed, with me,
I would die of happiness . . .

—*Fidelia González, museum guard*

2.

A Dangerous Season

Miami

More and more, Goyo lost himself in daydreams of revenge. As a group, Cuban exiles were ridiculed, dismissed as right-wing crackpots. Yet who knew better than they the truth of what that despot had perpetrated on their island, the lies that had calcified into history? To Goyo's dismay, his daughter was a blatant liberal who argued against the "futile" trade embargo. Every utterance of hers was an apologia for a moribund regime long sustained by the depth and breadth of world ignorance. Alina, like so many others, supported the oppressor while deriding the oppressed.

"Hey, Dad, how's it going?" His daughter entered the kitchen dripping seawater. Sand cascaded off her thick limbs and clicked onto the spotless tile floor. She yanked open the refrigerator door, scanning the shelves for animal protein. Alina latched on to a packet of boiled ham from which she rolled bright pink slices, wolfing them down with no evidence of mastication. "Want some?" She held out a floppy slice. His daughter attacked a cupboard next, pulling down a can of tuna, noisily opening it, and proceeded to dig out chunks with her briny fingers.

After seven months of living with his daughter, Goyo had nothing more to say to her. Once he'd been her sun and she a tiny, eager planet in his orbit. Now their differences were entrenched, defended like a Maginot Line drawn jaggedly through his luxury condominium. Alina was his flesh and blood, but she might as well have been a rhinoceros, a species Goyo barely understood. She had no regard for her safety, was indifferent to appearances, and was incapable of harnessing language to any socially appropriate use. How different she would've turned out had she been raised in a free Cuba. Ay, it sickened Goyo to think of the what-ifs. Dreams held too long and unfulfilled grew desiccated, pathetic.

Evidence of Alina's complexity surfaced only in her photographs, which, for a time, had made her highly sought after by magazines worldwide. Goyo remembered the fourteen-page spread she'd had in *National Geographic* two decades ago, a series on the Penitentes, a secret sect rarely photographed, whose members reenacted the crucifixion in the remote high deserts of northern New Mexico. What drew his daughter to such grotesqueries? Not once had Goyo seen her moved by ordinary beauty—a rosebud, the innocent face of a child, a pretty landscape. And now she was intent on chronicling every wart and wrinkle of his failing body!

Dark clouds billowed in from the southwest, from Havana, where Goyo's youth remained trapped. He recalled one particularly bad hurricane. It'd been late in December, already past the dangerous season, and he was home from Canada for Christmas vacation. The roar and force of the wind had sucked out his very breath. Goats and chickens—even a trotting pig—tumbled in the air around him. At Papá's ranch, a magnificent grove of date palms was uprooted like a bed of measly seedlings. Not a single lamp-post was left standing in Havana. Ocean fish and algae draped the rooftops. For weeks the island had the drowsy, luminous air of an aquarium.

Goyo spread his hands on the kitchen table and tried to push himself to standing. How useless his hands had become, reaching out for nothing and nobody most of the time.

"Let me help you." Alina encircled his waist from behind and lifted him out of his chair. "Where to, caballero?"

Goyo felt the heat of his daughter's tuna-breath on his ear. She was taller than he was now by six inches. It humiliated him to have to count on her for the simplest tasks. "To my office," Goyo croaked, burdened by the weight of his carcass on his deteriorated knees, his tumescent ankles.

"The doctors say you shouldn't be sitting in front of the computer all day—"

"I have legitimate business to take care of—"

"Reading crazy exile vitriol. You'll get another heart attack on top of everything!"

"Not that it would concern you but my building is—"

"Why don't you watch something other than Fox News—"

"Collapsing. Leftists were running the media long before that Herbert Matthews—"

"Made El Comandante out to be a hero. Uh-huh."

Goyo stopped to catch his breath. He was halfway across the living room, with its vast windows and rotating ceiling fans. In another thirty feet he'd be sitting comfortably in his office, its messy towers of paperwork mitigated by the beam of classical music that filtered in from a vintage radio. Goyo stayed hunched there for hours, messaging his online cronies, among them his older brother, Rufino, who'd been living in the same dilapidated bungalow in Coral Gables since 1966. The two of them got together once a year, at most. Their solidarity online rarely translated into sympathy in person; in person, fortified with a little Spanish rioja or a tumbler of rum, they fought like the bitterest of enemies. They rarely spoke about their younger brother, Marcos, except to agree that he'd been a dreamy, sickly boy who'd loved science fiction. Both Goyo and Rufino had been surprised when he'd volunteered for the Bay of Pigs.

"We need to talk, Dad."

Rufino's children hadn't turned out any better than his: the oldest boy had been killed by a London bus when he'd crossed against traffic; his daughter had gotten pregnant at fifteen and lived in Puerto Rico with her *great*-grandchildren; his younger boy, the most promising, had gone to medical school but became a psychiatrist, of all useless things, and married a browbeating, horsey-faced girl from Hackensack.

"Dad!" Alina snapped her fingers in front of his face.

"¡Qué carajo!"

"I've been trying to get your attention for the last five minutes. You went off into one of your fugue states."

"What is it you wish to know?" Goyo regained his composure. It was his best defense in the heat of battle. He'd had ample practice during the eternity of his marriage to a certifiable hysteric.

"We have to discuss your finances."

Not again.

"I don't have a clue what to do if something were to happen to you. I'm not after anything, I just want to help you get things in order. Like it or not, I'm all you've got."

Goyo refused to have this conversation. He didn't want to have it today, or last week, or the countless times Alina had brought it up since her arrival.

"What will happen to Goyito? Have you made arrangements for his care?"

"Provisions have been made, Alina. Now that's enough."

"Why is this such a taboo subject, anyway? It's not like any of us are immortal. Not even El Comandante." Alina patted her father's sweating forehead with a paper napkin reeking of tuna fish. "Here, sit down on the sofa."

Goyo felt feverish. The pressure in his bowels intensified, no doubt the result of the slow-cooked steel-cut oatmeal he was obliged to eat for breakfast. "Help me to the bathroom, hija," he rasped.

Alina tucked him under a burly arm and sprinted to the master bathroom, which his wife had retrofitted with a porcelain bidet and the plushest of cushioned toilet seats. After his daughter left him propped there, Goyo unfastened his pajama bottoms and settled in with the latest ¡Hola! magazine from his wife's ongoing subscription. Forty minutes later, he was caught up on the European royals (including details of the Duquesa de Alba's disastrous marriage to a man decades her junior) and the latest celebrity gossip. At least he wasn't reduced to wearing bedtime diapers like the tyrant.

Goyo heard the distant, tinny ring tone of "La Bayamesa," Cuba's national anthem. It was his son calling for the first of what would probably be a dozen times before noon. Poor Goyito. His bad luck had begun in utero. Bedridden for the last trimester of her pregnancy, Luisa was the antithesis of a blooming, expectant mother, and her condition only worsened after Goyito was born. She had no interest in holding or nursing their son (nursing wasn't customary in their social set, in any case), and she handed him over to an indifferent wet nurse for the first year of his life. The truth was that Luisa never loved Goyito. It was one of those miscarriages of nature for which there was no solution.

Alina knocked hard on the bathroom door, jolting Goyo. The

door creaked open, and her forearm slid into view, waving his cell phone.

"Por Dios, Alina, I've told you not to bother me when I'm in here!"

"It's Goyito."

"I know damn well who it is."

Her arm slid down the doorjamb and sent the phone skittering across the marble floor. It stopped a quarter inch from his lifted heel. Alina should've been a professional lawn bowler instead of a photographer.

"Hello, hello?" Goyo demanded, his lower back pinching.

"It's me." His son's voice was a dull, flat line.

"¿Qué tal, hijo?"

"I had that dream again."

"Which dream?"

"The one where I'm engulfed in flames."

Goyo was in no mood to plumb the depths of his son's psyche. "Have you told your dream to Dr. Recalde?"

"Yeah."

It pained Goyo to hear his son's voice sometimes. It sounded like death itself tolling for him.

"What did she say?"

"That every dream begins with a wish."

"So what is it you wish, hijo?"

"To kill myself."

"You know I don't like you talking like that." The plush toilet seat squeaked. "What would Rudy do without you?"

"Rudy has fleas. Fleas and aphids."

"Aphids?" Goyo unconsciously scratched his chest.

"They're everywhere."

"Listen to me. Have you taken your medicine?"

"The aphids took them."

"Cálmate, I'll call an exterminator. This is a problem that can be fixed."

"Dad."

"Sí, Goyito."

"Do you believe in reincarnation?"

"Of course not, I'm Catholic. Mira, I'm busy right now. Take your medicine and I'll call you back in an hour."

Goyo checked his watch and hobbled into the master bedroom, which was lavishly decorated in his wife's fantasy of an elegant boudoir: gilded chandeliers, mounds of tasseled silk pillows, brocade-laden tables displaying photographs, mostly of her, professionally taken and touched up, in silver-plated frames. Every inch of the walls was crowded with mediocre oil paintings except for the one Goyo had found, dust-covered, in a Guadalajara antiques shop. The painting turned out to be the lost work of a renowned Mexican modernist and was appraised thirty years ago for the princely sum of sixty thousand dollars. He'd thought of leaving this painting to his son. It might be less dangerous than cash or a trust fund. Goyo saw something of his son's fatalism in the painting, too, as if he, like the skeletal conquistador on horseback, had long ago bartered away his soul.

Goyito's hooliganism had begun even before his voice changed. At eleven, Goyito was selling marijuana to his fellow students and set fire to his school's garbage cans. At the military academy in Pennsylvania to which Luisa had insisted on shipping him off, he hot-wired and stole cars. At the aviation school in New Hampshire, the only flying he did was from his shabby kitchen, the headquarters, Goyo later learned, of the sixth biggest cocaine operation in New England. Luisa refused to visit Goyito in jail then or during any of his subsequent incarcerations, the latest for a heist of household appliances—Sub-Zero refrigerators, stackable washers and dryers—from the Sears warehouse where he was briefly employed.

Goyo shuffled toward his office, leaning heavily on his cane. He was worried about his brownstone, a five-story building on East Forty-Fifth Street, around the corner from the United Nations. For nearly fifty years, the building had been Goyo's chief source of income. But now it was collapsing, literally collapsing, its support beams rotting away, its hardwood floors buckling and sloping, its banisters wobbling. Its grumbling tenants included the convertible sofa store on the ground floor (owned by a crook who sold substandard merchandise), the Turkish restaurant on the second floor (run by a couple from Ankara who hadn't paid their rent since the shish kebab incident), and the occupants of the six more or less renovated apartments on floors three, four, and five, most notably ninety-two-year-old Mary DiTucci, arthritic and stone deaf in 5R, who paid a rent-controlled $312.56 a month with checks written in a trembling hand.

Now this same building, his golden goose in Turtle Bay, was on the verge of crashing down on all their heads.

Havana

El Comandante rearranged the covers and surveyed his room, which was outfitted with two flat-screen televisions and the best medical equipment on the island. Essential tomes of history and political philosophy—Aristotle, Hobbes, Hume, Kant, Marx—lined the mahogany bookcase alongside a complete set of his Colombian novelist friend's books, each signed and dedicated to him, including the one about Simón Bolívar's last river journey, which was inscribed: *To the only son of a bitch who ever dared come close . . . Affectionately, Babo.*

The tyrant was a great admirer of Bolívar, despite their tactical differences. Who else had had the balls to take on a fractured continent and battle, indefatigably, to make it whole? No matter that Bolívar had died, disgraced and disheartened, at little more than half the dictator's present age. It was his vision that mattered. How consumed Babo had been while writing that novel, employing a phalanx of researchers to fact-check his subject's every fart and sneeze. El Comandante had grown jealous, believing that Babo should be writing about the Cuban Revolution instead of Bolívar's fruitless efforts, and he'd waited in vain for his own colossal novel. That Bolívar book had rocketed Babo to stratospheric fame, cementing his transcendence from warty, toad-faced journalist to world-class literary prince and ladies' man. Given the choice, the tyrant had learned, most women chose poetry over power.

Over the years El Comandante had entertained Babo in every way an esteemed, high-profile defender of the Revolution could be entertained—bequeathing him a palatial seaside home and his own cinematography institute, utmost solitude when he wanted it, first-rate company when he didn't, and the best goddamn rum, cigars, lobsters, and pussy on the blue-green planet. Babo—el pobre was on his deathbed—remained loyal to the Revolution after all the turncoats had abandoned it like a love affair gone sour. When asked about his unflagging support for Cuba, Babo had famously retorted: "The Revolution might be a mangy, one-eyed cat, but it's our cat."

A cool hand stroked the tyrant's forehead. For a moment, he pictured his wife forty years younger, surrendering to him after the long trial of winning her heart. Delia displayed the confidence of a woman whose presence had once made grown men collapse to the ground and whimper: "¡Sálvame, mamita!" She was in her sixties now, thick-waisted after bearing him four sons, but her essential nature hadn't changed. To this day Delia girlishly pored over the Parisian fashion magazines sent to her by diplomatic pouch and never once complained about the tyrant's other women, or the children he'd recklessly sired (he despised condoms). She'd been content to stay sequestered inside their gated compound, hidden from public scrutiny during her most ravishing years, and devote herself exclusively to him.

"Mi cielo, how are you feeling?" Delia's guarapo voice had a hint of sand in it.

"Like hell itself."

"What is it, corazón? Tell me where it hurts." Her face was pure concern, the space between her eyes creased like a scrap of burlap. But what could he tell her? That every cell in his body was flickering its last? That the pain began in his toes, snaked up through his calcareous feet, burned through the veins and byways of his legs, his groin, his belly, his spine? An unfamiliar tide of defeat rose in his chest.

"I don't want to be old anymore."

"Ay, to me you're still El Caballo," Delia cooed.

El Caballo. How he'd hated that nickname! The singer Beny Moré had pinned it on him like the tail on a donkey, and it'd stuck for decades. The tyrant permitted no one but Delia to utter it in his presence. He looked up at his wife and tried to whinny like a stallion—this had been their signal for quickie sex, rough and from behind—but it devolved into another fit of coughing. Carajo, nothing was more demoralizing than being old and sick. He grabbed Delia's wrist. "I want you by my side when I go."

"You're not going anywhere, mi amor," she said. Then she turned and ordered El Huele Huele to administer a double dose of her husband's vitamin shots "to lift our commander's spirits."

The injection pinched the crux of his left elbow. The despot suspected that his caretakers were giving him more than B_{12} and magnesium infusions, but he'd stopped monitoring his health so closely. A pain in his chest cut off his breath, prompting another round of violent coughing. It sounded to him like machine-gun fire. He took sips of water from the glass Delia held to his lips, then sank back onto his pillows, exhausted. Of all his infirmities, the incessant choking bothered him most because it interfered with his ability to speak. If he couldn't speak, he couldn't cajole, intimidate, or command. Why, in his prime he could've persuaded Jesus Christ Himself off the cross and into armed revolt against His Father!

His old rival, Che, had suffered from chronic asthma, and this had slowed down the rebels in the Sierra Maestra. Half the time, Che was laid up looking like a goddamn saint. At least he'd had the decency to (finally) die young and photogenic while "exporting" revolution to Latin America, thereby becoming the face of radical heroism. That photograph—the one of him in a beret looking beatifically toward the future—was the most ubiquitous image of the twentieth century. Fifteen years ago an anthropology museum in Los Angeles had exhibited its infinite reproductions: refrigerator magnets, T-shirts, designer handbags, flip-flops, even neckties. Add to that a rash of movies and biographies and Che's myth was ironclad, larded as it was with lies perpetuated by the Revolution itself.

"What are your plans today, mi amor?" Delia asked, trying to recapture her husband's attention.

"You're asking me my *plans*?"

"Don't get upset, I'm just—"

"How about staying alive?" The spittle dribbled down his chin, but his wife tenderly wiped it off. Long ago, she'd learned how to handle his tantrums: indulge him like a two-year-old, kiss him sweetly, then bring him rice pudding or ice cream.* Delia slipped into bed next to him and patted his cheek.

---

* **Aviso:** The only manufactured product worth consuming in Cuba is ice cream, preferably mango.

"You're my handsome boy," she chimed.

"As handsome as Che?"

"Nobody, mi cielo, alive or dead, has ever been as guapo as you."

How it chagrined him to have engineered that asthmatic's canonization! By the time Che was executed in the jungles of Bolivia, he'd long outlived his usefulness to the Revolution. As an administrator he'd been a disaster, with no more diplomacy than a dung beetle. He'd grown cocky, too, refusing to stay in El Líder's shadow. Che had needed to die. The despot had merely facilitated the conditions. A Mexican poet of vacillating political allegiances once wrote: "Tell me how you die, and I will tell you who you are." Bueno, where the hell did that leave him?

The day he'd handed over the reins of power to his brother was the day he should've put a bullet in his brain. Not that Fernando wasn't doing a creditable job, but the man had the charisma of a box of crackers. What else could you expect from a textbook Communist? Put him onstage before a sea of lights and he froze up, squeezed out a few scripted words as though these pained him, then scurried off into the wings. He'd never been good-looking either. Fernando's features were artless, flat-bent, as if they'd been weathered down by the elements into a coarse Toltec statue. His eyes, though, were the eyes of a predator.

Unlike Che, Fernando had willingly spent his life as El Comandante's sidekick. It was where he felt most at home: watching his brother's back; eliminating those who would do him harm, real or not. Once in the Sierra Maestra, Fernando had thrown himself in front of an angry soldier threatening the despot with a Garand rifle. Now *that* was loyalty. In actuality, Fernando was the far more ruthless of the two. He never flinched when he killed anyone, and he slept like a baby. The tyrant liked to joke that, yes, Fernando slept like a baby but a baby with one eye open and a twitchy trigger finger.

During their guerrilla days, it'd been Fernando who'd insisted on a zero-tolerance policy for infractions deemed punishable by death: stealing, raping, or disrespecting the peasants who were helping them at great personal risk. At the first sign of trouble, the offenders were as good as dead. During the first weeks after the triumph of the Revolution, Fernando also organized the firing squads that rid the island of hundreds of Batista loyalists. In the years that followed, the despot talked his brother out of innumerable more executions. Fernando's greatest enemies? Poets. He considered them the most unscrupulous and degenerate of men and would've done away with all of them, if he could. Fernando couldn't abide complexity. He was 100 percent macho, too, even in the mountains where the rebels had suffered long stretches of abstinence.

That was what Cuba needed, more loyal machos like his brother.

Solidarity

Did you hear the one about the tree huggers who came to Havana during the Special Period and ate their hosts out of house and home? In those days, street vendors were disguising scummy mop threads with batter and bread crumbs and selling them as fried steaks. Por supuesto, they were chewy, but you have to understand: people were starving. Other descarados were melting Chinese condoms as "cheese" for pizzas.

Anyway, these tree huggers (they'd been living in the canopies of redwoods in California) got shitfaced one night on the island's fine rum and had the bright idea of smashing up their hosts' impeccably preserved 1950s television set and everything else they thought smacked of bourgeois decadence. The comemierdas left the place in ruins, stole the last of their hosts' toilet paper, and took off without offering to pay for a thing. So much for people-to-people diplomacy.

                                              —*Eusebio López, arborist*

3.

(To) Resolve

Miami

Goyo settled into his ergonomic chair and turned on his desktop computer. He put on the aviator bifocals that his wife had said made him look like a grasshopper. How bitterly she'd protested over the time he spent online, interspersing her moaning with ancient complaints about his long-dead mother. What Luisa had wanted, had needed more than oxygen, was Goyo's undivided attention—the one thing he couldn't give her. He was still shocked that she'd died before him. Her health had been far better than his, and Luisa looked many years younger besides, due to her penchant for plastic surgery. She'd begun with a discreet tummy tuck in her forties, progressing to successive and complex lifts to her face, breasts, and buttocks (all performed by Brazilian plastic surgeons at half the Miami price) and complemented by multiple liposuctions. Luisa had been cut, snipped, tucked, nipped, and sucked so often that her body looked stitched together from disparate parts. Coupled with an eating disorder that had her weight fluctuating a hundred pounds, the surgeries had left her prone to such unpredictable shiftings of flesh that nothing but a neck-to-ankle, extra-strength, beige body girdle could tame the unruly bulges.

At eighty-two, Luisa's face had been her crowning glory—radiant, lineless, frequently immobilized by Botox injections and plumped up with collagen. She'd spent the better part of every morning plastering her face with lavish creams made from the glandes of unborn lambs and meticulously applying her makeup. So obsessed had Luisa become with her appearance that she finally convinced Goyo to have a little work done himself during their last trip to Rio. The procedures—an eye lift, fat injections into his hollowing cheeks—had hurt like hell, and Goyo, stir-crazy and unbearably itchy, had ignored the plastic surgeon's instructions on sun avoidance and postoperative rest.

When Alina saw him shortly after his return from Brazil, she took one look and blurted out, "What the hell happened to you?" Never one for tact, she added: "Jesus, Dad, you look like a flounder." It was true. Goyo wasn't sure how or why it'd happened, but his eyes had somehow drifted closer together, then migrated, slightly, toward the right side of his face.

At a recent anniversary party for old friends, Goyo had been astonished at how youthful everyone looked until it dawned on him that nearly every octogenarian there was semibionic—artificial hips and knees, shoulder replacements, hair plugs, heart transplants, and a panoply of other age-defying enhancements. With the lights dimmed and the salsa "band" (in actuality, a liver-spotted singer with a synthesizer who did a passable imitation of Beny Moré) in full swing, the guests took to the floor and danced the night away, believing—if only for the two minutes and fifteen seconds of Pérez Prado's "Mambo No. 5"—that the Revolution had never happened.

Goyo's in-box was congested with the usual array of right-wing junk mail, penile enhancement ads, and phishing scams. His brother weighed in several times a day, too, ever hopeful about El Comandante's declining health: WE'LL OUTLIVE HIM YET, HER-MANO! Rufino claimed that his wife, Trini, a founding member of a bookkeepers' prayer circle that promised to work miracles with the IRS, had persuaded its members to devote the month's orations to ensuring the tyrant's untimely death. Goyo thought it ridiculous how religious fanatics believed they could sway the Almighty to do their bidding, as if they were divinely anointed lobbyists. God had been ignoring the Cubans' pleas since before the Wars of Independence. Why should He bother listening to them now?

Although not a victim of optimism, Goyo rarely succumbed to despair. If he was anything it was a Catholic pragmatist, which wasn't as contradictory as it sounded. Void, or paradise? Who really knew? Goyo continued to believe because the terror of not believing was worse. Above all, he tried not to let religion interfere with his common sense and took pride in analyzing events in as clear-eyed and dispassionate a manner as possible. Cuba's difficulties, in his opinion, had been exponentially compounded by its longtime status as a de facto colony of the United States. Goyo had seen the writing on the wall long before those barbudos took to the Sierra Maestra and *waited* for Batista to fall. A country can take only so much abuse before it implodes. The solution, sadly, turned out to be much worse than the original problem.

Goyo removed his bifocals and rubbed the bridge of his nose. He pulled a microfiber cloth from his desk drawer, polished his lenses, then turned back to the computer screen. A message bleeped in from his mistress, writing to him from the bank where she worked:

HOLA, MI TIGRE. HOW ABOUT A DATE THIS AFTERNOON? BESITOS Y
MUCHO MÁS, VILMA. This was followed by a winking smiley face
and a series of strange punctuation marks that eluded his compre-
hension. Goyo enjoyed Vilma's company—her love was a bright,
enameled thing—but their ardent frolicking often exhausted him
so completely that he was incapacitated for days afterward. MAYBE,
he typed back. I'LL CALL YOU.

Another message, the third of the morning, flashed in from
Goyito: SEND $50. DOWN TO MY LAST BAG OF CHIPS. Goyo logged
on to his banking account and transferred twenty dollars to his
son. He supported his namesake but only with the smallest incre-
ments of cash possible. Too much money overwhelmed Goyito
and made him do foolish things. Nine years ago, when he'd finally
won his disability suit against the state of Florida, the government
sent him a check for $22,000 in previously denied benefits. Goyito
ripped through that money in one blowout weekend of cocaine,
steamed lobsters, and whores.

During his brief stretches of sobriety, Goyito had held various
jobs and even managed to graduate from a fly-by-night college in
Brooklyn with a degree in finance. Not a pot to piss in, but the boy
had a degree in finance. After college Goyito had worked as a Wall
Street runner, operating on a high-octane combination of donuts
and amphetamines. Once Goyo had caught a glimpse of his son
on television wearing a garish yellow jacket and pumping his arm
at the day's closing bell. What Goyito had wanted, more than anything, was a fast-track fortune. If he hadn't become a drug addict,
he might've become a multimillionaire.

Thinking about his son upset Goyo, and he had no time to be
upset today, not with so many crises to resolve. In a locked compartment of his file cabinet, he kept a box of contraband chocolates
and his Chief's Special .38, one of two weapons he owned. The
other handgun, a Glock, he kept secured in the glove compartment

of his Cadillac. Goyo opened the gilded box of truffles and considered its contents—rich Belgian chocolates filled with ground nuts and flavored elixirs. Goyo popped a hazelnut truffle into his mouth, closing his eyes and savoring the silky gianduja on his tongue. His ringing cell phone disrupted his reverie.

"The whole thing's coming down like a house of cards," Johnny Esposito growled without preamble.

"How much time do we have?" Goyo imagined bricks of his cash sprouting wings in the vaults of Flagler Federal Bank and flying north to his contractor's pockets.

"A month, maybe two. You get some newbie buildings inspector coming anywhere near the place and they'll have it torn down."

Goyo swallowed hard. The brownstone had put his children through college (for all the good it'd done them), enabled him to live a comfortable retirement. "What now?"

"Reinforced beams. Concrete pillars from the basement to the roof. The building's gotta hang on those fucking supports."

"Can we do this without arousing suspicion?"

"Leave that to me," Esposito sniffed.

Goyo knew better than to inquire further. Esposito's contacts could magically make things happen overnight, or just as easily disappear. Inspectors, tax problems, collapsing buildings. Everything could be arranged for a price.

"What's it going to cost me?" Goyo fondled a truffle bursting with raspberry liqueur. If he didn't control himself, he might slip into a diabetic coma and Alina would be left to handle this mess. He put back the truffle.

Esposito laughed femininely, a soprano's laugh. "You don't wanna know."

"When can we start?"

"Pronto, comandante. I'll get my men working on this right away."

Goyo winced at the word *comandante*. Nearly every building in Havana was crumbling, but the tyrant had no tenant lawsuits to worry about, no inspectors cruising for kickbacks, no extortionist contractors draining off what remained of his retirement savings. El Comandante had even convinced UNESCO to restore the oldest part of the city as a World Heritage Site. Goyo had seen the photographs. It looked like it had in the fifties, when Havana had been on a par with New York or Paris, boasting world-class symphonies, theaters, ballet companies, an unmatched nightlife.

To remember all this was a heart-searing misery, but sometimes remembering was all Goyo could do. The litany rarely varied. The Revolution's early agrarian reforms had reduced his family's estates to seven percent of their former size. Seven percent. There was no future in seven percent. When his father's shipping line was also expropriated, the Herreras fled to New York. Goyo tried to make a go of it as an insurance salesman, but he couldn't earn enough money to pay the rent. Two years into his exile, he leased a dilapidated five-and-dime on First Avenue and introduced tropical milk shakes and Cuban sandwiches to mid-Manhattan. Eventually, Goyo bought the place and converted it into a diner, mixing in burgers and fries with his wildly popular island specialties. He also catered office parties for the United Nations delegates, delivering the food himself and making friends. He called it Minimax Café, after the Latin aphorism Minima maxima sunt. The smallest things are most important.

Goyo had done all right for himself financially. But everything else—the things people said money couldn't buy—bueno, with those he hadn't done so well.

It was barely eight o'clock and his stomach felt queasy. Goyo reached for a pink antacid pill. Most mornings he woke up at 4:00, convinced that he was having another heart attack. He consoled himself with statistics; if he made it to sunrise, the odds of surviving the day were good. Outliving the tyrant wasn't Goyo's sole reason for staying alive, but it damn near the topped the list. Besides, he didn't want to miss the pachanga in Miami when word spread of the tyrant's death. Other cities had disaster relief plans, backup generators, designated emergency shelters. Miami had a victory parade prepared to march down Calle Ocho on an hour's notice. The oldest exiles, now barely distinguishable from the dead, would miraculously spring back to life for one last fiesta with the news. When that hijo de puta finally kicked the bucket, everyone would be partying like it was 1959.

Galápagos

This is a very difficult country. Very stressful. No quieren reconocer que esto es un fracaso. An utter disaster. I waited years for an apartment in Havana until I couldn't wait any longer. I built my own place in between these two old mansions in Vedado. It's gloomy and narrow, but I shift a spotlight around to where I'm painting y me resuelvo.* At first the authorities considered me a squatter, then they tried to tax me out of existence. But I parked myself here and refused to move. I live with my kitty and a baby Galápagos turtle that a friend of mine smuggled out of Ecuador. Sometimes I take Piquito to the park so he can sun himself. They tell me my turtle will live three hundred years and grow to the size of a Volkswagen. But what's the use of worrying? Nobody knows what tomorrow

---

* *Resolver,* to resolve, is Cuba's national verb. This could mean anything from "resolving" a cake for a niece's quinceañera to "resolving" the Revolution's overreliance on imports.

—*Fulgencio Correa, grammarian*

will bring. If you chuck Piquito under the chin—like this, see?—he bobs his head. Ay, he loves that!

My paintings? Naturally, they have a sinister air. They're my hallucinations, my nightmares. Right now I'm working on a series called Buscando Carne en La Habana (Looking for Meat in Havana); meat, of course, in all respects. It's these disgraces that I'm driven to paint with my medieval palette. One disgrace after another. There are never any shortages of those.

—*Zaida del Pino, artist*

―᠒

Havana

The seas grew choppy as the winds intensified from the south. The international weather channel reported that a hurricane was gathering strength off the coast of Suriname, contradicting the predictions of that idiot meteorologist who'd reassured everyone of balmy days ahead. Carajo. How many sugarcane crops had been destroyed by hurricanes in the last sixty years? How many power lines downed, factories leveled, military installations laid to ruin? It was the one recurring disaster the tyrant couldn't blame on the Yankees.

His cohorts in Latin America whispered "yanquis" the way they whispered "fate," that dark obedience, as if the Cold War were in effect and run by superpower decree. Not that there weren't consequences to running afoul of the Americans—the tyrant knew that better than anyone—but their sanctions could be exploited for political advantage. Without the U.S. embargo, the Revolution couldn't have survived. It'd needed a common enemy to blame for its economic ills. In the end consumerism, not guns, would destroy Socialism. Microwaves and computers, motorcycles, iPhones, Omaha Steaks. Puta madre, his people would throw him out for a reliable supply of toilet paper!

The morning dragged on with the usual nonsense and syco-phants. El Comandante had seen and heard it all a thousand times before. If only Ceci Sánchez were at his side again, handling the crap. The irreplaceable Ceci had been his lover and loyal aide-de-camp in the Sierra Maestra. She'd taken care of his every need, down to relieving his blue balls. No other rebel was permitted to have a woman in the encampment, not that anyone envied his relationship with Ceci. She was exceedingly skinny, with no ass to speak of, and her teeth protruded unflatteringly during the rare times she smiled. Cuban men could put up with untold shortcom-ings in a woman, but a flat ass wasn't one of them. They felt a good culo to be their inalienable right, like access to potable water or a nightly shot of rum. A woman without an ass was called a rana, a frog. There was no worse insult.

Ceci had marched and carried her pack in the mountains like any good soldier. She didn't expect the royal treatment and was trustworthy and discreet. The woman proved to be a superb orga-nizer, too, and an invaluable liaison with insurgents all over Cuba. Her responsibilities didn't end after the Revolution, though her romantic relations with her famous lover did. During the rebels' victory parade across the island, women began tossing their under-wear and telephone numbers at El Comandante like he was Frank Sinatra or Elvis Presley. Overnight it became the ultimate in radi-cal chic to sport an unkempt beard, long hair, and a pronounced stink—and this in a country whose citizens had a mania for per-sonal hygiene.

He didn't know it then, but that long march to Havana, with its insistence of banners and speeches and ecstatic crowds, would prove the pinnacle of his power and prestige, as good as it ever got. After that, the grim business of governing began—battling

Yankees and Russians and traitors, the endless blood and gunpowder, expansions into Africa and elsewhere because the Revolution had to prove itself on the world stage. Lately, his enemies had taken to calling Cuba a basket case, a floating scar in the Caribbean Sea. He would die fighting their lies.

The tyrant had contemplated writing his memoirs but agreed instead to hundreds of hours of interviews with a sympathetic Spanish journalist. The resulting book—*Conversations in the Socialist Cathedral*—fell short of his expectations. El Comandante thought that if he were writing his autobiography he would arrange the chapters thematically, focusing on such crucial subjects as babalawos, the Russians, and his first wife, Miriam. Carajo, Miriam could fill a tome all by herself. The sight of her in her wedding gown walking down the aisle of the little church toward him . . . Bueno, that was the happiest moment of his life. It infuriated him to think that Miami, home to his most pestilential detractors, was the city in which he'd spent the first, unforgettable days of his honeymoon. Ay, Miriam! Her eyes had been like an ecclesiastical argument for infinity, and the rest of her . . . Coño, however hard he tried, it was impossible to forget her, impossible to forget anything about her—even her legendary culinary bungling. Who could resist her palomilla steaks,* fried to leather, which required every fiber of his jaw muscles to chew?

To his dismay, the beautiful Miriam expected him to provide for their family and supply the niceties that came with a bourgeois life.

---

* During the Special Period, I was asked, as chef of Cuba's most popular cooking show, to present a segment on palomilla steaks at the sentimental behest of El Comandante. Of course, I had to substitute pounded grapefruit rinds for the impossibly scarce beef and still make it appetizing for my viewers. The Maximum Leader confided in me at the time that he, too, had been denied beef along with, as he put it, "nearly every other goddamn pleasure known to man."
                                                    —*Hortensia Ramos, celebrity chef*

Why should he have to support one family, he'd argued with her, when history was offering him the chance to provide for an entire nation? Sadly, she remained stubbornly attached to convention and the demands of their newborn son. When Miriam's brother got wind of her situation, he arranged to have her put on Batista's payroll. His wife on his mortal enemy's payroll! Nothing had hurt or humiliated El Comandante more. She divorced him at his lowest point, during his imprisonment on the Isle of Pines. But enough! It was too agonizing to remember.

He licked his lips, which were cracked and tasted of medicine. The only person to do his life justice in print was a weasely former adviser, now exiled in France. He'd had the gall to publish El Comandante's life story as a novel. Ironically, it'd turned out to be the best thing that sorry-assed traitor ever wrote, a veritable magnum opus. To the tyrant's surprise, he'd been enthralled by his fictional counterpart—on a par with Hamlet or King Lear; flawed, but irresistibly grandiose and compelling. In short, he couldn't put the damn book down. Fictio cedit veritati, as those mothballed Jesuits used to say. Fiction yields to truth. The tyrant tore through the novel's thousand-plus pages during the better part of a mild spring weekend when his wife beckoned him from his hammock to taste her rice pudding.

El Comandante took issue with just one detail of that detestable defector's book: for the record, his pinga, fully engorged and ready for action, was not 6.2 inches, as erroneously reported, but a proud, thick, majestic 6.6.

—&

Babalawos

When the tyrant was still in short pants, his mother used to take him on surreptitious visits to a babalawo two towns away. It wasn't easy for her to escape her Galician husband for an afternoon, distrustful as he was of anyone who charged hard-earned pesos for a less than concrete exchange. Papá understood this: a hectare of sugarcane for a pair of superlative oxen; a cartload of mountain pine carved into so much rustic furniture; a day's backbreaking fieldwork for a day's meager pay. But sacrificing perfectly healthy farm animals for the dubious promise of spiritual betterment? That upset the balance of justice in his head. Not that he didn't frequently tip the balance in his favor with a meaty thumb. Business was business, after all. To Papá's mind, these country shamans did nothing but prey on an ignorant pueblo's superstitions and fears. All the same, he took great pains to avoid their wrath.

At the babalawo's home, dozens of candles had flickered on and around an enormous altar, illuminating pumpkins, gold chains, tureens, cowrie shells, decapitated doves, strings of beads, and a panoply of plaster saints. The babalawo told Mamá that her son had the fire of Changó in him, that he wouldn't spare his enemies on the playground or on the battlefield. Not long afterward, the young tyrant beat a schoolmate—an arrogant heir to the Bacardi fortune—to within an inch of his life for calling him what he undeniably was: un hijo de puta.

Later, when the rebel leader was ensconced in the Sierra Maestra, the island's babalawos prayed for his success, sacrificing rams, bulls, turkeys, and Guinea fowl in his name. And on the day he triumphantly marched into Havana with his band of ragtag men, thundering at the crowd of one million that had welcomed him to the great plaza, the same babalawos released a flock of white doves that soared and swooped over the people, signaling their approval. The god of fire, Changó incarnate, had ascended to power. So what if one of the doves trained to land on his shoulder took a shit on it? Fucking bird. Nobody was the wiser.

Verbatim Package Directions for Café Mezclado

"RECOMENDACIONES PARA SU ELABORACIÓN:

El agua a añadir no sobrepasará a válvula de la cafetera. El café que usted añada en el coledor nunca debe ser comprimido. Coloque la cafetera sobre la hornilla preferiblemente a fuego lento."

What they don't tell you: LIGHT THE BURNER, AND RUN LIKE HELL!

4.

Cemetery

Miami

Goyo brought violets. They would wilt in this heat, but they were Luisa's favorite flowers and he'd promised her when they were courting that she would never do without. In Cuba, violets had been a rarity—mysterious, delicate, otherworldly—and his wife had feigned similar airs. Now that she was dead, Goyo had vowed to visit her in the cemetery once a month; not often enough, he imagined Luisa complaining. Usually he came on a Tuesday morning to avoid the weekend rush and midday heat.

He placed the violets at the foot of her headstone—a pink Italian granite engraved with gold lettering—then set up his portable folding chair and a battery-operated CD player loaded with Enrique Chia's trademark boleros. Such "soundtracks" had heightened Luisa's sense of self-importance and provided her with narratives adaptable to her own life. After she'd discovered Goyo's early infidelities, Luisa had swooned and sobbed along to many a Julio Iglesias album. A desperate Goyo had considered (briefly) forgoing extramarital affairs altogether in exchange for his wife's promise to banish the balladeer's insipid songs from their home forever.

The fluttering of offerings to the dead—balloons, silk flowers, the papery scratch of a birthday streamer—contributed to the cemetery's serenity. The traffic on Calle Ocho was a low hum in the distance. The old-timers would be at Café Versailles holding court with their increasingly embellished stories. Goyo envied them. It was impossible for him to even remember a bad joke. This was a grave disability in Miami. That and his nonexistent dancing rendered him, in the eyes of his countrymen, a bogus Cuban. The exiles would be dissecting the latest news from Cuba, too. Hijodeputa.com had reported this morning that the tyrant was planning to address the United Nations in the fall. It was supposed to be a farewell address, though no one was calling it that, more like a last platform from which to mock his enemies.

To Goyo's knowledge, nobody but he visited Luisa's grave. Alina hadn't attended the funeral, and only a handful of his wife's Red Cross friends had shown up for the burial in their Sunday finery, gossiping and winking at him. Poor Goyito had driven down from Jacksonville, but he'd remained utterly silent and dry-eyed during the ceremony. To her dying day Luisa had believed that their son wasn't mentally ill but pretending to be crazy, as she'd crassly put it, for profit. "Aren't there easier ways for a clever boy to make money?" Goyo had argued back. But his wife was impervious to logic. After he'd tossed the clumps of requisite dirt on Luisa's coffin, Goyo was blindsided by a crushing, unexpected loneliness. Often, he dreamt that she still slept beside him. Luisa had been an agitated constant in his life for six decades—and damn it, he missed her.

An eclipse of white moths converged on his wife's grave. This would've horrified her. Among her many empty enthusiasms, Luisa had spent a great deal of her later years battling the inevitable mildew and moth infestations that came with living by the sea. Every now and then Goyo dug into his closet and pulled out a guayabera or a pair of slacks disintegrating with holes, and this made him miss her all the more. With her passing, Goyo had lost much of his own history. His wife's memory had been highly selective—for his concrete failings and her imaginary triumphs—but also for their early, tender love.

After her mother was buried, Alina told him a shameful story: that when Luisa was a little girl, her father would force her to watch him fondling himself in the shower, that her own mother would make excuses for him, telling Luisa that she needed to learn the ways of men. This had enraged Goyo. It also explained why his wife had struggled so terribly to give herself over to him. For the first disastrous weeks of their honeymoon, she'd insisted that they merely hold hands when they went to sleep. It'd taken Goyo a year of loving patience to coax Luisa to permit herself the pleasure he was capable of giving her. Who knew what other secrets she'd taken to the grave?

Goyo settled on his portable chair and pushed a button on the CD player. The sounds of "Quiero Volver" wafted over his wife's grave and up into the shading tamarind tree. *What's madness but nobility of soul at odds with circumstance?* Goyo recited this aloud, picturing his wife's puzzled reaction (he'd borrowed the line from one of Alina's poetry books). *Sometimes a man needs to go to extremes to test his convictions.* This line was his, as was what followed: *I can't wait any longer, Luisa. I must face my fears and become the man I know I can be. En fin, I want to be worthy of a fine elegy. I want you to be proud of me, mi amor.*

Who knew if Luisa would believe him? The two had lied to each other as a matter of course. She would've categorized her deceptions as feminine necessities: checking Goyo's mail and cell phone records, inspecting his credit card receipts. His wife hadn't spied on his e-mails only because she didn't know how to use a computer. She'd consulted santeras and fortune-tellers, too, for advice on how to get him back. Not that Goyo had ever threatened to leave her—well, maybe once or twice over her treatment of Goyito. The real problem had been that Luisa had wanted, unreasonably, to have him all to herself. She'd been incapable of emotional moderation, or the stony tolerance expected of a good Cuban wife. In Goyo's experience, American women were much more pragmatic about love, rarely exhibiting the melodramatic sensibilities of their Latina counterparts. Sometimes he longed for the strong, sensible girls from northern climes who'd understood the limits of his devotion.

Goyo skipped ahead to the song "Cuando Vuelva a Tu Lado." Luisa had tried to get him to dance to it cheek to cheek, but Goyo always felt like a hapless turtle fighting its way out of a paper bag. Now he pushed himself to standing and swayed to the music, sliding one foot forward then back. *This is for you, Luisa. For you, I'm dancing like an old fool.* He remembered the time his wife had shown up at his diner late one night and put on a recording by Olga Guillot. They'd danced their way into the pantry and made passionate love among the onions and industrial-size cans of tomato soup. Luisa had been a great beauty once, before her weight gains and corset-like girdles disfigured her body for good.

A small army of clicking beetles trundled across her grave. Goyo swiped at them with the tip of his cane. Last week his brother had told him that one of his great-grandchildren, the nine-year-old, was raising hissing cockroaches from Madagascar as pets. Cucarachas? This was inconceivable to Goyo. Couldn't the boy get a hamster or a Chihuahua like everyone else? Goyo reached inside his shirt pocket for the cigar he'd tucked there. He lit it and watched as the smoke ribboned to heaven. Maybe if he killed the tyrant, he might go straight to heaven himself. Ay, but there was little justice in the world. For him true heaven was the precious memory of his youth, of the earthly paradise he'd lost. Cuba had been his birthright, his home, and it'd been taken away from him—brutally, eternally. What was death next to such banishment?

Goyo considered the other graves, the statues of angels and gargoyles, the mausoleums and family crypts. So many heartbroken exiles were buried here, dreaming with their last breath of returning home to a free Cuba. At least Mamá had died in Havana, though nobody had envied her at the time. She'd only been fifty-seven. The doctors had suspected a heart attack, a family hazard. Above him, a pair of ravens drifted in the skies. The heat was growing unbearable. The sun bleached everything in its domain as it moved toward unforgiving noon. Goyo's cell phone rang. Coño, there was no escaping his son, even here.

"Rok-rok-rok . . . frahnk . . ."

"Goyito, is that you?"

"Rok-rok-rok—"

"Is that molar bothering you again?" Goyito's interminable dental problems frequently pushed him to unconventional expressions of pain.

"It's a great blue heron."

"A what?"

"That bird in the Everglades. It's a mating call."

"Are you trying to attract a female?" There were no passports for parenthood, Goyo thought, or for death.

"Listen to this: tsyoo-tsyoo-tsyoo-tsyoo-tswee . . ."

"Mira, hijo, I'm here in the cemetery with your mother and—"

"Guess what it is."

"I have no idea."

"A yellow-throated warbler. Okay, here's the last one. I've been practicing this one all morning: ta-ka-ta-ka-ta-ka-ta-ka-ta."

It sounded to Goyo like a maraca, but who knew what the bird was called? "I give up."

"A belted kingfisher! The longer the rattle, the more aggressive it's feeling. It's very territorial."

Goyo laughed. He envisioned the kingfisher, still wet and chattering on its mangrove branch. "That's very nice, Goyito. Is this a new hobby?" He didn't care what the hell his son did to pass the time so long as he stayed sober. Goyito was his dark angel, unfit for this world.

"Sort of."

"Ah, that makes me very happy. Let's hear another one."

"That's all I've got. I'm working on the black-capped chickadee and the ferruginous hawk. What are you doing at Mom's grave?"

"Having a conversation."

"Two-way?"

"Not exactly." His son sounded good, cheerful even. Maybe his shrink had adjusted his medications.

"Did you know that the entrance to hell is just a tiny hole in the ground?"

"Is that so?" Goyo's optimism sagged.

"No bigger than the size of a black bean."

"And how do you know this, hijo?" Goyo tried to keep his voice even. It wasn't possible to imagine Goyito's confusion, but he could try to offer him patience.

"I dreamt it."

Goyo heard his son grinding his back molars, popping his jawbone.

"Life and death aren't equal," Goyito added.

"I have to agree with you there." Goyo eyed the pink and white bougainvillea cascading over a grave twenty yards away. "It goes against what the Church says, but I suspect that life is a lot better than death."

"Whoa, then I'm totally screwed!"

"I didn't mean it like that, it's just—"

"Can you send me money for my tooth?" Goyito interrupted.

"When are you going to the dentist?"

"Next week."

"Then there's time. I'll call Dr. Yamada and make arrangements."

"I'm hungry."

"Bueno, eat something. Don't starve yourself." Recently, his son had embarked on a modified fast and was subsisting on liquid protein. In this, unfortunately, he took after his mother.

A cadaverous black dog nosed its way along the graves, limping on its back left leg. "Vete de aquí! Vete! There's a dog here, hijo. It looks like a pit bull. I don't want it digging up your mother's bones." The dog approached tentatively, its eyes on Goyo. Then without warning, it latched on to his mahogany cane. "Hijo de puta!" Goyo held fast to the curved end.

"Fifty bucks. Send me fifty bucks?"

"Twenty!" Goyo shouted. With a sharp tug, the dog got hold of the cane and trotted off with it, settling on some Cuban admiral's grave and having himself a good chew. "I'll call you back, hijo."

Now what? Goyo was sweating from the humidity and his battle with the dichoso mutt. A hummingbird flitted amid the bougainvillea. It looked like a gleaming ruby with wings, its beak a perfect curved needle. Mi madre, why was it breaking his heart? Time was no more than this, Goyo decided: a stray dog snatching your cane without permission or grace. Goyo wiped his forehead with a handkerchief. A drifting cloud gave him momentary respite from the sun. He stumbled after the dog, but it stood its ground and growled.

"Give it to me," Goyo commanded, stretching out his hand. If he couldn't get his cane back from this flea-bitten mutt, then

what hope did he have of killing El Comandante? The dog emitted a high-pitched whine. Goyo got a little closer. It sat upright
and offered Goyo its paw. He shook it, then reached for his cane.
"Good boy," he whispered. "You're a good boy. I'll bring you a
steak next time, okay?"

Charade

So there was this couple in Havana who'd been married forever
and devoted to each other like you've never seen. He'd been a
sociology professor at the university before they abolished the
department; she'd been a private French tutor until nobody
studied French anymore. During the Special Period, they had
next to nothing to eat, so every night they pretended to go to a
fancy restaurant and order a sumptuous meal. Would you like
the steak au poivre tonight? Oh my, look! They have stuffed
lobster tails and a bouillabaisse! They went through all the
motions: wiping their mouths with imaginary linen napkins,
toasting themselves with make-believe champagne in crystal
flutes, ordering blancmange for dessert. I heard this story from
their only son, an artist in Germany. He managed to emigrate
in the nineties and sent them money until they died "sharing" a
beef bourguignon.

—*Silvia Meléndez, glass blower*

5.

Rain

Mexico City

It was an interminable ride from the airport into the heart of Mexico City, where Babo was living out his remaining days. El Comandante had received the call late that morning: if he wanted to see his friend alive, then it was necessary to come immediately. The tyrant hated traveling, as he hated anything that wasn't under his direct control. It was a testament to his love for Babo that he made this exception. The filth and fumes of the capital's outskirts depressed the tyrant, and his limousine reminded him of a hearse. He decided against mentioning the resemblance to his wife. Delia would only contradict him, change the conversation to a more cheerful topic; in a word, irritate the hell out of him. He hadn't wanted her to come along today, but she'd insisted, something she almost never did, and so he'd reluctantly agreed.

When the doctors had first discovered the spot on Babo's lung, he'd overreacted, decamping from his villa on the Pacific Coast and cooping himself up in an ugly, pretentious high-rise next door to the best hospital in the country. El Comandante was surprised by his friend's apprehensions. The Babo he knew had lived fully and fearlessly, never hesitating to plunge headlong into battles for causes he believed in, be they political, literary, or romantic. It was midafternoon by the time the hearse pulled up to the luxury building. Rooftop snipers protected the uniformed doormen. This was what life had come to here. The rich could afford more protection than the poor, who were treated as so much cannon fodder in the war between the drug cartels and corrupt government forces. Woe to anyone who got caught in the crossfire.

El Comandante and his wife were escorted into Babo's building and up the elevator to his penthouse. Walls of bulletproof glass overlooked the city. Everything felt tightly sealed, vacuum-wrapped, airless. Babo's second wife, Gloria, to whom he'd been married thirty years, greeted them in her bare feet, her white linen dress absorbing the thin afternoon light. Despite her keen eyes and calm, ironic tone, she was something of an old hippie, if you could call the heiress to one of Mexico's petrochemical fortunes a hippie. Gloria was the opposite of the dictator's own wife, who had the good-natured sincerity of a puppy.

The atmosphere in the apartment was as somber as the decor. Gone were the wicker chairs and open-air patios of Babo's seaside home, replaced by stiff, cretonne-upholstered furniture. The three sat in silence as a maid served them coffee and petit fours, which Delia ate with abandon. Gloria didn't touch a thing.

"The doctors say he's in his last hours." Gloria lit a gold-tipped cigarette. She blew the smoke toward a chandelier and waited for it to dissipate before continuing. "I know he'll be happy to see you, Jefe."

"The truth is we—" Delia started, but she was cut short by her husband's glare.

El Comandante didn't want to risk Delia mentioning that they almost didn't come. Dying friends dispirited the tyrant.

"Do you think he'll recognize me?" he asked.

"I know he will." Gloria smiled one of the enigmatic smiles that Babo once confessed had hooked him like a helpless trout. That, and the fact that she gave the best head in all the Americas.

"I'd like to see him, Gloria."

"Claro, Jefe. Follow me."

He trailed Gloria down a dim corridor to Babo's study. It was here that his friend had insisted on spending his final days. He wanted, simply, to die surrounded by books. There were no family photographs, no souvenirs of his travels, no sign of his Nobel medal or snapshots of him with the great men of his day, the tyrant included; just books—his and others'—Babo's eternal friends, and a vase of hyacinths on the nightstand.

El Comandante approached his friend cautiously. He was relieved that Babo was alive but afraid that there was nothing left for them to discuss. In their heyday, their conversations had lasted for days, interspersed with fishing trips and the reverential hush that accompanied their smoking of fine island cigars. There were few subjects they hadn't broached, analyzed, laughed over, and argued about, all the while growing fonder and more admiring of each other. Not that there hadn't been a thorn or two. Once Babo stopped speaking to the tyrant for months over a rust-colored beauty they'd discovered on a visit to El Cobre's foundry. She was just Babo's type, too—pure liquefied mulata sugar. But at the last minute, the tyrant chose her for himself, pulling a revolutionary droit du seigneur. Every now and then the incident rippled through their friendship like a Cuban water snake.

Nonetheless, Babo had proved as savvy about politics as he was at writing about the darkest recesses of the human heart. It was a rare combination in a man of his accomplishments, and there'd been a time when the tyrant had envied his friend's gifts. (In truth, his envy still flared on occasion.) But Babo's unfailing good humor, his generosity toward the Revolution, and his unflagging personal loyalty to El Comandante had won him over. There wasn't another soul on the planet, save Fernando, whom he trusted as much.

"Hombre, what are you doing lying there like a beached whale?"

Babo opened his rheumy eyes and cracked a half smile. That initial spot on his lungs had developed into a tangled web of ailments impossible to unravel. As the afternoon light faded, Babo's surprisingly small study filled with shadows. Night's arrival would console El Comandante, at least until his exhaustion began to feed his paranoia and worsen his mood.

"Hijo de puta," Babo whispered, his grin widening a quarter inch. "Did they tell you I was dead?" The pale light gleamed off the side rail of his bed.

It seemed to El Comandante that something in the room itself, in the shelves of thick, silent tomes, in the collection of vintage typewriters and the fountain pens arranged in a perfect arc across Babo's desk, seemed charged in some imperceptible way. His friend's breathing grew labored, deliberate, as if he had to concentrate on it fully. A nurse who reminded the tyrant of his mother—dark-skinned with sinewy legs—held a handkerchief to Babo's mouth until he expectorated.

"Carajo, you look almost peaceful," El Comandante joked. "That's something we vowed never to become."

The old friends coughed companionably. The nurse poured each of them a glass of water, which their respective wives helped administer.

"All this love and we're still powerless against death," Babo said, regaining his composure. "In the end, I want to leave behind something imagined, not simply recalled."

The tyrant couldn't have disagreed with Babo more, but he was in no mood to antagonize him on his deathbed. No, he would much rather reminisce over his lurid, manic, garish, heroic, *lived* life than dwell on anything that even the great Babo could conjure up. It was action that fueled his ideas, El Líder thought, not the other way around. He was a man of action; action and appetites.

"Facts paralyze," his friend continued, a disconcerting rumbling emanating from his chest. "Imagination frees us."

El Comandante grew impatient. "But what good is imagination without action? No history is made. No lives are changed. Worthless." He registered the discomfort on his friend's face. "You deliver words. I deliver action."

"Words *are* action, mi amigo, as compressed and devastating as any bullet—or caress," Babo said with surprising vigor. "What do we have left except"—he paused—"the adventure of language between two wrecked ships."

"Carajo, everything you say is invention!" the tyrant countered.

"Couldn't I say the same of you?"

Son of a bitch. If Babo weren't so sick, El Comandante would launch into one of his infinite tirades. Instead he sulked.

"Have we forgotten how to laugh at ourselves?" Babo chided. "Then this must be the end."

The two remained silent for a moment, neither wanting to surrender to the other.

Finally, Babo blinked and changed the subject. "These days I prefer the language of rain."

"He's been praying for rain," Gloria interjected dully.

The tyrant turned to her. "And what have you done about it?"

"About what?" She inspected her fingernails.

"The rain."

"Mi cielo, they're in a drought," Delia protested. "Haven't you been listening to the news? Gloria, did you know we have the worst meteorologist in Havana?"

"This is your husband's last request and you haven't found a way to grant it?" El Comandante demanded.

"But, Jefe, how can I—"

"There are machines that can make rain. I could stand on the roof myself with a fucking bucket so that he might—"

"Don't get upset, Papi! This isn't something you can control!" Delia flushed with embarrassment.

The obdurate bells of Mexico City announced six o'clock, echoed by the grandfather clock in the hall. Socialism, or death? What was the damn difference? Babo remained placid in his bed, inhabiting the hour. Then, pink nostrils quivering, he requested his daily ration of chocolate tapioca and dispatched every last wobbly spoonful with enthusiasm. Visibly weakened by the effort, he collapsed onto his pillows and closed his eyes. Perhaps he was traveling back in time, to his childhood, to the river journey with his grandparents that had marked him forever.

The tyrant felt faint, though his heart beat wildly. Delia held a vial under his nose that smelled of Fernando's prison disinfectant. His brother had stayed behind in Havana, tending to emergencies: another hunger striker had tried to hang himself in La Cabaña; Fernando's daughter had imprudently called a dissident blogger "a sex-starved lesbian whore" on national television and was now combating a firestorm of international criticism; and, worst of all, one of the Damas de Blanco* had set herself on fire in the Plaza

---

* Who are we? Women who march to release our politically imprisoned husbands, brothers, lovers, and sons. I've been beaten, harassed, and twice jailed for trying to get my Carlos out. He sold illegal cigars, so what? How the hell else are we supposed to make a living around here?
    —*Jocelyn Matamoros, unemployed*

de Armas with rationed gasoline, like that monk in Vietnam years ago. Were the times really so desperate?

Drowsiness enveloped the tyrant. He didn't want to nap, but his body overruled him. With Delia's help, he settled himself in an overstuffed chair by Babo's bedside, sank his head to his chest, and, like his friend, fell asleep. The two snoozed together, leaving their wives to freely ignore each other. An hour later the men awoke with a start, almost simultaneously. The evening sky was hazy, reflecting the lights and smog of the city. Babo and El Comandante were pleased to find themselves still in each other's company.

"The moon dies with the night on its back." Babo's face creased with emotion. "I thought I had dreamt your visit."

"I'm no dream," the tyrant said, pressing his tongue against his palate. "Nor am I ready to repent or regret!"

Babo laughed a weak facsimile of his laugh. His mind was shorn of most wordplay, but his emotions remained fierce. "To the only son of a bitch who ever came close," he said, quoting himself.

"To the monarch of the word," El Comandante retorted, holding up an imaginary champagne glass.

In the spreading darkness the old friends surrendered to the ordinary happiness of being together, oblivious to the sounds beyond the study: the ringing telephone, a faraway television, the ticking of the grandfather clock, the few drops of rain moistening Babo's windowsill at last.

It was past twilight when El Comandante left Babo's side. What he least expected accosted him on the sidewalk: an ex-lover in red dreadlocks with a teenager—presumably their love child—in tow. Television cameras surrounded them. Supporters shook signs scrawled with accusations: EL COMANDANTE IS A DEADBEAT! PAY UP, PAPI! A cocktail waitress at the Meridian Hotel in the capital, Angela Reyes had flirted with him at a conference of Formerly Non-Aligned Nations (FNAN). It'd ended predictably—in his hotel room as his bodyguards waited outside. He might not have remembered her at all if it weren't for the threats Angela began sending him once she learned of her pregnancy. Next to her slouched a skinny, pimply teenager with multiple tattoos and piercings. There was no way in hell this punk could be his son.

The reporters stampeded toward El Comandante, but he and Delia ducked into the waiting limousine. Outside the tinted windows the crowd chanted: DO THE RIGHT THING! DO THE RIGHT THING! Delia had endured such sordid displays before but never said a word. This was one of the reasons the tyrant loved her, or at least felt sporadic surges of gratitude for her tolerance and discretion. The ride to the airport was miserable, slowed by the fierce rain. Entire neighborhoods of Mexico City were converted to mud and plunged into darkness by a sudden blackout. During the Special Period in Cuba, apagones had been a way of life. On street corners children with wild, squinting eyes peddled Chiclets alongside drenched newspaper vendors and peasant women hawking homemade tamales in plastic baskets.

El Comandante reached across the backseat for Delia's hand. It was cold and inert, and this enraged him. Over the years, the tyrant had refused all paternity tests. Cojones, *he* would decide which children were his. Hadn't he done right by Delia and married her, legitimized their sons? It'd taken twenty years because he'd waited until Ceci Sánchez, his compañera of the Sierra Maestra, had passed away. Yes, this was his Holy Trinity of women: Ceci, Delia, and his accursed first wife, Miriam. Unless he counted his indomitable— even in death—mother, who sometimes visited him during thunderstorms to argue politics. The rain came down harder. Lightning illuminated the night sky. At last, he and his wife arrived at the airport and climbed into the private propeller plane that would take them back to Havana.

Angola

What the hell are you looking at? That's what I really want to say, but I need your money more. Lost both legs and my eyesight outside Luanda with only a month left of my tour. Then I came home—to find what? A hero's welcome? A pension? My fiancée? Ha! One bad joke after another. I still have my dick, but what good is it? The Revolution used me, used thousands of us, then tossed us away. People say it's the same everywhere, but I don't believe them. In Cuba they want their veterans healthy and whole, devoted revolutionaries who'll still sing the national anthem. Fuck that. This country ruined my life, and it keeps on ruining it. Oye, can you spare any change?

—*Abel Padilla, veteran*

Miami

TIRED OF DOING NOTHING ABOUT THE TYRANT?

Yes, Goyo was tired and impotent and infuriated. How many times had he glumly reviewed his life—the fruitless years, days, and hours that he'd wasted *not* fighting to reclaim his homeland? He clicked on the e-mail. There were no explanations, only a map with a cross tucked deep in the Everglades; a date and a time, which happened to be three hours from now. Most likely the message wasn't meant for him, yet nothing had cut through Goyo's layers of equivocation more cleanly. He packed his unused gym bag with a change of clothes, extra underwear, socks, and a stick of deodorant. Then he fetched his Chief's Special .38 from the file cabinet and packed that, too.

Twenty-five minutes later he was pulling out of his parking garage and heading to whatever awaited him in the swamp. He was no longer young, but his hands were still steady enough for him to be a good shot. They—whoever "they" were—couldn't refuse to take him. His brother had died in the Bay of Pigs, his father had shot himself from grief, his first love had hanged herself over that tyrant. Goyo's hatred was incontestable, lavish beyond measure.

About a month after Papá died, he visited Goyo in the middle of the night. His father looked shrunken in his white linen suit, his cuffs frayed, his sallow face averted, mumbling under his Panama hat. "Where are you going, Papi?" Goyo cried out, but his father ignored him. Instead he checked and rechecked his pockets, growing increasingly despondent as he jangled loose keys and change. Goyo wondered if Papá was looking for his watch, the one with the thin gold chain. Of what use would it be to him in the afterlife? Then, without a word, he faded away.

The traffic was light on the highway that divided the northern perimeter of the swamp. Mangroves stretched as far as the eye could see, twisted roots emerging from the brackish water like a form of insanity. A snake crossed the road, its slide of muscles sheathed in stippled yellows and greens. Goyo calmed himself with images of the tyrant lifelessly splayed on a zinc-coated autopsy table. What was his own life worth if he wasn't willing to risk it for what he believed more fervently now than ever: that the despot must be killed and that he, Goyo Herrera, was the one to do it. Yes, he would become one with his fellow Cubans' dreams, restore wholeness after so many fractured years, celebrate their liberation together in the great plaza of Havana.

A sudden downpour forced Goyo to pull to the side of the road. He checked the e-mail's map against his larger one of the area. There were few roads and no specific address he could punch into his GPS. Goyo switched on the radio but got only evangelical stations extolling the virtues of the Holy Spirit. He lowered his window a few inches and breathed in the stench of the swamp. It reminded him of the San Isidro barrio back in the capital, home to brothels and knife fights and herds of illegal goats. A great egret stared at him from atop a clump of mangroves before taking off in slow motion, its magnificent wings like an archangel's.

Goyo felt his hands swelling, his feet aching. A mosquito bit him on the wrist before he could kill it. He rolled up his window and pushed the air conditioner to full blast. If he couldn't stand the heat now, how could he survive the swamp? Coño, he'd forgotten his bug repellent and a hat against the sun. Pa' carajo! José Martí hadn't ridden into battle lathered in sunscreen. What were these incommodities compared to the task ahead? When the rain let up, Goyo decided to follow the main road to Cypress Hammock and let his instincts take over from there. He peered into his rearview mirror and spotted a blue Toyota with New Mexico plates. He dialed his daughter's number and watched as the driver of the Toyota put a phone to her ear.

"Por Dios, Alina, what the hell are you doing here?"

"I could ask you the same thing."

"This is none of your business. Go home!"

"You left your computer on with that creepy message and—"

"I beg of you, hija, turn around and let me be!"

"You're going off the deep end."

"Enough!" Goyo hung up and pressed his foot to the accelerator. He would lose his busybody daughter if it was the last thing he did. There was nobody in front of him, and he pushed his Cadillac to sixty, seventy, eighty miles per hour. His car swerved on the slick road, but he held it steady. His cell phone rang and rang. Goyo had the impulse to shoot out Alina's tires, but he didn't want to injure her. If his daughter showed up at the encampment of coverts, there was no way they'd accept him. Goddamnit, she was gaining on him.

By the time Goyo reached the visitors' center, he was worn out from the strain of the chase. Alina pulled in beside him, got out of her car, and motioned for him to open his door. He refused. Before them a normal-looking family sat around a picnic table merrily cutting up a watermelon. Goyo disregarded his daughter's shouts and her kicks to his Cadillac, which finally caught the attention of a park ranger. Goyo drew circles near his ear in the universal gesture of "crazy." The ranger—name tag Cabrera, a scar from ear to jaw—brandished handcuffs, and a scuffle broke out. Goyo backed away and sped westward. By the time the cops subdued Alina, he would be deep in the swamp with his compatriots.

At a moldy outpost of a boathouse, Goyo commandeered a canoe under an alias and set off to find the band of Freedom Fighters. No longer would he evade his fate. It was close to noon, and the heat blazed around him like a web of flame. This must've been what his brother had endured at the Bay of Pigs. Poor Marcos, who'd broken out in summertime heat rashes, who'd sat in front of electric fans and bowls of ice to cool off, who'd rarely stepped outside their Vedado mansion with its frosted-glass doors and floor-to-ceiling shutters painted, at their mother's behest, with the lives of the saints.

The paddle split and splintered Goyo's palms, grew slippery with sweat. His skull throbbed from the advancing sunburn. Yet he was spellbound by the vegetation, the murky waters, the trills and whirs he couldn't identify except for the ospreys, which were identical to the ones in Cuba. Goyo had heard the Everglades called a river of grass, and he pictured its ancient flow beneath his canoe. It felt tideless, eternal. Its scum rotted in the sun; its reeking ferment enveloped him. He paddled toward wherever he found an opening in the mangroves. A bone wedged in some root appeared to be a femur, judging by its size and shape, and this unnerved him. He needed to rest for a few minutes, restore his energy. Goyo set down his paddle and, with considerable difficulty, slid to the bottom of the canoe. He laid his head against the warm wood of the seat. Exhaustion overtook him, and he slipped into a restive sleep.

In a dream, Goyo trailed Adelina Ponti to the Almendares River. Her dress was tight from her growing belly and cut low under the arms, which exposed soft excesses of breast. After the tyrant had impregnated her, she dropped out of the university and spent her days reading worthless romance novels procured from bookshops on the Calle de la Reina. Now she was crying alone under a blooming ylang-ylang tree. Goyo lamented the thousands of days he hadn't spent at her side. An afternoon shower cooled his brow. It trickled to his lips, reviving him. When he opened his eyes, a half-dozen men in fatigues stared down at him with mocking eyes.

"¿Hombre, que coño haces aquí?" their leader demanded.

The right side of Goyo's face felt on fire, and his throat was cotton-dry. "I am Goyo Herrera," he croaked. "And I am here to fight."

The men burst out laughing, but the leader stopped them with a slash of his hand. One of the soldiers sat on a stump with Goyo's gym bag slung over his shoulder. He was examining the Chief's Special .38.

"I got the message." Goyo's lips clung together as he spoke.

"Este viejo está loco de remate," someone dismissed him.

A burly man emerged from the ganglia of mangroves, advancing on Goyo like a hungry animal. The black mole on his temple looked pasted on. "Who the hell is this?"

"I'm tired of doing nothing," Goyo pleaded. "I can shoot. I'm not afraid to die."

"We have no time to waste, Herrera," the leader said, not unkindly. "You had cojones coming out here, viejo."

The sun continued its maddening glare. This wasn't how it was supposed to be. Around him the swamp gurgled and wheezed, attending to its grim business of decay. Goyo thought of how eventually everything would perish and decompose in this muck, far from civilization's reach. The distant roar of a helicopter prompted the men to vanish back into the swamp. Goyo stayed put, rocking in his canoe. The helicopter grew closer. The mangroves stirred from its intrusion.

"There he is!" The voice was unmistakable, amplified and crackling through a bullhorn. Alina descended from the heavens, as he had expected she would, in a cloud of emerald flies. Goyo had half a mind to turn over his canoe and sink into the hissing abyss. Instead, he tightened his thigh muscles as the rope ladder fell to within reach.

Somehow Alina had convinced the park rangers to leave Goyo in her care. The two said little to each other once reunited. His daughter had trailed him to the swamp in order (purportedly) to save his life. Didn't this mean that she loved him? Goyo wanted to be grateful, but he soon grew too enraged to speak. What next? Clamping a tag on his ankle like he was some goddamn endangered species? Sullenly, he agreed to follow her out of the Everglades. He flipped on the radio again. A news report was followed by a Haitian music program (he understood most of the Creole with his vestigial Canadian French) and a call-in show for troubled lovers.

Goyo had taken his beloved Adelina on three chaperoned dates, the last to a ravishing performance of Mahler's Fifth Symphony at the Gran Teatro de la Habana. Adelina was of Italian descent: her father a once-heralded bass baritone from Ravenna—that Byzantine city by the sea—who came to fame and fortune in the more indolent opera houses of the New World. A week after their symphony date, Adelina fell under the tyrant's spell and lost her senses. A year later she wrote to Goyo, asking him to meet her at the same theater, but he ignored her plea. By then he was engaged to Luisa and had hardened his bruised heart. His pride prevented him from ever approaching Adelina again, though not from sending her money. Only Carla Stracci, his longtime mistress at the UN, marginally reminded him of his beloved, not so much in appearance as in the small gestures: a delicacy of wrist; their charming, clinging syllables. Thinking of the two women weakened Goyo's already considerably weak knees.

As the theatricality of the Everglades gave way to the more groomed vegetation of south Miami, a bulletin announced that El Comandante had decamped to Mexico City to visit his famous writer friend, who was dying of complications from lung cancer. On an impulse, Goyo turned his Cadillac down a leafy side street of Coral Gables, then took the back way to the airport. He laughed to imagine the expression on Alina's face when she realized he was missing again.

The sky grew overcast. Thunderclaps boomed from the south. Goyo savored the relief a storm would bring, but he didn't want it delaying his flight. Of all the billions of variables at his disposal today, he'd chosen the most daring, and this pleased him.

The ticket clerk, a Mexican woman with elephantine legs, asked for his identification.

"I need to get on your next flight to Mexico City."

"No reservation?"

"Only with destiny," Goyo said, instantly regretting it.

"First-class, or coach?"

"What the hell, first-class!" Goyo couldn't contain his elation.

When he learned it would cost him fifteen hundred dollars, however, he switched to economy.

"Passport, please."

"¿Qué?"

"Your passport."

"Carajo, I forgot it." Goyo stood openmouthed. "Is there any way I can travel without it?"

"I'm afraid not."

"This is urgent, señorita. A matter of life and death. Can't you make an exception?" The last thing he wanted was to go home and face Alina.

"Perhaps you would like to travel tomorrow?"

"Tomorrow," Goyo said, sagging with the ugly spectacle of another defeat. "Tomorrow is too late."

6.

Almost Dead

Havana

El Comandante woke up with a start, his legs tangled in the top sheet. Damn these catnaps. Nothing was worse for courting ghosts. He'd had another dream about that hunger striker, Orlando Martínez, his head cowled in a yellow hood. With his bulging eyes and bony hands, that hijo de puta kept calling to him from the grave, twisting and hissing like a snake about to strike. Behind him stood a mob of Damas de Blanco, wailing like a Greek chorus. Insomnia was preferable to this torment.

His sleeping pills only perpetuated the nightmares. The long-dead Che had been popping up, foulmouthed and threatening to expose him. Other adversaries lined up to take their potshots: school yard bullies from Colegio Dolores, peasants he'd executed in the Sierra Maestra, a tremulous semicircle of forsaken lovers that included Adelina Ponti, with her face of pure sorrow. In one dream

Adelina stepped off a cliff into air saturated with a piano sonata, the pleats of her pink dress flaring like a sea anemone.

The tyrant fluffed a pillow and looked out at the sea. How many of his citizens would flee the island tonight under starry, hopeful skies? The Revolution had survived a crippling embargo, a full-scale military attack, shortages of every kind, but nothing on the order of what transpired after the Soviet Union collapsed. For the first time since 1959, people went hungry. Not even the high-protein soy blocks imported from China helped.* Looting broke out in the capital. The crime rate skyrocketed. Butchers were getting laid for a few ounces of skirt steak. Those lucky enough to work in tourism were courted like old-style caciques.

El Comandante appeared on television every night during the Special Period,** exhorting his countrymen to stay optimistic and redouble their efforts for La Revolución. Si finis bonus est, totum bonum erit. If the end is good, everything will be good. But the end was not good. In fact, it was nowhere in sight. When the number of suicides spiked, the tyrant unveiled—with great fanfare—the Psychoanalytic Clinic for Revolutionary Rehabilitation. It was meant to offer citizens an outlet for their miseries. But the hastily assembled therapists were required to keep detailed notes on every disgruntled patient before turning the information over to the authorities. Only a handful of citizens ever took advantage of the clinic's services. El pueblo, it seemed, was reluctant to

---

* People got violently ill from that Chinese soy. One of my neighbors even went blind! Only the dogs seemed to like the stuff, but the dogs here will eat anything. If it says HECHO EN CHINA, I don't touch it. Punto final.
                                              —*Héctor López, meat inspector*

** What a joke! We've never *not* been in a Special Period!
                                              —*H.L.*

unburden itself with "talk therapy." The only person interested in talking, they concluded grimly, was El Líder himself.

The tyrant's eldest son paid him a visit just before lunchtime. As a teenager, Emilio had accused him of purposely stunting his growth, as if this were in the realm of possibility. In their primes, Emilio was one inch shorter than his father. Now with the ignominious shrinkage of age, El Comandante was five inches shorter than his son.

"So what's going on in Iran?"

"You know as much as I do." Emilio had suffered a minor stroke, leaving one side of his face paralyzed. It gave him a permanently discontented air.

"No detonation yet?"

"They're awfully close." Emilio had spent nine years in the Soviet Union (when it was still the Soviet Union) studying nuclear engineering. He was the island's foremost expert on the subject. Puzzlingly, he also collected memorabilia from Nixon's 1972 presidential campaign, including buttons with the slogan *Sock it to me!* His brothers had studied engineering, too, but none practiced the profession. Estéban studied the mating rituals of Cuba's painted snails; Enrique wrote god-awful, state-sanctioned poetry (his latest title: *Sepals of Revolutionary Love*); and Eduardo refurbished old Chevrolets for illegal resale to collectors abroad. What a sorry brood. If it weren't for his wife's interventions, he would've tossed the lot of them off the island long ago. Fernando's children weren't much better. His eldest, a dull-witted sexologist with the shape and demeanor of a Russian tank, got into constant, fruitless cyberscrapes with Cuba's dissident bloggers.

"And the Israelis?" El Comandante asked. They'd been in lockstep with the Americans since before Batista.

"Apoplectic, as usual." Emilio inhaled deeply. "Mami tells me you're not feeling well."

"So you're on a mission of mercy?" The tyrant picked up the remote control and started channel-surfing. Europe's economy was tanking. Another loco had shot up a U.S. college campus. Twenty percent of American men between the ages of nineteen and fifty-four were unemployed. Not a word about him, or his revolution. "The Empire's days are numbered. You can hear the death rattle from here." He pointed at the window. "Close that for me, will you?"

His son forced out the plywood and let the window bang shut.

"Tell me, hijo. Do you think things were better before the Revolution?" The sun streaming in the window warmed his bones.

Emilio gazed past the seawall, as if following a departing ship. But there were no ships at this hour. Nothing left the harbor without his father's express permission. "I'm a scientist," Emilio said, then cleared his throat. "I think some things may have been better before but . . . most things are better now."

"What kind of goddamn answer is that?" El Comandante raised himself on one elbow. "If you're bullshitting me, then what's everyone else doing?"

"I just came to keep you company for a while." His son turned his attention to a TV report about skateboarding bulldogs in Los Angeles.

"Come closer," the tyrant rasped.

Emilio brought his face ten inches from his father's.

"Give me one of your cigars."

"You know the doctors—"

"Fuck the doctors! I'm asking you, man-to-man." He glared at his son until he reached into his jacket pocket and extracted a Cohiba lancero.

"Just don't tell Mami you got it from me."

El Comandante held the puro to his nose. "Give me a light."

Emilio handed his father a book of matches and crossed his arms. The hem of his guayabera was spotted with grease.

"Bola de churre," the tyrant said, and chuckled.

"¿Qué?"

"Dirtball. That's what they used to call me at Colegio Dolores."

Emilio shrugged and left without saying good-bye.

El Comandante and his two brothers had started out as day students at Colegio Dolores, the exclusive Jesuit boarding school in Santiago. To save money, his thrifty father had boarded his sons with a Jamaican family—a widowed piano teacher and her unmarried daughters. The women feigned airs of gentility, but they barely fed the boys, forbade them from playing outside, and forced them to do menial chores, including massaging the widow's arthritic feet. Abelardo, the youngest of the three, died of diphtheria before Christmas. By the end of that first school year, he and Fernando had lost a great deal of weight and their uniforms were in tatters.

It didn't help that they were the illegitimate sons of Papá's relations with their maid. At school, the tyrant contested every insult from his classmates with his fists, or by banging the heads of his opponents against the chapel's brick wall. His most memorable dispute involved Patricio Charbonell, heir to a sugarcane fortune, whom the tyrant forced at knifepoint to the edge of a school balcony with a rope around his neck as the entire student body watched, dumbfounded. If Father Bonifacio had failed to appear when he did, Charbonell would've surely ended up dangling lifelessly in the sunlit end of the Jesuits' courtyard.

El Comandante held up the forbidden cigar and licked it from one end to the other, deftly rolling it against his tongue. Tobacco was in his blood. His mother had been born to sharecroppers in the Vuelta Abajo. At fifteen she'd headed east to work, eventually ensconcing herself on Papá's rural estate. Mamá became famous in the region for her prized English roses and her ease with horses. The tyrant slid the puro between his lips. His hands trembled as he failed to light one match after another. Cojones. What man couldn't light his own cigar? The hardest thing for El Comandante to imagine about death was the lack of cigars.

Finally, the flame held and the fragrant smoke filled his mouth, coated his nostrils and throat. His eyes watered with pleasure as he sank into sacramental reverie. More than doctors or pills or purgatives, this was what he needed.

In the distance, rotting under the sun, stood the Art Deco hotel he'd converted into a political asylum. For a time, it'd housed many of the world's most notorious fugitives—Robert Vesco, Trotsky's assassin, deposed dictators of every political stripe. But the outlaws had grown restless in exile, issuing too many demands on the Revolution's flinty beneficence: coconut macadamia chip cookies, female bodyguards, Glenlivet single malt scotch. Power. None of them could live without it. The despot understood this better than any of them. Still, he'd kept the fugitives around so long as they remained a useful eyesore against capitalism.

El Comandante couldn't have said how much time had elapsed before a horde of his minders stampeded into the room, waving and shouting and pounding on his bed. The flames had ignited his mattress and feather pillows, engulfing him from all sides. The smoke obscured the ocean view. Carajo, he'd set the place on fire.

La Rusa

Ooooh, I love coming to Cuba! The men here know how to appreciate a woman like me. They are not afraid of flesh. Every

time I visit, I pick up a sexy black* man. Look at my honey—
isn't he a beauty? I bought him that gold medallion around his
neck. Mamita, he calls me, mi rusa preciosa. He loves the turn
of my ankle in red satin mules, the waves of my breasts and
belly flesh. Pareces una pintura de Botero, he whispers. They
are flashy, these cubiches, but cultured. Of course, I know it
won't last more than two weeks. Do you take me for an idiot?
The other tourists give me the evil eye when I bring my man
to the rooftop pool, but I know they're just jealous. Pasty,
querulous couples who fantasize about us when they make love.
Here in Havana, dorogoĭ, I am the star of the show.

—*Ivana Kuznetsov, Kiev jeweler*

Miami

Goyo clicked on to the exile website for the latest news on the
tyrant. El Comandante's fever had spiked since early morning and
he'd had another restless nap. For all the minutiae these morons
collected, why couldn't they simply inject the bastard with a lethal
dose of something or other and be done with it? An all-points bulletin interrupted the news as usual: a double agent had set the despot on fire! How badly Goyo wanted to believe it was true. His
housekeeper clattered into the office dragging a sloshing bucket

---

*I come to Cuba to be a man. In France, I cannot afford to keep mistresses, or live
like a king. Here I have two women. My Margarita is black and simple and she
knows how to please me. She smells like fresh, clean earth. My other woman is
more beautiful and light-skinned but she hustles me for this and that. Each dip in
her boyito has its price. Margarita takes what I give her with dignity and gratitude.
I don't love her, but I should.

—*Michel Durand, tire salesman*

and mop. A feather duster was propped in the back pocket of her cargo pants.

"So what's happening with the Old Goat?" Estrella had escaped Cuba two years before on a rickety boat piloted by her ex-brother-in-law. She was no fan of El Líder, but her bitterness was mere topsoil next to Goyo's geological hatred.

"One of our own set him on fire." Goyo sneezed from the stink of the ammonia. "He's almost dead."

"We're all *almost* dead." Estrella sniffed, then went off to clean the guest bathroom.

Goyo ignored his ringing phone for as long as he could before answering.

"Díme, hijo. Are you feeling any better?"

"I'm coming to see you, Dad. I'm bringing Rudy," Goyito announced, and hung up.

Would this hell never end? At times Goyo prayed that his son would die before him; nothing terrible, a quick aneurysm like his mother's. It pained him to admit that Goyito's death might be a lesser tragedy for all concerned. The guilt he felt over his son was unending, an arterial suffering. Without support, Goyito would likely become a ward of the state, or be left to fend for himself on the streets. That winter he'd been homeless in New York had been unendurable for Goyo.

Perhaps if he'd spent more time with his son when he was growing up, taken trips together, things might've turned out differently. When Goyo was five, he and his father had embarked on a train journey from Honduras to Belize. Accompanying them was an Englishman with business interests near Chetumal Bay. Goyo spent hours studying the Englishman's muttonchops and chewing the gum Papá dispensed to keep him quiet. For three days their train rattled through the jungle and along the Caribbean coast, past albino donkeys and chattering monkeys, past a village spit-roasting armadillos for its midday meal, past a man with a square box camera photographing a squat, melancholy couple on their wedding day. By the time the train pulled into Belize City, Papá had secured the shipping rights to all the bananas and coffee produced in the region. Within six months, he would become a very rich man.

Goyo stretched his legs under his desk. His whole body felt bruised, pummeled, like he'd been in a vicious fistfight. Prokofiev's *Peter and the Wolf* drifted in from the classical radio station. He'd played first-chair clarinet in the Jesuit school's orchestra, and he'd loved the part—ah, there it was!—when the cat lunged for the bird and missed. Goyo pushed himself to standing, then spotted his cane lying beyond his reach on the white tiles. He was gingerly bending over when his daughter walked in.

"What the hell are you doing?" she demanded.

Goyo would rather crack his skull than endure her assistance, but he had no choice. Alina picked up the cane and clamped his fist around the handle. Then she informed him that Goyito had called again to say that he'd been pulled over by a state trooper and issued a $240 speeding ticket.

"How fast was he going?" Goyo asked, not really wanting to know.

"Ninety." She extracted a handful of shelled pistachios from her shirt pocket and flung them into her mouth.

"The last time he was going a hundred twenty and landed in jail for a week. It took everyone I knew to get him out."

"Maybe you should've left him there." Alina's mouth churned with nuts.

"Por Dios, hija, you know he isn't well."

"That's been your excuse since forever. You've fucking crippled him with that attitude."

Goyo was in no mood to argue. The quarrels with his daughter left him depleted and resolved absolutely nothing. And yet he loved her. What else could he do?

"Did you hear that El Comandante is giving a speech tonight?"

"He's not dead?"

"What makes you say that?"

Goyo tamped down his disappointment. So the son of a bitch hadn't been burned alive. He was sick and tired of the false alarms. Coño, he'd better get busy. If Goyito was barreling toward him on the Florida interstate, then he'd try to welcome him like a prodigal son, Great Dane and all. First stop would be La Carreta to pick up some roast pork, black beans, fried plantains, an assortment of desserts (they both had a sweet tooth). They'd have a fine feast, talk warmly, familiarly, as if tragedy hadn't struck long ago. Goyo dialed his mistress's number.

"Mi amor, I thought you'd never call," Vilma purred.

He heard the clackety-clack of her computer. It wasn't rudeness that kept Vilma typing, but multitasking. These days people thought nothing of answering their cell phones on a lunch date, or texting and talking simultaneously while keeping an eye on whatever wide-screen TV was in the vicinity. Even doctors' waiting rooms had them now. There was no escaping the meaningless stream of information.

"Vilmita, I won't be able to see you today."

"Not yesterday? Not today?" Clack, clack, clack. "You don't love me anymore?"

"My son is coming to visit. I have to pick up some lechón."

"Tell me the truth, Goyo. Is there someone else?"

"Claro que no, mi reina, it's just that—"

"Then I'll meet you at La Carreta in twenty minutes." Click.

Vilma would probably want another quickie in his Cadillac. Lately, she'd been insisting on elaborate role play: the sheikh and the harem girl; the girls' field hockey coach and his star player

(Vilma had brought the puck). What next? Cavorting with sea mammals? Goyo didn't know how much longer he could brave her exhausting charades. He longed for the sweet idleness of holding hands or even a straightforward missionary position, tough as it was on his knees.

Goyo turned off the radio and navigated down the marble hallway. Even with his antiskid slippers, he had to watch his step. Safely in the bedroom, he tugged off his pajama bottoms, balanced on the edge of the bed, and pulled on navy blue slacks, a white polo shirt, and his red jacket. Thanks to Luisa, his every ensemble in Miami was a patriotic statement. Wallet, keys, a comb through what remained of his hair, and he was ready to go. For their fiftieth wedding anniversary his wife had made him sit for a couple's portrait, a dazzling deception of optical illusion orchestrated by Luisa to make her look twenty years younger. He'd looked like her dirty old uncle.

His car was parked in its new, cheaper spot in the southeast corner of the garage. Luisa had been appalled when he'd driven home the mustard-colored Cadillac with its black leather interior—a killer bee, she'd called it—but it'd been on clearance and was heavy as a tractor. He felt secure in the car, as if the industrial heartland had been welded into its every inch. Besides, his father had always bought Cadillacs. Goyo turned on the ignition, twisted his torso, and draped his arm over the seat as he backed out. Then he steered the behemoth down the narrow, twisting ramp and into the obliterating Florida sun. With a push of a button, the air conditioner roared to full blast.

As he cruised down Crandon Boulevard, Goyo took note of the civic improvements on Key Biscayne: newly planted palms in the median, a refurbished playground, the traffic light that had supplanted an obstructed stop sign. Even the community center had a fresh coat of paint. Such evidence of progress buoyed Goyo, gave him hope that, against all odds, people could work together for the common good. He regretted his own missed opportunities to make a difference. His daughter was right, he thought glumly. No worthwhile epitaph would ever be chiseled on his tombstone.

Vilma was waiting for him, posing beside her orange Honda. She wore a clingy beige dress decorated with a V-shaped cluster of rhinestones that looked like a flock of migrating birds. Vilma loved flash, exulted in it. Coño, just look at how she sashayed toward his car! Her locomotion was a form of genius particular to Cuban women, expressly designed to torment every male beholder. Watching his mistress move toward him on high heels, gathering force like an impending hurricane, made Goyo roll down his window and release a slow whistle.

Vilma slid into the passenger side of his Cadillac.

"Your place, querida?" he crooned.

"I can't. Mami is playing dominoes with her friends."

"To the beach then?"

Vilma pulled the seat belt across her voluptuous hips and breasts. There was a stretch of the state park that would be deserted this time of day. Goyo turned down the road strewn with pine needles and found their preferred spot. He kept the engine running for the air-conditioning and turned on an oldies station that featured Cuban classics from the forties and fifties. A bolero scorched the close air of the Cadillac. *Soy ese vicio de tu piel que ya no puedes desprender, soy lo prohibido / Soy esa fiebre de tu ser que te domina sin querer, soy lo prohibido . . .*

Vilma slipped off her rings and bracelets, tucking them into the glove compartment, and unpinned her dyed blond hair. Then with a swift flick of her wrist she unzipped Goyo's trousers and deftly massaged him to life. Ay, the woman was sublimely dexterous! Goyo closed his eyes as they kissed, picturing Vilma as an eight-armed Indian goddess bestowing her lusty pleasures upon him. At this moment he wasn't the least bit concerned whether his mistress was after his money, or expected him to put her half-wit son through chiropractor school, or pony up for her aging mother's mounting medical bills (la pobre had Alzheimer's). In her merciless beige dress, so tight it looked like a lusciously dimpled second skin, Vilma could ask nothing of Goyo that he wouldn't willingly, gratefully, give.

An hour later Goyo was back at La Carreta buying roast pork and desserts for his son. He felt vaguely ashamed, as he often did after an assignation with the sexpot bank teller. Fortunately, none of his meager thespian skills had been required to consummate the act. Luisa had often accused him of being attracted to trashy women, and he couldn't deny it. Shame was erotic. He had the Jesuits to thank for that. But Goyo was also blessed with a good lover's ample sense of what was beautiful. To him, every woman had something: a graceful neck, fetching knees, sultry lips. Even as a young man, he'd preferred his lovers maduritas. In his opinion, women were at their best after forty.

The bakery counter girl at La Carreta's—boyish, with cartoon orange hair and smelling of pound cake—talked Goyo into buying bread pudding, coconut flan, and enough flaky guava pastries to feed a baseball team. Carefully, she packed everything into a glossy white box, then penciled her number on the back of his receipt.

"I'm sure you'll be happy with your selection."

"Señorita, I already am."

One of the benefits of being old and rich in Miami was that the social odds were decidedly in his favor. At his wife's funeral, a couple of her covolunteers from the Red Cross had had the audacity to jump-start their flirtations. To his credit, Goyo had remained a chaste widower for nearly three months before taking up with the irrepressible Vilmita. Mentira. He'd made an exception for Mrs. Anderson, a former Rockette who'd shown up at his condo eight days after Luisa's burial wearing a sequined pink leotard and fishnet stockings under her mink coat. God bless Mrs. Anderson.

Goyo settled into his Cadillac, checked the mirrors, and sidled into traffic. In the four and a half seconds that it took him to straighten his wheel, a black Camaro with tinted windows slammed into him from behind. The impact jolted his spine and sent his Cadillac crashing into the air pressure pump of the Shell station. The pain radiated from his sternum, where the seat belt had struck. His sacrum flared with needle points. Blood oozed from where he'd bitten his tongue. Goyo's fists stiffened on the steering wheel, and his right foot was stuck to the brake, as if a curse had frozen it there. The driver of the Camaro jumped out, swearing a blue streak.

The ambulance arrived, sirens wailing. Against his protests, the attendants lifted Goyo onto a stretcher and slid him into the back of the ambulance like a corpse. They checked his blood pressure, injected him with who knew what, and strapped his legs down, all the while discussing the prospects of Los Crocodilos, the city's second-string baseball team, a source of heartbreak to its many violence-prone fans. There'd been talk of pitting Cuba's national team (an all-star lineup that included Bobby Relleno, a once-in-a-generation pitcher who'd be cleaning up in the States given half a chance) against an American one, but exile leaders had put a stop to that tentative thawing of bilateral relations.

As the ambulance sped across the causeway that connected Key Biscayne to the steaming maze of Miami's streets, the pain seared through Goyo's body. He tried to distract himself with baseball memories. In Honduras, he and his friends had played with broomsticks and bottle caps that they'd bundled together with rubber bands. Later, he played on his school teams in Cuba and

in Canada, occasionally distinguishing himself with outfield heroics: leaping into the bleachers to intercept a ball, and once pulling
a Willie Mays over-the-shoulder catch (before there was a Willie
Mays) to triumph over the execrable Montreal Moose.

Goyo was growing drowsy. The attendants must've given him
a sedative. Through the back door windows he spotted a pair of
herons, elegant against the blustery Miami skies. As he slipped into
unconsciousness, he began to dream that he was wandering around
a sepia-toned city wearing Old Testament robes. His left big toe
was blackened with fungus and his wife's perfume suffused the air,
a floral amalgam so potent that it'd made his eyes water in close
quarters. "Luisa, is that you? I've come to join you, mi amor!" He
might as well cover his bases. Goyo missed his wife, but he wasn't
looking forward to meeting up with her in the afterlife, not after
today's boisterous romp with Vilma.

A tropical island floated into view, chalked with cumulus clouds.
He longed to reach it, but there was no cliff to leap off, no sea to
traverse. Then as if propelled by a giant spring, Goyo found himself
streaking through the clouds like a cannonball. Coño, I'm flying,
he thought loud enough to hear. He raised his arms to temper the
turbulence, but a whacking pressure kept them at his sides. His
robes ballooned in the wind, and Goyo realized, to his mortifica-
tion, that he wasn't wearing so much as a jockstrap. An enormous
bird—a raven or a vulture, he couldn't tell which—with feathers
so sleekly black they looked oiled, appeared out of nowhere and
cruised beside him. Goyo tried to wave, hoping it was friendly
and disinclined to peck at his vulnerable flesh. A row of hooked
umbrellas, also pitch-black, droned by.

"Dad!" Goyo felt two sharp slaps against his cheeks. His head
felt like a pile of broken bricks. Slowly, his eyes fluttered open to
find his daughter's large-pored face hovering uncomfortably close
to his own.

7.

Prime Time

Havana

Fernando strode into El Comandante's room without knocking. He was in full military uniform after his meeting with the Joint Chiefs of Staff. The lot of them had been ordering an immoderate number of cut-rate tanks and artillery from North Korea. With 10 percent of the island's population employed by the armed forces, Fernando considered these purchases a necessary bulwark against unrest. His goal: to keep the Revolution rebellion-proof by achieving the perfect ratio of military personnel to civilians. Unfortunately, he was less interested in other aspects of running the country. The economy was in a shambles, the hospitals had no aspirin, and nobody got what their ration books promised except for their monthly quotas of sugar and rum.

"You had an accident?" Fernando asked tentatively.

"¡Que tonto! You think I deliberately set myself on fire?"

"Cálmate, hermano. Who did this to you?"

"Have you seen the news?" Reports of the conflagration had been immediately broadcast on the Miami exiles' news stations.

"Same old lies." Fernando smoothed his mustache.

"How did they know about this in ten fucking seconds?"

"I'll look into it right away."

"I want everyone investigated." The tyrant felt the stirrings of another conspiracy afoot, and he wanted it quashed before it got out of hand.

Fernando's back was ramrod straight. He was a veritable fountain of youth next to his ailing older brother. By nightfall, he would find out who was behind the news leak and have them arrested.

"How the hell am I supposed to relax when their spies are watching me take a crap and smoke my last cigar?"

Fernando's eyes drifted to the wall clock.

"I want to talk to the people tonight. Clear out all other programming."

"Do you think that's advisable?"

It was Thursday, and there'd be complaints over the cancellation of the wildly popular telenovela from Argentina. The lead actress, a callipygian hellion from the Pampas, played a nymphomaniac chef who wielded a meat cleaver like a martial artist.

"What excuse can you give me, Fernando? That our people would rather watch *Gaucho Love* than listen to me?"

"I don't like seeing you so agitated. You need to rest."

"I'll be fucking resting for eternity!"

Fernando had suffered countless of his brother's tantrums over the years. To say anything else at this point would only invite more abuse.

"The people need to know that the Revolution must go on, with or without me." El Comandante pulled at his beard. "Those gusanos will undo everything, change the street names, tear apart our history."

"That won't happen, I promise you—"

"Who'll take over once we're gone, Fernando? When we die, so will the Revolution."

"The Revolution will never die. The people will—"

"The people will sell us out for a bar of soap!" the despot cried, spittle flying.

During the worst of the Special Period, after the Soviet Union collapsed and its five billion dollars in annual subsidies to Cuba along with it, when basic necessities were scarce and the plumpish populace lost, on average, twenty-two pounds (statistics were kept on such matters), what Cubans complained about most bitterly was the lack of soap. The Revolution was brought to its knees, its citizens forced into prostitution (often for a few hotel toiletries), because the government couldn't keep them squeaky clean.

"You underestimate them—"

"Or a cell phone. Or a plate of dichoso pork chops! We might convince everyone on this island that the sea is red, but let's not deceive ourselves!"

"If I believed you, I'd put a bullet in my head." Fernando lowered his voice. "You're overexcited. Let me take care of this."

El Comandante shifted onto his right hip, then changed the subject. "And what's this I hear about plans to build luxury casinos in Varadero?"

"It w-will attract a higher caliber of tourist." Fernando stuttered when he was nervous. He didn't dare tell his brother about his preliminary talks with the Mexicans.*

---

* **Radio Bemba:** Fernando is looking to partner up with Mexico for a share of the drug trade. But you know what they say: cartels = organized crime; government = disorganized crime.

"We're not that desperate yet. Cancel it."

"But—"

"I said cancel the casinos. We're not goddamn Monaco here! Whatever happened to going green, anyway?"

"We'll never be in the black by going green," Fernando quipped.

"Cojones, you sound like a captain of industry."

"Hermano, we *are* the captains of industry here."

His brother had been succumbing to too many bourgeois indulgences of late—Rolexes, hot tubs, golf, and now casinos. Some Communist ideologue he'd turned out to be. El Comandante didn't bother asking about the disastrous real estate reforms already under way.

"And the Bay of Pigs reenactment?"

"We're having trouble getting those old planes to work." Fernando avoided his brother's gaze. "Besides, no one wants to play the bad guys."

"Who the hell gets to decide what they want to do around here?" El Comandante struggled to sit upright. "Listen to me, Fernando. Everything must be perfect. Down to the combatants' stinking underwear. Do you hear me? The eyes of the world will be watching us again."

"I'm on it," Fernando whined, then turned around and left.

Let him sulk, the tyrant grumbled. The Revolution's party days were over. The sooner Fernando realized this, the better. The two were overly attuned to each other's moods. It'd begun when they were boys and Fernando inexplicably stopped talking. For eight months he relied on his older brother to speak for him, to say Fernando hurt his knee, or needs to take a shit, or wants vanilla ice cream. One day they snuck into a neighborhood cockfight, and the favored rooster swiftly decapitated the other and plucked out its eyes in the first round. "Puta madre, did you see that?" With those words, Fernando rejoined the ranks of the articulate. Now cockfighting was making a comeback in the capital. The best ring, by all accounts, was in Regla. Fernando wanted to shut it down, but the despot advised him to wait and strike when the ring was more flush with cash.

A pair of dazzling peacocks strutted and shrieked in the gardens below. The birds had been shipped from Madagascar at his wife's request. El Líder studied their tremulous, iridescent plumage. These two had been impressing each other for years without a single female to distract them. When he'd complained to Delia about being surrounded by maricones, she'd nibbled on his ear and said: "Mi amor, you know as well as I do that boy animals are prettier than the girls." Who was he to argue?

A stack of fresh reports was piled high on his desk: annual nickel production, last winter's lobster harvest, revisions to the elementary school curriculum, tobacco exports to Switzerland, illegal marijuana production in Oriente, the trade imbalance with Mozambique, an exposé on the cross-dressing babalawos of Camagüey, another on Baracoa's illicit moonshine operators. (Five people had died from the sweet potato liquor.) How the hell did he know what was true anymore? People told him only what they thought he wanted to hear. Nobody had the nerve to say that this plan was unsound, or that most government employees didn't bother to show up for work on any given day. Cuba was riddled with corruption, hustlers, parasites; plagued by a culture of sinecure, amiguismo, back-scratching, ball-scratching. If you didn't lie, cheat, or steal* you were considered stupid or incredibly naïve. If you happened to be a genuinely honest, hardworking revolutionary, you came under the worst scrutiny of all: accused

---

* *Stealing* is an ugly word, Papito, but I ask you this: when I steal your entry fee from the state, why do you call that "theft"? Everyone here works for slave wages, so I ask you: who's robbing whom?
    —*Yvette Aguirre, Partagás factory tour guide*

of being a spy, a sellout angling for some negligible advantage over your neighbor.

Seagulls soared along the shore, peering down at the glinting sea for fish. El Comandante took a swig of cognac from a flask hidden in his nightstand. It disheartened him to be so infirm and uncommanding. If only he could resuscitate the spirit of the early days, when the literacy campaign had taught a million peasants to read. Or figure out how to become a martyr, if he wasn't already too damn old for that. In the fifties, Orthodox Party leader Eddie Chibás had shot himself in the stomach on his weekly radio show over a stupid political embarrassment and had become an instant saint. How Cubans loved their martyrs, roasting them over the fires of memory like suckling pigs!

The tyrant fixated on a crack in the ceiling. It looked, dispiritingly, like the state of Florida. For decades he'd ruled the country by jeep, traveling to its remotest corners to oversee the installation of electric generators, or the building of sugar refineries, or to slap the back of every last worker at a copper processing plant. His tireless work used to inspire his people. Not anymore. He felt cheated. So much effort, and for what? To watch his island sink into mediocrity and wholesale thievery? Each brick filched from a construction site, each vial of medication sold on the black market was a slap to his face.

The abuses got more outrageous every day. Just yesterday he'd heard that prison buses were being rented out for weddings, quinceañeras, and beach shuttles. That three tanks' worth of oil from human remains (stolen from the Guanabacoa crematorium) were being sold on Havana's streets as cooking oil. That everyone—rappers, cartoonists, school children—was mocking the moringa, a miraculous plant he'd taken great pains to import from India to feed the people. Black market hustlers had even gotten ahold of the pesticide from the campaign against dengue fever and were auctioning it off to the highest bidder. Nobody on the whole goddamn island did a lick of work but complained all day about the lack of fucking mops. His were a people sans rigueur, as Napoleon might've put it. They expected the country to prosper without sacrifices on their part.

How the hell could he *not* take it personally?

El Comandante coughed up a knot of phlegm and summoned El Conejo with the push of a button. His principal adviser appeared without delay, nose twitching, teeth so severely splayed that they invited both revulsion and pity. El Conejo didn't keep notes, relying instead on his computer database of a brain. In nineteen years of service, he'd forgotten nothing, nobody, not a single salient detail entrusted to him by the tyrant. The man couldn't be blackmailed either, because he'd never been known to so much as blink with carnal interest at another living creature.

"Find out what's going on with those hunger strikers. I want a full accounting." People were surprised at how soft the tyrant's voice could be in private, too; so opposite his public thunder.

"A sus órdenes, Jefe."

Towels

Everyone thinks just because I work at a resort that I'm rolling in money. But the tourists who come here don't leave tips. Since they're on prepaid package tours, it doesn't occur to them to leave me so much as a miserable peso for cleaning their rooms. So here's what I do: short them a towel and pretend it was they who lost it. The hotel charges fifteen dollars for a lost towel, so it makes sense for them to pay me a peso or two to "find" it. If the guests indignantly refuse (only the Germans refuse), they'll still be charged and I'll get my cut from the front desk.

—*Idalia Ferrer, chambermaid*

⎯ꕥ⎯

Havana

Every public appearance by the Maximum Leader required the efforts of dozens. If he didn't look perfectly groomed and lucid—tremor-free, no slurring of words or faltering of any kind—the rumor mill worked overtime churning out more lies. The latest outrage making the rounds would be ludicrous if it weren't so poisonous: that the tyrant was, in fact, already dead and the government was using a body double to maintain stability. But the lies that irked him most took aim at his manhood: that cancer had eaten away two-thirds of his balls; that his pinga had shriveled to the size of a Vienna choirboy's. Maybe he should drop his pants on television and show those bastards what he still had between his legs!

Around him, the TV station was on high alert. Everyone was running back and forth and talking at once. His nephew Javier was the producer in charge of this mayhem. An ambitious little man with a theatrical streak, he was the opposite of his taciturn father. Whenever El Líder looked into his nephew's eyes, he saw someone who wanted to stand in his shoes before he'd stepped out of them.

"Por favor, Comandante, look this way." The makeup artist moved El Líder's chin an inch to the right and patted some foundation on his nose with a spongy wedge. She'd been entrusted to make him look as healthy and youthful as possible by minimizing his liver spots, lightening his under-eye pouches, tinting his lips and cheeks with a touch of color. Endless mariconería, but he submitted to these indignities for the sole purpose of deflecting viewers' attention from his battered appearance to the substance of what he had to say.

A violent debate broke out over the degree of formality appropriate for El Comandante's first speech in fourteen months. Should he stand in military dress behind a podium (with its added assurance of support), or appear relaxed on a sofa, more like the commander in chief emeritus? If this was going to be his swan song, the tyrant decided, then he would go down—if he was going down—like a soldier. A staff physician injected him with vitamins while a nurse spooned cough suppressant into his mouth. His dentures were pinching like the devil, but there was no time to adjust them.

If there was any grumbling about the bumping of the Argentine telenovela, nobody dared say so to his face. Often, he wished that Cuba could grow rich again. The despot recalled the fleeting possibility some years back that the island might be sitting atop huge oil reserves. Before the exploratory drilling even started, the United States had filed a slew of lawsuits, claiming that the oil, should it exist, belonged to them. In the end the reserves were far smaller than El Comandante had hoped and far too costly to drill. As his best economist told him: "Trying to extract it would put us all back in loincloths."

A trio of perfumed wardrobe assistants helped the tyrant into his uniform. The jacket was heavy with medals. Why was it that the most beautiful women worked in television? For a time, El Comandante had preferred the taut angularity of ballerinas (Cuba produced the finest dancers in the world). Yet for all their grace and passion under the floodlights, they proved inhibited in bed, too critical of their bodies. To them, an ounce of fat was the stuff of tragedy. He'd devoted a great deal of thought to what constituted the perfect woman. He had his proclivities, of course—blondes with blue or green eyes, tiny waists, ample hips, and the younger the better. Women over forty, with rare exceptions, were best viewed fully clothed or in the dark, though many were good for the game all night long. Ay, to have seen Delia as a seventeen-year-old in a tight white bathing suit strolling along the beach at—

"Jefe, I have the news you requested."

Irritated, the dictator turned toward his adviser. "I'm about to go on the air."

"Infiltrated by foreign agents. Potential fiasco." El Conejo barely moved his lips when he spoke. His consonants were mere fumes. "The Church, too, is involved."

"That asshole Mexican bishop?"

"Along with the Pope and peninsular agents." El Conejo's nostrils flared.

The tyrant had underestimated the international impact of those goddamn hunger strikers. He didn't know who was worse— those idiots starving themselves, the bloggers spewing lies, or the Damas de Blanco subjecting themselves to daily beatings and arrest. Those bitches might turn out to be most dangerous of all. Hadn't the Mothers of the Plaza de Mayo brought down the generals in Argentina? And those Mirabal sisters, murdered under Trujillo, had set in motion his demise. Assassination plots he knew how to handle. Armed insurrection. Political dirty dealings. But unarmed women? Men starving themselves in the name of freedom? Damn it, he'd have them force-fed if it came down to it. Not a single one of them was going to croak on his watch.

"Let's get this show started." He thrust his cane at an underling and hobbled to center stage. The lights brightened and the cameras rolled. El Comandante barely waited for the last notes of the national anthem before he broke in: "Nobody, do you hear me? Nobody will steal this revolution away from us. I'd prefer to see it in ruins than sold off, piecemeal, to the highest bidder. The day is coming, ciudadanos, when your faith in our great society will be tested."

Damn it, how he loved to hear his voice fill a room; nothing was more powerful to him. Nothing sounded more like Cuba than his voice. It was bigger than him somehow. Oceanic. Invincible. He was two people: him and his voice. Fuck them all, he thought.

"I'm well aware that there are persons at home and abroad who've been plotting, under the guise of empty martyrdom, to embarrass our revolution in the eyes of the world. Listen to me well, counterrevolutionaries and imperialist coverts: your tricks will not be tolerated! Not by me nor by the legions of good revolutionaries who continue to carry on in the spirit of Che!"

The dictator looked directly into the eye of the biggest camera, which was moving in for a close-up, black and glossy as a Cyclopean owl's. He shifted from one leg to the other, felt the grind of bone in socket, imagined himself flying through the air, a basketball at the tips of his fingers, rotating light.

Carajo, where was he?

"Next month, we'll begin the first in a series of historical reenactments of our revolution, to remind ourselves—as well as our friends and enemies around the globe—how hard we've fought, how much we've been willing to sacrifice for our goals. Never in the history of mankind has one small country accomplished such gargantuan deeds. Not only here at home, where freedom and prosperity have reigned for nearly six decades, but abroad, where we've sent legions of our doctors and nurses and teachers, who've struggled, and continue to struggle, in solidarity with our friends and fellow revolutionaries."

El Comandante touched the microphone on his lapel. It was round as a beetle, reminiscent of the Ministry of the Interior's antiquated bugs. A screeching echoed through the studio, and the soundman jerked off his headphones. The tyrant preferred the bulbous, old-fashioned microphones, the ones he could adjust and tap and caress while his next volley of thoughts coalesced. Tonight he wanted to strike fear in his listeners, renew their unswerving dedication.

"Do you think the reactionary Yankee henchmen do what we do? Why do their slums teem with poverty and the unemployed? Why do their people die from a lack of basic health care? Why do millions of their homeless roam the streets? Why, ciudadanos, are the poodles in Beverly Hills taken to plastic surgeons for tummy tucks? Profit, and more profit, that's why! It is profit, not justice, that motivates the capitalist scum—and they will step on, overthrow, murder, or destroy anyone who gets in their way. Necessities that we provide to each and every one of you free of charge cost infinitely more than luxuries for a few. Think about it: you can buy a thousand bicycles for the price of one brand-new Cadillac!"

Fernando made a chopping motion at him from the wings, but his brother ignored him. Focus, the tyrant reminded himself. Focus.

"These historical reenactments, ordered by me, will bring to life the most illustrious days of our revolution. The inaugural event will be a solemn remembrance of our triumph at the Bay of Pigs. Never before had the imperialist colossus to the north been defeated, much less by an adversary a fraction of its size, with a fraction of its fighter planes, ammunitions—"

A tremor skittered up the back of El Comandante's leg and spread to his buttocks, which began twitching like a rumba dancer. A milky substance occluded his vision. Focus, focus.

"What the Yankees hadn't counted on was that our material deficiencies were nothing compared to our surplus of determination—the determination of a people unwilling to behave like the slaves they kept enchained for centuries. The Empire's days are numbered. Do you hear me? Numbered! But . . . but . . . our revolution has only just begun!"

Something pink swirled behind his eyes, a fleeting iridescence. He heard his mother singing at twilight, a plangent song from another century. *Bésame, bésame mucho / Como si fuera esta noche la última vez / Bésame, bésame mucho / Que tengo miedo a perderte, perderte después . . .* *

"So I am here tonight, ciudadanos, to exhort you to fight like those brave men and women at the Bay of Pigs, who saved you from a fate still suffered by millions around the world and who—"

A cramp seized his other leg and his breath came in ragged bursts. The tyrant forced himself to continue. "Furthermore, it has come to my attention that shameful irregularities and abuses of our resources are taking—" And then he passed out.

---

* This is our most lucrative song. We pick out the fattest, ugliest tourist we can find in La Plaza de Armas and love her up with it. Tony plays guitar, Miguel has the voice, and I put on my Panama hat and move in for the kill. When she opens her purse to give us a tip, I get a good look at what's inside. More songs, another tip. A kiss or two, another tip. You never know where it might end. If she insists "No más," we move on to the next one. Later, we divide the spoils.
                                                                    —*Luis Rivera, hustler*

8.

Sugarcane

Miami

Perhaps it was the heat and agitation of these last days—the Everglades; his son's incessant phone calls; the vigorous rendezvous with Vilma in his Cadillac; the rear-ending by that balsero in the stolen Camaro (the accident had made the evening news and revived the debate over elderly drivers, a hot topic in Florida); his daughter's badgering him about finances; the continual pricking and prodding by the medical staff since his arrival at the hospital some hours ago—but Goyo had had enough. He scowled at the mule-faced nurse and refused to roll over for another injection. No, no, y no. The ensuing silence magnified the hum and whine of the medical machinery.

"Dad, don't be difficult." Alina crossed her arms, gearing up for battle. She pushed aside a pair of monstrous cameras hanging from her neck. "If you keep up the militant psycho act, they're going to transfer you to the loony bin."

Goyo didn't move a muscle. The nurse placed her syringe on a metal tray with a ping and left the room. Victory. But the pain, carajo! His leg was immobilized in some plastic contraption, and his blackened toe looked twice its normal size. The doctor told him that he'd probably broken his leg when he hit the brakes, but Goyo found that implausible. Alina pulled out what looked like a huge metal spider from her shoulder bag and unfolded a tripod. She positioned the larger of the two cameras on it and aimed the lens at his face. Let her take his picture. She would get nothing from him but a spectral trace. He had more important things to do.

"He's coming up," Alina announced.

"Who?" Goyo smoothed the front of his hospital gown and shifted to a more comfortable position.

"Goyito. I told him where to find us."

The phone rang, and Goyo reached for it. It was the hospital receptionist complaining that his guest was insisting on bringing in a Great Dane. "You better talk to him."

"For God's sake, Goyito, leave Rudy in the car. The hospital has rules. You can't bring a fucking dog in here!"

Goyo instantly regretted speaking harshly to his son. Who knew what might set off another bout of self-destruction? He'd read somewhere that a proclivity for suicide was genetic, a deep cellular longing. Why had some men jumped out their windows after the 1929 stock market crash while others patiently rebuilt their fortunes? His father had lost everything at the onset of the Revolution, but there were thousands like him who hadn't killed themselves, who'd worked as janitors or waiters, biding their time until they could grow rich again. But when Papá decided something, nobody could stop him.

"My father was the king of Cuba!" he blurted out to no one in particular.

Goyito stood in the doorframe carrying a dwarf areca palm in a terracotta pot. Its fronds gave him the appearance of sporting waxy wings, an ecological innocence. He looked heavier than the last time Goyo had seen him, and he wore a malodorous, salmon-colored tuxedo from the seventies with a ruffled shirt, matching cummerbund, and scuffed-up sneakers with the laces untied.

"Jesus Christ, who did this to you?" Alina looked her brother up and down.

It pained Goyo to see his children together. It redoubled his sense of failure.

"Come here, hijo. Give your father a kiss."

Goyito shuffled toward him, stiff as a mannequin, and set the potted palm down at the foot of the bed. His wrists jutted out of his too-short sleeves. He extended a hand, like the Pope offering his ring to be kissed. There were dimples where the knuckles should be.

"It's a pretty little palm tree, Goyito. Gracias." Goyo brought his son's stubby hand to his cheek.

An afternoon thunderstorm erupted, rattling the hospital windows. An hour ago it was coasting over Cuba.* A flock of parakeets chattered in the coral tree. Goyito narrowed his eyes, as if trying to decipher the birds' litany of injuries. His son could be

---

*It hadn't rained in weeks when the mother of all thunderstorms hit. Rain slashed our village, then big chunks of hail fell like God Himself was throwing stones at us from heaven. My two chickens were too stupid to run for cover, so I dashed out to look for them and found them dazed, one of them bloody, under Violeta, my neighbor's cow. I rescued them and ran like hell through the mud, holding my gallinas close all the way home.

—*Heriberto Montuyo, campesino*

stubbornly inarticulate, but he understood every chirp and bark in the animal kingdom. Goyito began sweating profusely, as if some internal faucet had been turned on. Rivulets dripped off his forehead, slid down his neck, wilted the ruffles on his shirt. All color seemed to wash out of him.

"Alina, call the doctors!" Goyo shouted. His monitors twittered, red lines spiking.

"I-I-I wanted to come for the funeral," Goyito stammered. There was a gap where his front teeth used to be.

"What funeral, Goyito? Nobody has died here. Alina, what did you tell your brother?"

"What the fuck—" she sputtered.

Goyito's eyes teared up, but he betrayed no other emotion.

"Ay, hijo, you're just tired from your trip. Alina will take you home so you can rest. She's going to pick up some lechón y pastelitos for you and Rudy."

"I'm going to *what*?"

"Por favor, Alina. Let's not argue for once. If you won't be of help, then just go away." Goyo waved her off with a flutter of his wrist. With much clanging and muttering of obscenities, Alina collected her equipment and left.

Goyito looked down at his feet, then climbed onto the hospital bed. He put his damp, shaved head against his father's chest and fell instantly asleep.

"Now that's a good boy," Goyo said. "You rest now, you rest." He stroked his son's head, bristly with stubble, felt the punctual beat of his heart. A vein, thick as a varicose, snaked up the side of Goyito's neck. His nostrils seemed enlarged, too, as if he were sucking in more than his share of oxygen. Goyo unbuttoned the top of his son's shirt and tried to tug off the tuxedo jacket. A crusty elbow peeped through a tear in the sleeve.

The summer he'd turned twelve, Goyito had slept excessively. Goyo couldn't have imagined what was wrong at the time. It turned out that his son had been experimenting with powerful barbiturates. Back in Havana, nobody he knew had taken drugs or had any idea how to obtain them. In his day, the debauchery of young men was of another sort altogether. Rum, yes. Women, yes. All-night carousing, yes. But drugs? That was something that happened only in Hollywood gangster movies.

Lectures he had given Goyito. Man-to-man talks. Sermons to nowhere. He'd even hit upon the idea of ranking decisions like Olympic medals: gold, silver, and bronze. The more gold decisions you racked up, the better off you'd be. His son had ridiculed the analogy. Bribes and threats hadn't worked either. Nor had the brief episodes of physical violence that Luisa, questioning Goyo's manhood, had shamed him into. The first time Goyo punched his son, he blackened his eye. The second time, he dislocated his jaw. The third and last time, he broke Goyito's arm. That third time, Goyo also put a pistol to his son's temple. He wanted to scare him, and he did; the boy shit his pants. He was fifteen and, Goyo believed, still salvageable. The next day Luisa threw Goyito out of the house with a laundry basket of his dirty clothes. He went down faster than anybody could've imagined.

A fire itched under Goyo's patchwork of bandages. He should sue that son of a bitch balsero in the Camaro, but what would that get him? The tattered inner tube that the sorry bastard had floated on to Florida? Goyito's legs slowly bicycled in his sleep. Tears seeped from his eyes, moistening his collar. Goyo could intellectualize his son's suffering, get heartsick about it, puzzle over it. But understand it? Never. This was what pained him most.

Excerpts from a doctored recording of El Comandante's voice circulating in Havana:

> Este es un país de tontos y de idiotas . . .
> Un país grosero e insultante . . . y contrarevolucionario. Nunca en ninguna época ningún ejército en ninguna parte del mundo luchó contra un pueblo de cientos de miles de delincuentes comunes . . .
> Este país es un asco, aunque sea bien grosera la palabra . . .
> El sistema ha fracasado. ¿Quién tiene la culpa de eso?

> This is a country of fools and idiots . . .
> A rude and insulting country . . . and counterrevolutionary. Never at any time has an army in any part of the world had to fight against a population of hundreds of thousands of common criminals . . .
> This country is repulsive, although that's a rude way of putting it . . .
> The system has failed. Whose fault is that?

Havana

The tyrant awoke in the middle of the night inhaling the verdant sugarcane.* It was the smell of his childhood, of the acres and acres

---

*What you see here in Trinidad was once the heart of the sugarcane industry. I treat these old mills as archaeological sites and excavate evidence of the lives lived—and lost—inside their boundaries. It's my life's work, but I've been

of swaying stalks, of the pealing bells calling the cutters to the fields. Everything had tasted of sugarcane then, stank of it; down to the coarse soap he scrubbed his neck with, down to his morning shit. Sugarcane had been his family's bounty and its curse, a microcosm of everything that was wrong with Cuba. It'd brought slaves from Africa, destroyed the island's forests, depleted its soils, and rendered the land useless for other crops. It'd made kings of a few and paupers of most, hurdled the economy through booms and insufferable busts. In the remote corner of Oriente where Papá had ruled over his fiefdom of sugarcane, his sons had been princes.

The hospital room gradually came into focus. Myriad tubes connected the despot to drips and computer monitors that turned his hands blue in the reflected light. How he hated this place! It reminded him of his near-lethal gastrointestinal troubles years ago. What was left of his large intestine was prone to infection, trapping food in its creases and folds, which bubbled out painfully at the slightest provocation. Sometimes the pain got so bad that the dictator swore off solid foods for weeks at a time.

The winds tossed the canopies of trees, casting wavering shadows against the walls. After a lifetime of insomnia, the tyrant could gauge the time of night as easily as he could the day. By the inky quality of the skies, he guessed correctly that it was a few minutes past four. The hour of grace would come just before dawn, when the night gave way to the stippled pinks of first light. Soon the morning papers from Europe would arrive along with the daily digests from Asia.

---

slowing down on account of my Parkinson's. The medicines knock me out, and I'm good for maybe two hours a day. The rest of the time, I shake like a leaf. Nobody's interested in my research anymore. What my students want more than anything is to get as far away from here as possible, away from the sugarcane that predetermined their lives.

—María Estela Arza, historian

"Ssssst!" he called to the guards standing outside his door. Neither looked familiar, and this put him ill at ease. "Who the fuck are you?"

"Lieutenant Perico Rojas, sir!" The short, warty one snapped to attention.

"Captain Benancio Cuevas!" The other was lanky and rawboned.

"Are the newspapers in yet?"

"No, sir!" they answered in unison, salutes frozen.

"What the hell happened to me?"

"Happened, sir?"

"Why the fuck am I here? Have you overheard the doctors say anything?"

"No, sir!"

Carajo, these buffoons wouldn't have lasted two days with him in the Sierra Maestra. Only once did the tyrant leave the mountains in four long years: to attend Papá's funeral. El Comandante had been the most wanted man on the island, so he went to the funeral disguised as a Jesuit priest. He saw it all now as if neither time nor geography separated him from that hot July day: his chafing collar, the creaky procession of horse-drawn carriages, the campesinos dressed in their Sunday best, Papá's mausoleum shaded by a copse of flamboyan trees.*

All his life, death had pursued him without success. After the

---

*The flamboyans call to me with their outlandish orange blossoms. How I'd love to climb in one and stay forever, like the count in that Italian novel I love. Now and then, I'd lower a tin bucket for books and Serrano ham, but mostly I'd just watch the pageantry of this vibrant, decaying city. As I write, the Revolution is in its last gasp. What will come after, nobody knows.
—*Cristina García, novelist*

Missile Crisis,* his enemies said he'd gone mad, that he wouldn't be satisfied until he blew the world to smithereens. It infuriated El Comandante to recall the balls-cutting humiliation of the Russians' betrayal. When push came to shove, they dealt him out and negotiated directly with the Americans. On the world stage he'd been discounted as a bit player. Difficult as it was, he'd survived that insult—and then he kept on surviving.

～☞

The Russians

It'd taken El Comandante the better part of three decades to understand the Russians—not their psychology, exactly, which was the same for powermongers everywhere, but how to read them. Most of his difficulties stemmed from the language barrier and the interference of translators who, however meticulous, ended up complicating the proceedings. The tyrant was at his best one-on-one, draping an arm over his listener's shoulder, offering a fragrant cigar from his private cache.

For him, the art of persuasion was akin to good lovemaking: rapt attention (however temporary), a few enhancing details (rum, orchids, fruit), seductive whisperings that paved the way for the royal screwing to come. Sex was better when a woman wanted to be screwed. One couldn't just go through the motions. Bueno, it was the same with sensitive political maneuverings. It'd been a hell of a challenge with his ill-tempered Soviet allies. After untold hours of language lessons, El Comandante could utter nothing in Russian beyond a few basic

---

* **Q**: Did you know there's no mention of the Missile Crisis at the Museo de la Revolución or in Cuba's history books? **A**: What missile crisis?

pleasantries. With six linguistic cases and the resulting infinity of verb possibilities, he could never tell who the hell was coming or going.

In the eighties, the tyrant had hired a gorgeous young translator—Cuban mother, Russian father—who'd spent her formative years in Moscow. Carmen Novikov was a fantasy pinup of cross-cultural womanhood: blond, blue-eyed, caramel-skinned with torpedo breasts and the most luscious hips on either side of the Atlantic. It was all he could do to stay focused on whatever negotiations were at hand. The lilt of Carmen's voice, the zzzhhh of her consonants, the way her lips pressed together when she was silent, as if holding back the words corralled in her mouth, drove the tyrant to contemplate a different manner of revolution. Just once did he have the pleasure of nestling his chin on the perfumed curve of her shoulder to ask: "Lily of the valley?" Carmen had the good sense to slip away and pretend she hadn't heard him. Eventually, she married an Indian diplomat while on assignment in Berlin and gave birth a year later to underweight fraternal twins in Bombay.

For El Comandante, the most frustrating aspect of dealing with the Russians was getting them to reveal state secrets. No matter how drunk or compromised their position (Cuba's vaults were bursting with their lumbering sexual exploits, thanks to State Security), the Russians kept their mouths shut. Nothing was more alien to the island's national character. That was why those braggart exiles couldn't get anything off the ground. Put two of them in a room and you immediately got a conspiracy, or un relajo total. An hour into planning a commando raid, everyone in Miami would know about it, down to the abuelitas shopping for yuca at Publix.

From the early days, the tyrant had battled his own secrecy-challenged ranks with terror. In the Sierra Maestra, loose lips were dealt with swiftly, by firing squad. Fernando had convinced him of that. If his followers weren't 200 percent behind him, they were most likely against him. To this day Cuban spies had infiltrated the highest ranks of the CIA and the Pentagon without blowing their covers.

A good number were retired with generous U.S. government pensions. The intelligence they'd gathered, e.g., who'd killed President Kennedy, Jimmy Hoffa's whereabouts, et cetera, had proved invaluable for the Revolution as well as for the Soviets, who'd turned out to be as clumsy in espionage as they were in bed.

—⁂—

Miami

It was barely dawn when Goyo woke up with shooting pains down his back. His son was spread-eagled on the hospital bed, his left eye open and eerily flickering from left to right, as if reading an invisible text. El pobre exuded a foul, garlicky odor, most likely from all the junk food he ate. Yet despite his girth, Goyito seemed impervious to aging. Half a century of cocaine and buttermilk donuts and, physically at least, he remained imperturbably hale. His son should leave his corpse to science, because nobody, in Goyo's opinion, had ever submitted his body to as much abuse and survived.

Goyo rolled his stiff neck from side to side but only succeeded in straining it further. Coño, he was tired of being old. In the natural world, dying was more dignified. When a wolf's time came, there were no legions of money-grubbers trying to profit off its passing. The wolf went deep into the forest and surrendered its carcass back to nature. Since he wasn't a wolf, Goyo had thrown his lot in with the Catholics for the same reason he bought Cadillacs: tradition, reliability, and the promise of running forever. He didn't know how much time he had left, but he was dead set on outliving his nemesis. He'd settle for an extra hour, ten minutes, anything—but he wanted, *needed* that bastard to die first.

Goyo put a gnarled hand on his son's sleeve. "Buenos días, mijo."

Goyito's closed eyelid fluttered and he smacked his tongue against his palate. Without a word he climbed out of bed, dug up a scroll buried near the twisted roots of the dwarf areca palm, and thrust it at his father.

It appeared to be a list of some sort, but Goyo couldn't fathom its meaning. *What I believe,* it began. *That I can speak to dogs. That they don't listen to me. That women are impenetrable. That children should like me.*

Goyo hesitated. "Is this an assignment from Dr. Recalde?"

His son stared back glumly.

That the good things in life are bad for me: mothers, malted milk balls, cocaine. That there is a God but He's ignored me. That a family awaits me. That one morning I'll wake up dead and that will be without pain.

"What is this, hijo?"

"A poem."

If his son had said he'd been moonlighting as a drag queen on weekends, Goyo couldn't have been more surprised.

A nurse squeaked in on rubber-soled shoes, carrying a breakfast tray of oatmeal and pineapple rings in light syrup.

"Do you have buttermilk donuts?" Goyito asked as she retreated.

Goyo pulled out his cell phone and dialed Alina's number. She picked up on the third ring.

"Jesus, it's six in the morning."

"We're done here."

"That goddamn dog chewed two legs off the dining room table. I forced him out on the balcony, but he howled at the moon for hours."

"Come and get us, hija," Goyo said. "Your brother and I are going to New York."

AUGUST 13–15

TROPICAL FORECAST: The threat of heavy rain
continues. A tropical storm warning is in effect for the
eastern part of the island. Maximum sustained winds are
near 65 kilometers with higher gusts up to 165. Dangerous
waves will persist in the north and south-central coasts.
I don't know about you, but I'm staying home to watch
the latest episode of *Gaucho Love.* Como siempre . . .
el último meteorólogo en La Habana.

9.

The Visit

Havana

It was long past midnight and the tyrant couldn't sleep, not a wink. It was a wonder he hadn't suffered another intestinal attack after the knockdown fight with his brother. Fernando had revealed—with surprising nonchalance—that the impending Bay of Pigs reenactment had been transformed into a goddamn musical. No planes, no beach landings, no decisive battles against the mercenaries. Not only was it a musical but it was now in the hands of a gay theater director who'd publicly denounced the regime. This was burlesque, pure grotesquerie! The remains of a birthday hat and ripped tissue paper lay strewn near his bed. Delia had given him his birthday gift early: a ludicrous child's telescope, ill-suited for anything but voyeurism.

El Comandante lit a Cohiba. After nearly self-immolating last month, he'd given up all pretense of giving up cigars. Now he smoked three or four daily and didn't give a damn what anybody thought. He balanced the puro between his thumb and forefinger as he tottered along the foot of his bed. The smoke engulfed his leonine head, penetrated his beard, the deadly expression in his eyes. His anger toward Fernando surged anew. Did his brother think him a fool? He should never have trusted him again after he'd pissed away three million dollars on that joint-venture zombie movie. Fernando still defended the film, insisting that the flesh-eating zombies were supposed to be Yankee-backed dissidents trying to destabilize the country. What did he care that nobody understood the social satire? They'd been laughed out of every film festival on the planet, including Karachi's.

The tyrant sat at the edge of his bed and looked down at his bare feet. They were thickly veined, the skin dry and cracked. A blood clot adorned his big left toe like a garnet. To think that he'd once marched for days on the pads of his once-sturdy soles. At his peak, he'd known omnipotence, a holy opprobrium. Now it was zombies and queer theater directors, insurrection on all fronts. How could he possibly leave the Revolution in the hands of these imbeciles? Revolution and art, he'd decided long ago, were fundamentally incompatible.

To cancel the stupid musical would be to risk public humiliation, something the regime couldn't afford. On the other hand, he couldn't permit Fernando to blatantly undermine his authority. El Comandante had demanded a historically authentic invasion, complete with vintage B-52 bombers, mercenary boats, and a cast of thousands. The extravaganza would dazzle their international guests and ensure that the Revolution's version of events survived. Now what the hell did he have to look forward to on his birthday?

He called El Conejo. "I want to see the dolphins," he ordered. Visiting them always calmed him down.

"A sus órdenes, Jefe. When should I arrange a visit?"

"Immediately."

"Immediately?"

"Do I need to use profanity?"

"I'll come for you shortly."

The tyrant savored the moment. His whim would ruin the nights of a dozen or so of his minions. It was useful to test their loyalty now and then, though he'd learned from experience that the most publicly loyal were also the most likely to betray. But if the commander in chief—the hell with Fernando, *he* was still in charge—wanted to visit the aquarium at two in the morning, so be it. Twenty minutes later, he was climbing the steps to the dolphin house. A group of underlings accompanied him: the youngest of his personal physicians (on probation for trafficking in antibiotics); the ministers of the interior and agriculture; three veterinarians, including an expert on cetaceans; and a couple of comemierda generals.

El Comandante entered the ultramarine room and waited for a bodyguard to adjust his portable leather chair. He would much rather spend his days right here in the aquarium than in the stifling, modernist house his wife had insisted on filling with backbreaking Danish furniture. There wasn't so much as a footstool in the whole damn place. The tyrant swiveled to face the gigantic tank. Once he'd dreamt of capturing a two-hundred-ton blue whale and putting it on display in Havana, but experts had quickly dissuaded him. Blue whales were an endangered species, and their size made them next to impossible to capture. Besides, to look into a blue whale's eye, they said, into its great wink of eternity, could drive a sane man to madness.

The dolphins sidled up to the glass to gaze, brine-eyed, at their most ardent fan.

"Start the show," El Comandante barked.

The lights dimmed, and a trio of lithe divers—two men and

a bespangled woman with chapped, forlorn feet—slipped into the water wearing wet suits but no diving equipment. The divers worked in close harmony with the dolphins, gracefully kaleidoscoping into hearts, spirals, and hexagons to the gyrating rhythms of Los Van Van's greatest hits. Their routines reminded the tyrant of those old Hollywood movies with the swimming starlet Esther Williams (he'd had a crush on her as a young man), except that this music and choreography were far superior.

After a difficult series of jumps and twists, one of the dolphins nuzzled the female diver and waggled its prodigious tail. The dictator clapped his hands in delight. "Ha, that's a new one!"

Everyone present breathed a sigh of relief. With any luck, no one would be upbraided tonight; no one dismissed, or incarcerated for real or imagined crimes.

"That one's getting fat," El Comandante said, singling out the dolphin named Betty. Recently, he'd resuscitated the Revolution's fitness-for-all campaign from the dark ages. Nobody embraced the idea, least of all Cuba's gym teachers, who were as overweight and underaerobicized as everybody else.

One of the veterinarians, a doleful fellow with concave cheeks, stepped forward. "She's pregnant, Comandante," Dr. Gutiérrez explained, clicking his rubber heels.

The tyrant brought his hands together, fingertips touching. "Is she in your charge?"

"Sí, Comandante." Dr. Gutiérrez blushed to the tips of his ears, as if it were he who'd impregnated the sorry creature and was now facing her father's wrath.

"Where was her chaperone, eh?"

Everyone remained silent. Mistaking El Comandante's intentions had proved a fast path to oblivion, or worse.

"¡Idiotas!" he burst out, laughing.

The divers energetically resumed their routine, rushing a few backflips. During the finale, the errant Betty torpedoed around the gigantic tank, coquettishly flapping her tail. It seemed to the tyrant—and he was never wrong about such things—that the bitch only had eyes for him.

———◦‿⌒———

No sooner had the dictator returned from the aquarium than the morning's troubles resumed in full force. The crashing euro meant fewer tourists and trade. Imports to Cuba had fallen 37 percent, ravaging the economy. For months, headlines around the world had been proclaiming the death of the Revolution. Fernando's attempt to lay off more government workers had backfired. Protests were breaking out in Guantánamo and other cities that the army couldn't fully contain. By every conceivable measure, it was all a fiasco. Only in Cuba, El Líder thought miserably, did citizens expect to survive without working—and moreover, feel entitled to not working.

He rang for his breakfast: oatmeal, stewed fruit, multigrain toast that tasted like sawdust. Today was his birthday, goddamnit, so he demanded a cafecito* and heaped in six teaspoons of sugar. More bad news. There was a record rice shortage in Asia. Cuba's sugarcane harvest was expected to be worse than last year's. The ever-optimistic *Granma* printed the schedule of festivities to be held in honor of the tyrant's eighty-ninth birthday—parades in Holguín and Camagüey; a dance festival in Trinidad; a workers' rally on the steps of the Capitol at noon; and, most infuriatingly, the premiere of *Bay of Pigs: The Musical!* in Cienfuegos.

---

*The coffee tastes better since they started mixing in the chickpeas. It was too bitter before. I don't know if the coffee in Baracoa is different than in Havana, but I'm telling you it's smoother. Let me make you a cup and you can judge for yourself.

—Magdalena Alvarez, truck driver

That he didn't already have Fernando's head on a platter over this abomination attested to his weakness. It was impossible to fight everyone at once. If only he could be like that Bruce Lee, kickboxing his way through a hundred men. Early on in the Revolution, the tyrant had battled his own family first to mute criticism of his policies. Papá's hacienda was nationalized before any others. His cousin's sugar refinery was handed over to its workers. After the Revolution took control of the banks, his mother publicly criticized him for displaying "bad manners," adding: "This is not how I raised my son." The tyrant couldn't make her understand that when it came to building a nation, niceties were not a priority.

Besides, next to the Soviets he was a model of civility. For years El Comandante had endured their endless, vodka-fueled banquets—everyone two-fistedly shoveling in heaps of caviar, sturgeon, sheep's-cheese sandwiches, balyk (the highly prized dorsal sections of salted or smoked salmon), and those beastly pies, heavy enough to use as artillery shells. What the hell were those pies called? Kulo-something-or-other. Kulo-ban-skas. No, no. Kulebyakas. That was it. Colossal, stupefying pies stuffed with oily fish, congealed meats, cabbage. How he hated that stinking sour cabbage! Like eating out of a urinal. Kitchen sink pies. Why, he'd half-expected to find wrenches or chunks of farm machinery between their leaden crusts. His stomach, at least, had been iron-clad then.

Once, the tyrant had so mangled a toast in Russian that it sent his Kremlin cronies—with their galoshes and greatcoats and dull, barking basses—into paroxysms of laughter. He'd meant to say: "I salute, with fervor, the young men and women of great Mother Russia, whose future in this land is bright." Instead it came out: "May the lamb-clad maidens of Mother Russia enjoy their bright morning sprats." Oh, everyone laughed heartily over that one. The mirthless wives with their heaving acreage of breasts. The snub-

nosed state accordionist, who doubled over with tears in his eyes
and stopped playing for a full five minutes. The foreign minister joked: "Our Cuban friend knows as much about Russia as a
pig knows about oranges." More ah-ha-ha! El Comandante never
attempted to say anything in Russian again.

Outside his window, dawn slowly dissolved into day. A squad-
ron of pelicans flew close to shore, dive-bombing the surf for fish.
How he would love nothing more than to spend the day fishing
like them. A cramp tightened his belly. He winced and shouted for
an attendant. An unfamiliar, goggle-eyed man in a pin-striped suit
answered his call. The tyrant's sphincter froze.

"Who the hell are you?" he said, balking.

"Compañero Vásquez."

"You're no compañero of mine. Where the hell did you get that
suit?"

"It's the one you wore for the Pope's visit. How handsome you
looked. The ladies flocked to you anew."

The stranger spoke perfect Spanish but with a foreign accent
that the dictator couldn't place. The son of a bitch was probably
CIA. "What do you know about it?"

"People underestimate you at their peril." Vásquez grinned, displaying a double row of crowded, discolored teeth. "Permit me to
wish you the most felicitous of birthdays."

"What's your business here, Vásquez? I can see you're not
armed."

"You were expecting an assassin then?"

"I'm always expecting assassins. How the fuck did you get my
suit?"

"Let's just say . . . the world recycles its gifts."

The tyrant reached for the buzzer that summoned El Conejo.
He would boil that rabbit's head with parsley for this breach of
security.

"It's no use, Jefe. All connections have been temporarily sev-
ered." Vásquez grinned again, drumming the air with pallid fingers.

"So you're here to kill me." El Comandante eyed his nightstand,
where he kept his trusty Browning. Calmly, he opened the drawer
and grabbed hold of the pistol. It was a touch dusty but otherwise
ready for action. He aimed it at Vásquez.

"There's no need for that, Jefe."

"I'm counting to three."

"You'll be counting longer in eternity."

"You're the one who's going to eternity, hijo de puta. One . . ."

"Put it down and I'll tell you why I'm here."

"Two . . ."

"It's about your after—"

"Three."

El Comandante pulled the trigger. The shot erupted with a
deafening blast, tearing a hole in the visitor's thigh. Through it, the
tyrant spied the bookshelf where he kept his signed first editions
of Babo's novels.

"Afterlife," Vásquez repeated without a hint of aggression. "You
were trained by the Jesuits, no?"

The tyrant studied his still-smoking pistol. His thumb was
bleeding where the hammer had hit it. His shoulder hurt like the
devil, too. El Comandante looked up at Vásquez and felt ice in his
chest. Was it heartburn, or fear? It'd been so long since he'd actually
been afraid of anyone that he barely recognized the signs.

"My legacy *is* my afterlife, idiot. Here on the island, with my
people."

"Then you don't believe in the transmigration of souls?"

The despot was tired of playing games. He slapped his own
face, trying to wake himself up from this nightmare. Those fucking
sleeping pills were to blame.

"You shot me through the leg and I'm still here." Vásquez waggled a finger through the charred hole to illustrate his point.

"That proves only that you're a figment of my imagination. You don't exist, asshole. Listen, hand me a cigar from that box over there."

Vásquez, or whoever he was, lifted the mahogany lid of the humidor and removed a puro. He held it to his nose. "De primera."

"Take one for yourself," El Comandante offered, and Vásquez did.

Vásquez struck a light by snapping his fingers and held them first to the tip of the tyrant's cigar and then to his own.

"Nice trick." The tyrant was enjoying this now, surrendering to the fantasy.

"You don't have much time left, Jefe," Vásquez said, blowing immaculate smoke rings toward the ceiling. He puffed out his cheeks and with a few quick contortions of his lips, blew out a smoky replica of the Greater Antilles.

"Tell me something I don't know."

"Your death will be heroic."

"I would expect no less."

"You have many enemies."

"Are you one of them?" the tyrant asked, repositioning a pillow.

"Jefe, trust me. I'm your ally."

"Then enough chatter, Vásquez. Have some respect and shut the fuck up."

The two of them sat smoking for a while in silence. This Vásquez was no amateur when it came to handling a fine cigar. El Comandante's respect for him grew. It was difficult to make new friends at his age. People either shunned him out of fear and hatred or groveled obsequiously out of the same fear and hatred. To sit companionably with this stranger mitigated the weight of his loneliness somehow. Bueno, if Vásquez was the Devil, at least he'd be assured of decent company in hell.

"Where did you say you were from?"

"I didn't." Vásquez was working on a wispy chart of the solar system.

"You an astronomer?"

"I suppose you could say that."

"A reader of stars then?"

"If you wish."

"Carajo, it doesn't matter. You feel very—"

"Dare I say 'brotherly'?"

"Jesus, I want to fucking ring his neck for what he's done. There isn't a soul on this island I can trust anymore. But you probably know that already."

"I do."

The smoke lazily encircled them.

"So how much time do I have left?" El Comandante tapped an inch of ash off his cigar into a Venetian glass ashtray.

"This business of time is tricky. Nowhere in the universe is it as divided and wasted as it is here."

"You mean in Cuba?" The despot pushed himself up onto one elbow, ready to take offense.

"Don't get your hackles up, Jefe. I meant on this planet." The last of Saturn's rings disintegrated. A replica of the Milky Way followed.

El Comandante grew drowsy. He didn't have the same stamina for staying up all night and shooting the breeze. "I'm eighty-nine years old today."

"Again, my felicidades." Vásquez stood up and delicately stubbed out his cigar. The hole in his leg had vanished. "It's time for me to go."

"Come back anytime," the tyrant offered with genuine hospitality. "Don't worry about protocol." He cackled at his own joke, and saliva collected at the corners of his mouth.

Vásquez disappeared through the closed door. The dictator inspected his room. Everything remained the same except for the smoky constellation near the ceiling—the North Star, Orion, the dippers, large and small. He finished his cigar. The morning stood still. The same pelicans hovered by the shore, diving for the same translucent fish. The same clouds cast their gauzy shadows on the sea. If he closed his eyes, El Comandante mused, might he stop time indefinitely?

Soon he dozed off. He dreamt that it was daybreak and he was floating in the air like one of the pelicans, gazing down on his near-naked, lifeless body. It was displayed, unceremoniously, on a metal operating table. His corpse sported a winter hat with earflaps like his Russian comrades used to wear. People gathered around him, parasols flaring open against the sun. Two or three men came closer, sniffing like stray dogs, their faces edged with malice. They pointed at his sagging chest, the slackness of his thighs, his gouty, unsheathed feet.

A seamstress with pins in her mouth pushed through the crowd and began to take his measurements, as if for a new suit, except that she measured extraneous details: the distance between his radial ears; the length of his incisors (she pulled back his cracked lips to check); his fingers, stiff as flagpoles; the at-rest dimensions of his penis nestled against his bloated balls. A beam of light suddenly illuminated his corpse. The steel table beneath him rose heavenward—up, up, up into the feathery clouds—before reversing direction and dropping like a broken elevator. The crowd scattered as the steel table cratered the ground. No one was left at his grave site—if, indeed, it was his grave site—except for Compañero

Vásquez, dressed in a sulfur-colored suit and twirling a gold-tipped walking stick.

"Amigo," Vásquez called to him, exuding sympathy, "we mustn't take pity on our own misfortunes."

~⁊

Limbo

I studied to become a lawyer only to realize that there is no point to this career. What can you do as a lawyer here when the laws are arbitrary and change from day to day? You can lose your house, your job, your reputation, if the state decides this is your fate. That's what happened to my Tío Rolando, a thoracic surgeon, after he applied to leave the country. He's become a pariah. His children can no longer attend school. Officially, his whole family doesn't exist. They'll live in this limbo for as many months or years as it takes for them to escape. Now I'm studying to become an air traffic controller. The work isn't subject to interpretation. The plane lands safely, or it doesn't. There is no ambiguity. No margin for error.

— ***Margarita Bofill, aviation student***

10.

Myths

Durham, North Carolina

Goyo settled on a garish cushion next to his son and watched the seminaked harlequins slither up and down the glistening poles. There were seven dancers altogether, but Goyo was fixated on the skinny, pliable one. She looked soft in spite of her acrobatics, boneless, as if any man could shape her flesh to his needs. Goyito was wearing a Mexican poncho and a bear mask, an outfit he claimed protected him from malevolent forces. His Great Dane, the indomitable Rudy, waited in the parking lot in Goyo's newly repaired Cadillac, the windows open, a chewed rawhide in the mangled backseat. How the hell had they ended up in this strip joint on the outskirts of Durham, the obesity capital of America, on a jag of father-son debauchery?

The tempo picked up as the dancers, long-legged variations of one another, approached the cheering patrons in Rockettes fashion.

They kicked their legs high, leaving nothing to the imagination. Goyo found this display distasteful in the extreme. A woman's treasure wasn't meant to be paraded in such shorn, unseemly quantities. It seemed to Goyo that what this dancing offered—if such gyrations could be called dancing—appealed not so much to the audience's groins as to their feeble hopes. As a theatrical production, it was a disaster.

His son cheered the women on along with the other men, who summoned the dancers with ten- and twenty-dollar bills. Goyito had singles, which he held out in threes or fives (he had a fear of even numbers). He was probably not much different from the strip club regulars—neither talented nor burdened with superior intelligence nor extraordinary in any way. He had one unpardonable zeal: cocaine. All the rest was shaped by habit and a paucity of imagination.

Goyito thumped the cocktail table with the heel of his hand, rousing the curiosity of the boneless girl.

"Hi, Papa Bear," she growled, baring teeth so tiny they might've been her milk teeth. Boneless Girl's nacreous flesh seemed to shimmy in every direction at once.

Reluctantly, Goyo thought of his son's penis. It hadn't been circumcised—only the Jews in Cuba were circumcised—but the boy, in a drug-addled frenzy, had attempted a do-it-yourself circumcision at sixteen.

A string of vermilion lights flashed, signaling the dancers to retreat. Hips and breasts blooming with cash, they launched into a disco number. Goyo escaped the smoky club and hobbled outside. Cement clamshell fountains furred with mold framed the entrance. The parking lot was packed with locals and drive-through travelers. Goyito had begged his father to take him to Durham en route to New York so that he could enroll at the Rice House. Luisa had spent many months and thousands of dollars shedding extra pounds at its weight-loss program.

The night was oppressively humid. Goyo's every gesture seemed to indent the air. He closed his eyes for a moment, watching the pink quivering of his lids under the bright parking lot lights. Then he reached into his guayabera pocket for the cigar he'd been saving. He lit a match and held it to the tip, puffing until the compressed leaves embraced the flame. The smoke soothed his throat, seeped through his nostrils, rolled along his palate.

A fragrant scrim enveloped him. To surrender to a good cigar was to deny time's tyranny. As he smoked, Goyo had the disconcerting feeling that he was mirroring the tyrant's movements. Back at the university, people had often mistaken the two of them. They'd both been tall and handsome then, and were known to drop Latin aphorisms into casual conversations. But Goyo had been a political moderate in his youth, the opposite of that firebrand thug who was always on one hit list or another. Everyone knew he'd murdered a fellow student over some barbaric nonsense.*

The unfamiliar sounds of the North Carolina night unsettled Goyo. He couldn't identify a single birdsong, and the crickets ground out an alien whirring. Above him, at least, the skies were embossed with the same moon and stars. The older he got, the more vividly his memories of Cuba returned—its dialects, its minerals, its underground caves, its guajiros, its hummingbirds, its fish, its chaos, its peanut vendors, its Chinese lotteries, its cacophonies, its myths, its terrors. Maybe this was what happened when a man approached death; senility and longing conspired to

---

*The student's name was Patricio Canseco, and he was the tyrant's most dangerous political opponent, dangerous only because he'd grown extremely popular. Canseco's assassination set the tone for the tyrant's later intolerance of his enemies.

—Adolfo Ochoa, historian in exile

overtake reality. Perhaps Cuba had become nothing but an imaginary place, unrelated to any truth. Goyo looked down at his feet, which loomed closer every day. Coño, there was no denying his diminution. He recalled, much chagrined, how his daughter had ridiculed his wished-for epitaph: *Here lies a Cuban hero.* The last thing he wanted was to die another forgettable, brooding exile in the heart of discontent.

A stirring at the edge of the parking lot caught Goyo's attention. A pudgy creature waddled out from a tangle of weeds. Its striped tail was unmistakable. It turned to face him, point-blank and accusatory, as if to say: Et tu, Goyo? The raccoon reminded him of his old social studies teacher, Father Antonio Beixet, with his triangular Spanish face and parchment skin. The Spaniard's favorite saying was Fortes fortuna adiuvat. Fortune favors the bold. At one of his high school reunions, Goyo learned that Father Antonio had died from septicemia in 1973, at a retirement home for Jesuits in rural Indiana.

A plane blinked across the moon's path. What would Father Antonio have thought of him today? What sort of life had he led, with its myopic concern for money and material comforts, its fundamental cowardice? The sacerdotal raccoon sat on its hindquarters, frozen, its front paws outstretched like calipers. Goyo's cigar burned, unsmoked. He spat a speck of tobacco off his tongue. He was on his way to New York, to the United Nations, where the tyrant would speak next month. The distance between the mortal and the divine, Goyo thought, might still be bridged with one decisive act.

~&

Island Blogger 1

Have you noticed how many of the children of our so-called
leaders live as exiles in Spain, France, or the United States?
The offspring of our elite, with all their privileges, don't choose
to live in the society their parents built. Why? Because real
revolutions, good citizens, don't last over half a century . . .

~&

La Cabaña

El Comandante scrutinized the hunger strikers lined up before
him—skeletal misfits with protruding ribs and gray, sunken cheeks.
Their leader, Orlando Martínez, had succeeded in starving himself
to death, increasing the media spotlight on the survivors. They were
ordinary men, for the most part, a choir of nobodies. Here in the
most feared penitentiary in the Caribbean, dissidents were meant
to perish anonymously, like the thousands before them. Instead the
six (now five) hunger strikers had become martyrs, their stories and
images disseminated worldwide.

The ragtag prisoners stood facing the tyrant in the warden's spar-
tan office, its only adornment a framed photograph of the Maximum Leader himself. Each dissident displayed the usual marks of
torture—cigarette burns, broken ribs, gouges and wounds of vary-
ing shapes and depths—on his bare torso. None had caved yet under
the psychological pressure. It was critical to get the upper hand
with these morally righteous wretches, El Comandante thought.
They were infinitely more difficult to deal with than garden-variety

thugs and drug traffickers. The hunger strikers' bodies had become contentious political terrain and a public relations debacle for the Revolution. He wasn't going to let these malcontents beat him at his own game.

At first the despot matched their silence with his own, waiting for one of them to crack. An almost imperceptible electricity united the men, but they didn't exchange so much as a glance. Who knew what these five had in common? Juan Collante, a former copper factory foreman. Rigoberto Alves, the baroquely disgraced physics professor who'd tried—and failed—to escape Cuba fourteen times. Carlos Matamoros, a Havana hairdresser and seller of fake Partagás cigars. Mario Benes, a war hero from Angola who'd left his cushy colonel's job in the provinces to fight the Revolution from within. And the kid, barely nineteen, Antonio Zaldívar, an emaciated street hustler turned informant turned dissident.

"I am here," El Comandante began slowly, "*not,* as you may believe, out of hatred, or disdain, or fear—don't flatter yourselves there—but out of concern." He paused to let this sink in. "I, too, was imprisoned once, reviled and abandoned. One's flesh, one's spirit remembers such things. No one came to me, as I am coming to you today, to offer forgiveness and redemption. Perhaps, like you, I would've been too proud to accept such gifts. In those days I was blinded by rage and a sense of my own destiny, of our island's destiny. I'm sure you would agree that my passions were not misplaced?"

Only the kid dared look at him, shaking a skinny leg with impatience. The tyrant decided to ignore the impudence. He ordered the heavily cologned warden and all military and prison personnel to leave the room. El Comandante wanted to be alone with the dissidents. Of course, he would've preferred to speak to each of them individually—divide them, conquer them—but he had neither the time nor the stamina for that. Once in the Sierra

Maestra, he'd devoted an entire night to convincing one of his own delinquent soldiers (he'd stolen a pig and seduced a peasant girl) that he must die by firing squad at daybreak to make credible the revolutionary cause.

"I am a part of you, inside you, in your bloodstream—and I'm not going away," El Comandante continued. "You won't escape me, even in death. So why not choose to partake of life, to join me in making history?"

This seemed more than the hunger strikers could bear. They twitched and looked at the floor, the ceiling, anywhere but at him. Finally the kid erupted, his face distorted by rage: "The only history you've made on this fucking island is shit."

"Cállate, estúpido," the copper foreman hissed.

El Comandante smiled. Already, he was chipping away at the group's primary resolve—to refuse to engage with him. This was progress. Now it was time for a little provocation. "Punk," the tyrant sneered. "You're too weak to even jerk off."

"I'll fucking show you who can't jerk off!" Antonio yelled, and pulled down his prison pants. His cock was huge and purplish hard. "Let's see what you've got, faggot!"

A pair of military police stormed in and dragged away the hustler, his penis bouncing off their thighs, his insults echoing against the ancient stone walls: *Este país es una mierdaaaaaa* . . . El Comandante shrugged off the incident as if it were nothing more than an inconvenient stirring of dust. "The, eh, incommodities you've suffered in prison are nothing compared to what you're inflicting on yourselves, on the Revolution that nurtured you. Our bodies are fragile—I know this better than any of you—and it won't be easy recovering from the trials to which you're submitting your kidneys, your livers, and most especially your hearts."

The tyrant signaled with a wave of his hand, and the banished personnel returned. "Are we ready?"

"Sí, Jefe." The warden practically saluted. He was the son of a rehabilitated Batista henchman, and devoutly pro-revolution. He'd lost a leg to diabetes but still moved with the vigor of a biped.

"Follow me," the tyrant said in his most seductive voice. It was the voice that those who knew him feared most. The voice that ordered men thrown from helicopters, hands and feet bound, into the Caribbean. A merciless voice.

With the warden at his side, El Comandante led the unlikely procession through the prison, past fetid labyrinths of cells where inmates gnawed on their own flesh to stave off hunger. They shouted out to him, begged him for clemency, cursed and praised him in equal measure. It was a vision of hell, a stench for the ages. Carajo, Fernando had assured him that they'd cleaned up the place for his arrival. Prisons were his brother's bailiwick, the part of his portfolio he'd once enjoyed most. The tyrant hadn't set foot in here since the onset of the Revolution. Their worst political enemies had waited within these walls before their summary trials and executions. Not much had changed.

The dissidents shuffled together behind El Comandante, ankles enchained, moving as one tentacular beast. Their destination: the warden's private dining hall, where a rustic banquet table was set with china and water and wine glasses and a dusty arrangement of plastic daffodils. With a sweep of his arm, the tyrant invited the hunger strikers to lunch. The guards unfastened the prisoners and forced each one to take a seat. As the waiters poured the Spanish rioja, the despot sat at the head of the table, beaming with self-satisfaction. The first course was a steaming ajiaco chock-full of green bananas, yuca, and chunks of pork. El Comandante dug in, lifting a spoonful to his lips.

"Mmm, delicioso. Mamá used to make this every Sunday when I was a boy. Won't you try some?" He looked placidly from one man to another.

The tension in the room spiked lethally, but the prisoners said nothing. A row of electric bulbs glared down on them from the ceiling, and a stuttering fan overhead suddenly stopped. An open floor-to-ceiling window overlooked the sea but, strangely, admitted no breeze. The stifling dining room and the agonizing fragrance of the stew made the hunger strikers all pour sweat. Not a single one picked up a spoon. After an interminable moment, Juan Collante lifted his water glass to his lips and sipped in silence. The others followed suit.

El Comandante dabbed his mouth with a white linen napkin (it could easily have doubled as a blindfold) and ordered that the next course be served: lobster-stuffed avocados. The prisoners' nostrils flared as they struggled to ignore their appetizers. Most of the lobsters caught off Cuba's coasts were exported, or reserved for tourists. The odds were high—the tyrant relished the thought—that these troublemakers hadn't seen a lobster in decades.

Without warning, the physics professor rose to his feet and stretched his arms wide, as if being fitted for a crucifix. His eyes were burning, feverish looking. The guards made a move to restrain him, but El Comandante held them off with a raised finger.

"Does the professor have something to impart to us?" the tyrant asked, spearing a hunk of lobster with his fork.

Rigoberto Alves broke out in loud laughter, knocking over the untouched rioja and his lobster-stuffed avocado. "I prefer my lobster grilled with butter sauce," he pronounced. Then he flapped his arms, the wingbeat akin to a turkey vulture's or a great brown pelican's, and raced to the window overlooking the sea. Without hesitating, he threw himself out of it, wheeling into the air with astonishing grace, hovering for the length of a holy incantation, the summer day's haze outlining him as if he were a shimmering, stained-glass saint. Alves dropped three stories and landed, chin first, in a spray of blood and bone, interrupting the prisoners in the courtyard, who were practicing for a much-anticipated Sunday soccer match against the guards.

"He chose his own penance," El Comandante said tersely, recalling how Che used to dine at the firing squads. "No sense in ruining a perfectly good luncheon." He signaled to the waiters, who brought in an enormous earthenware casserole of chicken and rice festooned with asparagus, roasted red peppers, and petits pois. They served heaping platefuls to the pale, shaken dissidents.

The ex-colonel stood up and took a clumsy step toward the tyrant. His legs were short for such a tall man, and his left hand was withered from an army accident. His people had been cane cutters and tenant farmers back in Oriente. Without the Revolution, Benes would've been nothing. His ingratitude was particularly galling.

"You wish to make a statement, Benes?" The prison visit was going better than El Comandante had expected. All he had to do was show up and the hunger strikers self-destructed one by one.

Benes cleared his throat, endlessly it seemed. "When I get out of here, dead or alive," he said, his voice cracking, "I will tell everyone about the barbarity of your so-called revolution. Far and wide, to the living and to the dead, I will tell the truth: that you are a manipulator of facts and men, anything but a true revolutionary—"

"That's enough, Mario!" Collante interrupted him.

"No one gives a shit what you have to say," El Comandante said, reaching for a roll and meticulously buttering it. "In fact, no one gives a shit what any of you have to say."

"So why the hell are you here?" the hairdresser lashed out. "Your time is over, viejo. History has already issued its verdict: your revolution is a fracaso!"

The tyrant cut into a seared chicken breast bursting with the subtle taste of saffron. He had them where he wanted them—agitated and impotent. Their resolve was waning, he could sense it. They were feeble, ravenous, worn out.

"Bring cerveza," he ordered the waiters, who quickly placed an ice-cold beer before each dissident.

El Comandante studied his opponents' eyes, glazing but still wary. It was the time of day when the entire island came to a standstill in deference to the sun. Soon the dissidents' hatred would lapse into exhaustion, as hatred invariably did. Collante picked up his empty water glass and raised it toward the waiters, who didn't move a muscle. They would drink the beer or they would drink nothing. The tyrant scraped up the last grains of rice with his fork. His appetite was unusually robust today, fueled by the pleasure of battle. "We must make our peace with the necessity of dying." He paused, glancing toward the window. "But remember this: you won't create a new solar system in which I am not the sun. Even after I'm gone, the heat of my presence will be felt."

"You have no feelings except ambition and vanity!" Matamoros shouted.

"Where would any of us be without ambition or vanity?" El Comandante retorted with a tinge of exasperation. If he didn't keep his emotions in check, he might be tempted to throw the lot of them to the sharks and invite more grief upon his regime— and just when he was trying to restore its tarnished reputation. He must deflect their hatred as he had the countless assassination attempts against him.

A fly buzzed over the dissidents' untouched plates. At last, the foreman could no longer hold himself back. "The world you are leaving us is broken, Jefe," he said quietly. "Let another generation try to make something from the ruins. As it is, we're all sentenced to death."

"You're an intelligent man," El Comandante said, trying to contain his fury. "What are you doing with these losers?" An errant cockroach scuttled near his foot, and he crushed it, almost absently, with the toe of his heavy black boot. He snapped his fingers for dessert, a coconut flan baked in the shape of the island and floating in a sea of caramel syrup. After the waiters served each man a generous portion, the despot requested a box of cigars. "No calories there, pendejos," he laughed. "You can light up with a free conscience."

A knock on the door interrupted the luncheon. The prison dentist, Doctora Tomasa Firmat, strode in with her black bag of drills and amalgams and a low-level euphoria that resulted from her free access to anesthetics. Once a month she visited La Cabaña with the express purpose of extracting teeth. On the days Dr. Firmat appeared, the screams in the prison were more dreadful than usual.

"Good afternoon, Jefe," she said cheerfully, a mustache of perspiration glistening on her upper lip. Circles of sweat also dampened the underarms of her white physician's coat. "I'm here to check on one of the hunger strikers."

The tyrant looked around and noticed, for the first time, that the left side of the foreman's face was terribly swollen. El Comandante savored his flan, watching as the no-nonsense dentist withdrew a clawlike instrument from her bag. She bent over Collante with a dramatic flair and inserted the metal claw into his mouth. Collante moaned, pitiably, to the creaking, sucking sound of bone separating from flesh. A moment later, the triumphant dentist brandished the infected molar, bloody roots and all. The prisoners stared at one another, then down at their desserts. What more awaited them at this interminable meal? El Comandante cleaned his plate and, rubbing his stomach, made a show of refusing seconds. La dentista cauterized the site where Collante's tooth had been, stuffed a wad of sterile gauze in its place, bid everyone a good day, and departed with her drills and clinking implements.

Collante held his cheek with one hand and reached for a proffered cigar with the other. The tyrant was pleased to see that the foreman would not refuse a Cohiba even after his ordeal. Following his lead, the hairdresser and ex-colonel each tentatively took a cigar. They lit them and leaned back against their chairs, enveloped in clouds of smoke. The cigars seemed to soothe their jangled nerves, tamp down their hunger pangs, their proclivity for self-destruction. A man didn't kill himself, El Comandante knew, while smoking a good cigar.

The tyrant stifled a yawn. He was overcome with drowsiness after the heavy meal. "Your legacy," he said, "is a negative imprint that will fade in a matter of weeks."

"One can't predict the caprices of history," Collante mumbled as he pulled the bloody gauze from his mouth. "Sometimes the paths of logic and folly are one."

Since when had this asshole become a philosopher? The tyrant refused to be lectured at by someone whose very education was made possible by the Revolution. The waiters cleared the hunger strikers' plates. They would take the leftovers home to their families. It was one of the perks of the job.

"Take them away," El Comandante ordered, finishing his cigar, and the guards reappeared to enchain the prisoners and escort them back to their cells.

11.

Birthday

The South

The morning was so hot that only children moved with any semblance of energy. Goyo had walked these same streets with Luisa twenty years ago wearing squeaky new sneakers—the first pairs either had ever owned. They'd started exercising gradually, trudging along the nearby college's symmetrical paths. Wealthy, corpulent dieters from around the world lumbered alongside them like so many dinosaurs. On rainy days the lot of them trooped over to the indoor shopping mall, forming a colorful parade in their size quadruple-X sweats.

Goyo drove his son to the Devil's Diner, renowned as the best place for a last meal before commencing the Rice House diet. The diner's cinnamon buns were legendary, each larger than an infant's head. Goyo and his son slid into a red vinyl booth and accepted the photo menus from the waitress. The offerings verged on the pornographic: caloric sundaes erotically glistening with pecans; slabs of ham like a chorus line of delectable thighs; deep-fried Oreos smothered under scoops of candy-flecked ice cream. Across the ceiling, giant ventilation shafts sucked up the copious grease fumes.

Goyito selected breakfast specials numbers three and seven: six fried eggs, a double portion of cheese grits, two cinnamon buns, a pound of country ham, home fries, a stack of flapjacks, a basket 'o biskits [*sic*], bottomless orange juice, and a pot of coffee. Goyo ordered a half grapefruit with a bowl of raisin bran (to help relieve a two-day bout of constipation). He shook out his medications onto an oversize napkin and swallowed the pills with a glass of tomato juice. When their orders arrived, Goyito calmly and meticulously devoured his breakfast. His focus was impressive, his manners impeccable. His lineless face seemed outside time. He wielded his knife and fork with aplomb, dabbed his mouth at regular intervals, and dispatched his grits like soup, decorously tipping the bowl away from his torso.

Goyo scrutinized the other customers, who also were tucking into manifold platters of food. His son, at five four and nearly three hundred pounds, was among the largest. Goyito called over the waitress and ordered a slice of pecan pie à la mode for dessert. Weeks had elapsed since Goyito had professed a desire to kill himself. He wasn't on the streets, or in jail, or in a mental hospital with his arms straitjacketed across his chest and a rubber clamp between his teeth. This, at least, was progress. Outside, a pair of boat-tailed grackles hopped and screeched under a crepe myrtle's blossom-draped limbs. Goyo tried to catch his son's eye, but he was too busy delicately scraping the last of the pecan pie off his plate.

At the Rice House, Goyo wrote a sizable check for his son's weight-loss program. He signed his name at the bottom of a stack of paperwork next to Goyito's spidery scrawl. Sometimes Goyo guiltily wished for another son, one he might've loved without reserve, with whom he might've been friends at this stage of life, a son he could brag about to his friends, who had, above all, a capacity for happiness. Goyito had been the most sensitive in the family. When he was a boy, his nerves seemed to trail from his body like fibers of light. What else, Goyo lamented, could he have done to save him?

Soon Goyito would submit to the rigors of eating the daily fare of hundreds of millions of Asians. Their dietary habits formed the basis of the Rice House's "revolutionary" approach to eating: a modest portion of white rice topped with steamed vegetables and "seasoned" with specks of animal protein. Only Americans, Goyo thought, would pay thousands of dollars to be meagerly fed, spartanly housed, and monitored by humorless nurses.

Goyo joined his son for the inaugural meal. They sat at a table with a voluminous woman from Dallas and a goateed Venezuelan who, despite his considerable bulk, gave off a playboy air. It turned out that the playboy was heir to an oil fortune in Caracas. His self-professed downfall: sweet fried plantains. He admitted to eating them by the boatload. The mood was grim during the first course, a scant bowl of vegetable broth. It was tasteless and needed salt, but no saltshakers were permitted. At the other tables, the regulars had the unmistakable gray cast of prison inmates. Goyito consumed his broth with the same imperturbability he'd displayed toward his grits.

The rest of lunch—white rice, dry-grilled eggplant, a microscopic portion of minced chicken—worsened Goyo's disposition. He'd paid twenty dollars as a guest for this unspeakable meal, which had cost the Rice House thieves less than fifty cents. This was on top of the forty-three dollars he'd shelled out for brunch, the thirty-five-hundred-dollar deposit for Goyito's first two weeks here, and the kennel-and-kibble fees for Rudy at a local pet resort.

Everything about the place depressed Goyo. The shabby clapboard structure painted a minimalist gray. The bulbous TV set from the seventies. The garden, colorless except for a few anemic tomato vines. The not so subliminal message was clear: *tame your excesses*. If this were a country, Goyo thought, its citizens would be clamoring to emigrate.

After a dessert of mealy sliced pears in sugar-free syrup, it was time to get back on the road. Goyito buried his head in his father's chest. No matter that he was loco de remate, his son loved him with a child's vast innocence. The two walked arm in arm to the Cadillac and together adjusted a droopy side mirror. Goyo could've used a nap, but he was anxious to continue his trip. As his son frantically waved, Goyo pulled down the gravel driveway and onto the sleepy streets of Durham, then out toward the interstate that would take him to New York.

A hundred miles flew by as Goyo sped through the dense foliage of the South. He wanted to make it to the suburbs of Washington, D.C., before nightfall, check into a nice hotel, order a top sirloin from room service. He fiddled with his XM radio, scanning its two-hundred-plus stations. A Yankees game was under way—another dead heat with the Red Sox. The Yankees pitcher threw behind a right-handed slugger, and the Red Sox bench emptied as the batter charged the mound. Goyo remembered his own days as a third baseman—that triple play he'd made, catching the ball, stepping on third, throwing to first before the stumbling runner could get back. The crowd had gone crazy. *Go-yo! Go-yo!* For twenty-four hours he dreamt himself into the majors—until the next game, when he caught his cleat on the pitcher's mound running to position and flopped 360 degrees. He got his second standing ovation in as many days.

At a gas station in rural Virginia—his Cadillac was an unrepentant guzzler—Goyo noticed the billboard for an indoor shooting range down the road. Five pickup trucks filled the lot. Goyo extracted his Glock from the glove compartment and slipped it into his waistband. Leaning hard on his cane, he headed inside. He tried not to think of the arguments he'd had with his daughter over his possession of weapons. During their last debate, she'd stopped him cold with the question "Is there a gun that can't kill the owner of the gun?" Alina might be crazy, Goyo thought, but she was whip smart.

A couple of country boys idled behind the counter. They were respectful enough, gushing their "yes, sirs" and "sure things." The freckled one did most of the talking. Goyo examined the assortment of firearms on display: AK47s, twelve-gauge shotguns, .357 Smith & Wesson Magnums. He was tempted to try one of the semiautomatics, but he wasn't here to play. "Give me thirty rounds of nine millimeters," Goyo said, trying to countrify his accent a bit, though the clerks had probably seen his Florida plates on the security cameras. They asked him to fill out a disclaimer stating that he wasn't mentally incompetent, a fugitive from the law, or involved in a violent domestic dispute. Then he surrendered his driver's license.

"Nineteen twenty-nine." The freckled boy whistled. His expression matched that of the longhorn sheep trophy on the wall behind him. Where the hell had they hunted that? Goyo declined the boy's offer to load the magazine. For years he'd kept his Glock tucked under the diner's cash register. He'd never shot anyone, but he'd waved the gun around enough times to spread the word that he was packing. When you rehearsed something long enough, its reality became more likely. After what'd happened in Cuba, he wasn't about to let some punk take anything else away from him.

The blasts from the other shooters jarred Goyo, even with his ear protectors on. In one booth, a sloppy-looking woman shot off a rifle, muttering: "Oh yeah, baby, you gonna pay." Goyo set up at the far station. He steadied his shoulder against the cinder-block wall and pushed five rounds into the magazine. He sent the target out forty feet, farther than the deadly accuracy the Glock promised at closer range. A cramp pinched the arch in one foot, but he ignored the pain. The Glock felt solid in his hands. He straightened his right arm, stabilizing it with his left, both thumbs forward. Then he lined up the sights, and exhaled. One easy squeeze should do it. Así. Straight to the heart.

~ ❧ ~

Havana

When El Comandante awoke from his nap, he found his brother waiting at his bedside, eyes bloodshot from drinking.

"Cojones, help me to the crapper." This was as close to an olive branch as the tyrant ever offered.

Fernando jumped to readiness and guided him to the toilet. "We've got a birthday rally at the Capitol," he said, standing guard as the despot took a shit. "Everyone and their canaries will be singing you 'Happy Birthday.'"

El Comandante half-smiled.

"Of course, you'll want to say a few words," Fernando went on, encouraged. "Then we're going to fly you to Cienfuegos for—"

"Pa' carajo—"

"I brought Mejías here to give you assurances."

"You what?" The tyrant reached for his bathrobe.

"Give him three minutes of your time. If you're still against it, we'll cancel the whole thing. But remember, people have come from all over the world to celebrate with you. The presidents of Mexico and Brazil are here, leaders of seven African nations, ambassadors and foreign ministers from another twenty-four. And there's a big Hollywood contingent."

"Who?" El Comandante couldn't contain his curiosity.

"What's her name? The one who rode that mechanical bull in—"

"That was years ago, Fernando."

"Believe me, she still looks great. I saw her at a reception at the Hotel Nacional last night. She asked for you."

"Everyone asks for me."

"She used your first name."

The tyrant softened. "How did it sound?"

"What?"

"My name. In her mouth."

"Puro guarapo, hermano. Puro guarapo."

They both laughed. Despite Fernando's more straitlaced nature, the brothers had occasionally shared lovers in the early days of the Revolution. Their tastes overlapped just enough to have made these arrangements interesting. For a time, Fernando had been obsessed with Maria Callas. Poor bastard. He never worked up the courage to invite her to Cuba, much less try to seduce her. If the tyrant had felt the slightest attraction for that Greek diva, he would've shown Fernando how it could be done. No woman—not even the greatest soprano in the world—was out of his reach.

He rolled his eyes. "Bring in the fool then."

Fernando retreated before his brother could change his mind and returned with Orestes Mejías. El Comandante took inventory of the man. So this was the faggot who'd dared defy him with his counterrevolutionary plays? Mejías's face was pear-shaped and disfigured, no doubt from prison beatings, and his skin had a typhoid tinge. He wore baggy, checkered trousers and yellow shoes with rubber treads, obviously black-market purchases. His left eye was bruised shut, but the right one, a muddy green, looked around the room with anguish. It seemed to take in everything, down to the crooked straw in the tyrant's watered-down orange juice.

It'd taken the island's best detectives three weeks to track down Mejías, half starved and eaten alive by mosquitoes in the Zapata Swamp, a stone's throw from the Bay of Pigs. The playwright had been surviving on crabs.* He had cojones. That much the despot would give him. Not like the vast majority of maricones he'd had locked up in concentration camps in the sixties. Most of them had fucking died of melodrama. Not a single one ever changed his sexual orientation, no matter how many "reeducation" denials they'd signed.

Mejías said nothing at first, biting his knuckles until they bled. Then, as if electrically prodded, the playwright released a flood of words. The new musical, Mejías insisted, would be a showcase for both El Líder and the Revolution. Blah, blah, blah. The more he talked, the more the bastard's confidence grew. Yet there was something wrathful in his expression that the tyrant mistrusted. Who would give a damn if one of Fernando's bodyguards cracked the pervert's head in two? What was the worst that could happen? If Mejías double-crossed them in the end, they could simply tie him up with dinner napkins and throw him to the sharks.

Gradually, the playwright wound down. His cheek twitched and his breath whiffled out wordlessly, like a mourning dove's wing. Down below in the courtyard, the tyrant's twin grandsons were coaxing their cat to walk on its hind legs. They'd taught Angola other tricks—offering its paw, sitting, rolling over. Delia

---

* The crabs are running this time of year. We catch them at night when they cross the Ancón Peninsula, from the ocean to the bay and back. Our crabs are as big as a man's fist and very tender. The paladares charge tourists fifty times what they pay us. A few years ago, a giant cangrejo punctured the tire of a Swedish woman's car and sent it skittering into the sea. They say la sueca drowned, that her body was never found. Sometimes I fantasize that the crabs will rise up and fight back— an army of them, claws waving, refusing even us.

—*Gumersindo Pérez, crab catcher*

liked to joke that Angola had been a Doberman pinscher in a previous life. "And you were a fancy poodle," El Comandante had teased his wife, to which she contested: "¿Y tú, mi amor? Definitely a sheepdog. Ay, you never stop bossing everyone around!" A crash of dishes erupted from the kitchen. Gusts of frying meat wafted through the open window.

Fernando opened his mouth to speak, but El Comandante cut him off with a papal gesture. "I've heard enough. You may proceed. But watch yourself, Mejías, or you'll be sleeping with the fishes." Then he turned to Fernando: "Let's hope you're not warming a serpent on your breast. Facilis descensus Averno."

⁓

Rural Virginia

Goyo hadn't forgotten how to shoot a gun—his skills were too ingrained for that—but he'd forgotten the visceral pleasure of pulling a trigger. As he aimed at the target, he imagined the tyrant at the business end of his barrel. This made it easy to shoot "him" in the heart fourteen times in a row. Over the years, Goyo had sharpened his skills with regular visits to shooting ranges in the suburbs. Once he'd taken Luisa to his regular range in Fort Lee— he'd wanted her to learn the basics in case something happened to him—but she'd left trembling and unable to fire a shot. Goyo knew he was capable of killing. If he ever came face-to-face with El Comandante, there'd be no discussion, no second thoughts, no mercy. He'd shoot the bastard dead.

A soft rain fell as Goyo drove through the Virginia countryside. He liked the distorting effects of the rain on his windshield, how everything appeared moist and magnified, like his best memories.

The rains here were nothing like the torrential autumn storms in Cuba, where the water sluiced through the streets like rivers. The tropics were defined by excess: too much light, too much rain, too many mosquitoes and caudillos, avalanches of grief. A convoy of refrigerated dairy trucks roared past him, most likely headed to New York. When he'd been a part of the city's hurly-burly, he'd taken its wonders for granted. Miami was a village by comparison.

Goyo pulled off the interstate to a drive-through place and bought himself a chocolate-dipped ice cream cone. It would have to tide him over until he got to Arlington. He wanted to arrive before dark, after which it would become difficult for him to read the road signs. He'd programmed his GPS to take him to one of the better business hotels in the area. His days of staying on flimsy, spine-torturing mattresses were over. Lo barato sale caro. What's cheap ends up expensive. His father had taught him that. Papá had also taught him to seize pleasure when it presented itself. Because the real juice in life was fleeting, he'd said, hallucinatory, essential for dispelling the long stretches of mundane.

A slate-gray storm obscured the sky. Lightning cleft the horizon. Goyo flipped through the radio stations again, stopping at a Metropolitan Opera recording of *Faust*. He pictured the twisted face of Mephistopheles booming: "Here comes eternal remorse and eternal anguish in everlasting night!" For a time in the seventies, Goyo had secretly taken singing lessons. It turned out that he had a decent baritone—alas, the most common voice—but he didn't pursue it further. Another passion discarded in the name of security. He turned up the volume on the opera. If Mephistopheles were to appear before him now, would he do as Faust did and take the Devil's deal?

A clock chimed inside the hotel's oak-paneled lobby. The sounds of a fox-trot drifted in from the lounge, where the bartender, burly as a gorilla, refilled the equidistant bowls of nuts. Goyo settled on a leather banquette near the bar and ordered a crème de menthe on the rocks. Around him a bunch of ruddy road warriors, fat from expense accounts, drank or played billiards, the balls clacking sharply on the baize-covered table. Above the liquor bottles, a flat-screen television murmured the news. The Middle East was in a shambles. Another ethnic uprising was convulsing Rwanda. A tornado had torn through Kansas, just like in that movie Goyito and Alina had loved as children. Carajo, he'd forgotten it was El Comandante's birthday. Footage showed celebrations all over the island—no doubt with people they'd forced to the events with threats of reprisals. This was ruining what was left of his day. Goyo swallowed a third of his drink. Not even his sister-in-law's prayer circle of Miami accountants could hasten the tyrant's demise. Every santero and babalawo in Miami also had been called upon to use their sorcery against him, but nothing had worked. The hijo de puta had become immortal.

A man in white robes walked into the bar looking like Lawrence of Arabia. Goyo must've stared at him a moment too long because the fellow sat down next to him and ordered a Corona with a twist of lime. The stranger removed his turban, and his curly, reddish hair sprang to life.

"You didn't think I was really an Arab, did you?" he drawled.

"Are you in theater?" Goyo ventured.

"Working on a PhD in sociology." He took a swig of his beer. "Where are you from, man?"

Goyo pointed to the TV screen, now showing a frenzied conga line weaving its way through the streets of Cienfuegos in anticipation of the tyrant's arrival. "A cursed place, a place where treachery is the common currency."

"You a poet?" Lawrence tossed a handful of cashews into his mouth.

"Oh, nothing so useful as that." His back pain was flaring up, and his mending leg throbbed. "Are you going to ask me what you should do with your life?"

"How'd you know?"

"One learns more from being old than from being the Devil." Goyo sighed. "What would you rather be doing?"

"Playing the trombone."

"The trombone?" In every concert band he'd ever played in, Goyo had disliked the trombonists most.

"It's a very underrated instrument."

Goyo shrugged. "Then take off those ridiculous sheets and become a trombonist, young man. Now could you please help me up here?"

Switch and Bait

Look at me: eighty-three years old and still peddling straw hats on the streets. My wife makes them with the sewing machine I've kept working for her since 1952. Did I tell you that I'm on the waiting list for new dentures? The ones I have are too big for me and hurt my gums. Mira, the teeth are so huge, especially the incisors, that everyone—even my own great-grandchildren—calls me Dracula. Don't think this doesn't hurt my feelings. I am, above all, a sensitive man.

I cut sugarcane for many years, but today the fields are in ruins and we import food that nobody can afford. How can you live on a jar of olives? Even good olives from Spain. Everything, down to the bread on our tables, comes from abroad. That's why I'm out here under the hot sun selling hats for a peso. Sometimes I change my price and tell a tourist the hats cost two pesos, not one. That's two pesos convertible (CUC), or forty-eight pesos national money. Today, some fat cow from Miami fought me over the switch and bait, so I let her have the damn hat for one.

—*Faustino Diliz, street vendor*

12.

Monkeys

Havana

The day was sweltering as the tyrant climbed onto the steps of the Capitol building, the heat a thick ache inside his skull. He was working up the gladiatorial energy to address a crowd only a third the size Fernando had promised him. Most of those present had been bused in from the provinces, tempted more by the opportunity to visit Havana than to listen to another one of El Comandante's long-winded speeches. All of them had already seen him on multiple occasions. Cuba was small, and the tyrant had visited every corner of it, shaken everyone's hands twice over, kissed each new generation of babies, bored one and all to tears with his trademark tirades.

A comparsa tried to pump up the excitement with its drums and Chinese cornets. A sea of birthday signs bobbed before him:
¡FELIZ CUMPLEAÑOS! ¡QUE VIVA EL JEFE! ¡CIEN AÑOS DE REVOLUCIÓN!

El Comandante braced himself against the podium. Numbness crept through one foot, and he stamped it to prevent it from falling asleep. "¡Buenos días, ciudadanos!" he croaked. (Last month, a British newspaper had described his voice as "tobacco tinged with dirty, moonlit gravel.") "Thank you for coming to celebrate my birthday today. But more important than my statesman's age," he said, pausing for effect, "is the fact that we, as a people, as a dedicated revolution, are still alive and well."

Impromptu dancing broke out in the back of the crowd, where the ¡SALUDOS DE SANTIAGO! signs were thickest. A few supporters waved from balconies, or were perched in the park's deciduous trees. The tyrant could always count on the party faithful from Oriente to rise to any occasion. Historically, anything important that had ever happened in Cuba—in politics, culture, or music—had begun in Oriente, himself included. They were his people and he knew how to handle them, knew how to handle all the islanders. No one else could do what he did.

El Comandante waited, letting everyone have their fun, before leaning in to the microphones: "¡Que viva La Revolución!"

"¡Que viva!" the crowd roared back.

Near the front, a good-looking guajiro carried a girl on his shoulders. Years from now, she would remember the day she got to see the last great strongman of the Caribbean. The tyrant beckoned them to the stage, and security went nuts, walkie-talkies squawking. What the hell was El Caballo up to now? The crowd parted as the man pushed forward, a look of disbelief on his face. He took to the stage, the girl still on his shoulders, and shook El Líder's hand.

"Tell me your name."

"Jacomino Rey," he said in such a deep, sonorous voice that it made the women swoon.* "This is mi hija, Clotilde."

---

* **Basso Profundo.** He says only one word to the ladies, one word that emerges from his endlessly seductive throat, a sound they can squeeze with their pussies.

El Comandante loosened a microphone from a cluster on the podium and brought it to the girl's lips. She was maybe five years old, missing a tooth, and her hair was neatly cornrowed. "How old are you, Clotilde?"

"Cinco," she lisped, and the crowd went wild.

"Did you know that today is my birthday?"

She buried her face in her father's neck.

"I have a special favor to ask you, Clotilde. I would like you to sing me 'Happy Birthday.' Could you do that for me?"

The girl nodded and immediately began singing to him off-key. It was a perfect moment, like so many he'd savored during his decades in power; in sync with an adoring public on a glorious summer day. Ay, why deny it? Every once in a while his scalp itched for a crown. He waited for Clotilde to finish before shouting: "¡Patria o muerte, venceremos!"

At the edge of the crowd—everything significant always happened along the edges—El Comandante spied a group of protesters waving posters with . . . what? Caged monkeys? ¿Qué carajo? Security forces quickly descended on the miscreants and dragged them off. A shot rang out from who knew where, and people screamed and went running in every direction. Jacomino hit the floor with his daughter as a posse of bodyguards pulled the dictator down the Capitol steps. Undeterred, the congueros kept playing like it was the last party on earth.

"Why the caged monkeys?" the tyrant demanded.

El Conejo, imperturbable as ever, settled next to him in the backseat of the Mercedes. "They're protesting the use of psychotropic drugs against political prisoners."

For years, El Líder had sent Cuba's best medical students to the

---

It's a form of hypnosis, his voice, rumbling toward them like temptation itself, catching them for an hour, or an afternoon.

former Soviet Union to learn the art of making antidissident drug cocktails. Few approaches had proved as effective, in the long run, as turning his opponents' brains to mush. Also, by being sequestered in mental institutions, the dissidents slipped under human rights radars. The motto chiseled at the entrance to La Mariposa, the island's most notorious asylum: "There is no greater misfortune than the loss of reason."

"Who shot off the gun?"

"It was stolen from a militiaman in Sagua la Grande. I'll have more information for you shortly."

The tyrant looked out the tinted window of the sedan. It sped by ceiba trees and decaying balconies, past la esquina caliente, where men argued sports all day long (and needed licenses to do so), past the broken sidewalks and cobblestones of Old Havana. Last week, two depraved citizens shook their fists at his passing car. How long before they dared curse him to his face? Along the malecón, skinny boys in rags jumped off the seawall, trying to outdo one another scavenging for bottle caps and fishing hooks* and rusty coins. What would their revolution look like ten years from now, or twenty?

When his sons were little, Delia had procured for them a pet bonobo from Africa. The filthy, insolent creature had humped the furniture, stolen the despot's cigars, even sat in his armchair, waving and chattering like a third-rate politician. This had delighted everyone but him. "Send it back to the fucking jungle!" he'd ordered his wife. Later, he found out that Delia had donated the

---

*__Trabajito.__ To catch a big fish, it takes a few fishhooks, not to mention other key ingredients I'm not at liberty to discuss. The target of my efforts has gotten too audacious, too arrogant. He makes fishhook paintings that sell for obscene thousands abroad. If you live by fishhooks, I say, then you die by fishhooks.
—*__Anonymous__*

sorry beast to a zoo in Montevideo, where it continued to entertain gawkers with its antics.

"I want to see those posters."

El Conejo bent over his cell phone, gleaning more details about the disruption. Security forces had rounded up 276 people in fifteen minutes, most of them randomly. After their release, word would spread of the Revolution's continuing and unsparing interrogation methods. Fear would send deeper taproots into el pueblo's fragile psyches. Terror, El Comandante knew, was the best taskmaster, delegating the bulk of his regime's dirty work.

Back at his compound, the tyrant examined the placards retrieved at the rally. The most egregious displayed a grainy photograph of a chimpanzee dressed in military fatigues pasted above the headline ANTI-EVOLUTIONARY! Another showed a group of sullen-looking monkeys behind bars wearing metal caps bursting with unruly electrical wires. The caption: RESIST BRAINWASHING! The most insulting poster featured a grinning chimp in a jaunty beret, mocking the slogan BE MORE LIKE CHE! El Comandante felt the slow tolling of an impending migraine. He was disgusted by this latest evidence of unrest—and on his birthday, no less.

Arlington, Virginia

Goyo's hotel room was perfectly anonymous, decorated in masculine shades of beige and brown. There was an excellent mattress, a faux-marble bathroom with high-quality amenities including a discreet three-pack of condoms. Perhaps he should live out his days in a full-service hotel like this; forget the upkeep, the condo fees, the persistently noisome neighbors. No point in leaving his money for his children to squander. There was a giant flat-screen television, but he couldn't bear to watch any more footage of the despot's birthday festivities. He ordered a steak from the overpriced room service menu, medium rare with a double portion of mashed potatoes and a slice of peach pie. Then he washed his face and dried it on one of the thick, spotlessly white towels.* In the hotel directory, an ad for a psychic healer caught his eye: SEÑORA VÁSQUEZ. BILINGUAL. NO PROBLEM TOO BIG. On an impulse, he called the number.

"Good evening, Señor Herrera."

"Are you Señora Vásquez?" Goyo asked, startled that she knew his name.

"Yes. I'll be right up after your dinner." The dial tone blared.

Goyo's lower back burned from the long drive north. He dug into his suitcase for a couple of aspirin, then lowered himself onto the bed. Room service knocked and rolled in his meal. The steak was excellent—except for the sautéed mushrooms he hadn't requested. Señora Vásquez appeared at the door as he was finishing the last bite of peach pie. She wore a bold-print shift and carried a knapsack, from which she extracted a candelabra and a rusty gridiron. Then she whipped out a pack of Tarot cards and began shuffling and dealing them like a casino pro.

"You are suffering from severe myocarditis," she pronounced. "This condition will determine—"

"Perdóname, señora," Goyo interrupted. "But won't you ask me

---

*Towels are the biggest scam going in Cuba. I took a group of American students to Trinidad for a week, and on our last morning there, just as our bus was getting ready to leave, the hotel manager came running out to tell us that there were three towels missing from our rooms. "Go back and double-check the number," I yelled at him. When he disappeared into the lobby, I turned to our driver. "¡Arranca y vámonos!" We spat gravel all the way back to Havana.
          —*Dr. Linda Howe, Spanish literature professor*

any questions?" He wanted to inquire about his son's future and his collapsing building and, most crucially, the odds of him succeeding in killing the tyrant.

"That won't be necessary." One globular eye stared at him; the other continued reading the cards. "You will circle back to the original wound."

Goyo ground his back molars. What was this raving nonsense going to cost him? He kicked himself for not negotiating a flat fee in advance.

"Twenty dollars for the first ten minutes. Prorated thereafter," she said. "What you must do cannot be accomplished with a watering can."

No shit, Goyo wanted to say, but he kept his mouth shut. He noticed the diamond cross nestled in her cleavage, her black hair lacquered into a chignon at her neck. Her fingers were lengthened by long, flawless nails. She looked like someone capable of cursing him with durable maledictions.

"You must not hesitate."

"To do what?" Goyo broke in, exasperated.

"To fulfill your incurable fate." Señora Vásquez flipped and rearranged the cards. "It is certain because it is impossible. Look here," she said, tapping an acrylic nail on a gloomy-looking knight. "Destiny has put a spear in your hand. The ranges of disloyalty are great."

Goyo squirmed. "I don't understand."

"This is what I can offer you. You don't have to pay me if you find this unhelpful." A madly twittering parakeet appeared on her shoulder out of thin air. "Now, now, Renata, calm down," the psychic crooned, stroking the tiny bird's head.

Goyo thought twice before reaching for his wallet but decided to play it safe and handed the gypsy two twenty-dollar bills: one for her time, the other as insurance.

"Call me if you have any more concerns." She pocketed the cash and left.

It wasn't just the forty dollars he'd stupidly wasted that gnawed at Goyo but the countless minute decisions that had led him to the end of his pointless life. Carajo, why hadn't he met Adelina again at the Gran Teatro when she'd asked him to? Hadn't her request been tantamount to an apology? His whole life might've changed course right then and there. He rooted around in his toiletries for Luisa's expired sleeping pills and climbed into bed. After she'd died, Goyo had sorted through a mountain of her personal belongings: crocodile handbags, designer suits ranging from petite to obese and imbued with her perfume, unguents and eye serums, a thousand shiny tubes of lipstick. He was half-crazed by the time he had it all carted off to the American Cancer Society.

As he dozed off in a medicated haze, his phone rang. It was Goyito, begging him to return to North Carolina to pick him up. Was there no peace for him even at this hour?

"They're trying to poison me! They put LSD in my rice!"

Goyo was too exhausted to argue. He'd heard from the Rice House director earlier in the day that Goyito had been caught distributing buttermilk donuts to his fellow dieters. That wasn't all. Evidently, his son was also selling amphetamines in the form of diuretics and running a jigsaw puzzle racket. When it came to self-destruction, Goyito was a one-man Category 5 hurricane.

"Tomorrow, hijo. Tomorrow," Goyo slurred, then fell asleep.

In the last of several feverish dreams, Goyo attended a lavish ball at the Catedral de San Cristóbal, its archways hung with swags of valerian. The guests were dressed in nineteenth-century finery—bejeweled women in cerise gowns, men in top hats and tailcoats. Chandeliers flickered vertiginously as the clatter of a thousand Spanish fans filled the air. A bald man in a Venetian mask presided over the festivities on a carved peacock throne, holding a scepter with a slowly spinning globe on its tip. Goyo drew closer to the globe. It was a perfect replica of earth, complete with snowcapped mountains, swaths of dense jungles, the ruffled surf of miniature oceans.

His mission grew clear. "I've come for the scepter." Goyo's voice squeaked like a choirboy's.

The Satan fixed him with a stare. He lifted the scepter, and the spinning globe stopped. Goyo looked around him. Giants with halberds guarded the exits. As he lunged for the globe, the floor gave way and he dropped for what seemed an eternity . . . Through a slit in the curtains, the moon streamed its radiance into his eyes. Shadows he couldn't account for marred the walls; whisperings seeped up from the plush carpet. Was he between worlds—a foot in this one, another in death? He worked up the courage to speak, to dispel the nightmare: "I am Goyo Herrera," he gasped. "And I am still alive."

Cacharro Chino

The car was a Geesley or a Gasless or a Ghastly—who the hell knew?—and it was my rental from Havana to Trinidad. Every indicator on the dashboard was useless. The speedometer flew to 220 kilometers per hour with each tap of the brakes. Or hovered at zero. Or wandered, haphazardly, to other erroneous speeds. The fuel gauge stayed on full, so I had to guess when to put in more gas, which cost an outrageous five dollars a liter. According to the odometer, the total mileage for our ten-hour round trip was 13.5 kilometers. I'm not even going to talk about the potholes. Or dodging the cows, goats, horses and buggies, chickens, vultures, three species of crabs, aggressive hitchhikers, Russian tractors, or rope-toting cowboys. Ask Pilar and Linda. They were with me.

—*C.G., novelist*

‿❧

Matanzas Province

The helicopter noise was infernal. Even with his protective head-gear, the chukka-chukka roar of the blades drowned out the tyrant's every thought. As they coasted over the hushed decay of the Zapata Swamp, he spotted an alligator surface then dive beneath the mangroves. El Comandante used to take VIPs snorkeling along the magnificent coral reef nearby. The Russians had looked like sloppy lobsters with their flabby, sunburned guts. Today, the sky was glazed a porcelain blue. The weatherman* had predicted rain, but that fool couldn't separate thunder from his own farts. Regrettably, he was the last meteorologist in Havana. The rest had defected to Miami.

The pilot flew low over the countryside, over its helices of palms and crumbling concrete huts that had replaced the sturdy bohíos with their thatched roofs and swept-dirt floors. "¿Todo bien, Jefe?" Captain Nicasio Correa was a stocky, hirsute man whose hairline merged with his wraparound sunglasses.

Inland, two old sugar mills still stood: the Covadonga, where his father-in-law had worked as a young man before siring the

---

* Ese tonto has been around since el año de la nana. I can say this much for him: he's consistent. If you expect the exact opposite of what he says, you'll be okay.
—*Basilio Machín, tobacco farmer*

ravishing Delia; and the Australia, converted into his military headquarters during the Bay of Pigs, then reconverted into El Museo de La Comandancia. *On this day in history, Yankee imperialism suffered its first great defeat in the Americas!* The tyrant had soothed himself to sleep many a night with those words, knowing that if he accomplished nothing else in his life, his place in history was secure. His mother-in-law, who'd lived in the area all her days, could identify every species in the swamp—pygmy owls and herons, water hens, purple gallinules. As a girl, Delia had loved to watch the crabs scuttle onto the roads and beaches during the massive spring mating frenzy. The crabs, she said, had made her horny as hell.

El Comandante pointed to a spit of land at the edge of the swamp. "Put her down right there, soldier."

"But the President said—"

"I'm in charge here!" he shouted over the noise.

"Yes, sir." The pilot landed the helicopter, as if on a bull's-eye.

The rotting stench was overpowering. "Over there was where the largest concentration of enemy troops landed," the tyrant said, indicating a beach across the bay. By the end of that first day, Cuba's air force had sunk a landing craft and two transport ships, the *Río Escondido* and the *Houston.* A freighter owned by that Galician bastard Arturo Herrera was also badly damaged and most of its crew killed. Four mercenary B-26s painted to look like the Revolution's planes were shot down; two more were crippled.

El Comandante gazed into the distance, lost in reminiscence. Diversionary tactics had forced him back to Havana in midbattle. Infuriated that he'd been lured away from the action at Playa Girón, he raced back to Pálpite. There he and his men came under artillery fire from the mercenaries' stronghold in Playa Larga. Although antiaircraft batteries had recently arrived from Russia, nobody knew how to operate them. Their first attempt to take Playa Larga failed. His troops suffered heavy casualties, mostly from among the young recruits of the Militia Leadership School battalion. But the impact of their attack forced the enemy to withdraw at dawn.

The tyrant was soaked with sweat, and the pilot fought off a cloud of mosquitoes. "With all due respect," Captain Correa said, "we should push off or we'll be meat for these pests in no time."

El Comandante relived the acid energy of those long ago April days. El Duque, one of his most trusted men from the Sierra Maestra, had raced to the swamp in his Buick, an ancient bazooka in the backseat. Without orders he took charge of the eastern front and managed to recapture a village from the enemy before being captured himself. Brave men like El Duque no longer existed in Cuba. A year later he died of a malignant goiter. When the doctors tried to remove it, the hero's head came right off with it.

"Let me help you into the helicopter," the pilot offered. "They're waiting for you in Cienfuegos."

The tyrant climbed back aboard as the helicopter's blades stirred a wide circle of cow lily leaves. Fernando had promised him a gaggle of starlets from abroad—Spain, France, Hollywood, all revolution-friendly places. El Comandante enjoyed charming these beauties, even at his age. A moderate dose of Cuban flattery translated to baroque devotion anywhere else. Before long they'd be feeding *him* chilled oysters from their fragrant fingertips. Yes, he was quite the master of hospitality, but the true geniuses, in his opinion, were the Arabs. Even the lowliest Bedouin in his blinding white burnoose welcomed a stranger to his tent with cardamom coffee and dates.

At the Cienfuegos airport, a crowd waved more birthday signs: MAY YOU LIVE TO 100! YOUR IMMORTALITY IS OURS! HEROES NEVER DIE! Who the hell came up with this shit? A swarm of elementary school children sang him "Las Mañanitas," and a pixie with hairsprayed curls plunked something out on a portable harp. The province's best marching band followed with a mambo a todo meter. Everything in this godforsaken country turned into a dance party,

El Comandante thought glumly. Nobody wanted to buckle down and do the hard, anonymous work of building the Revolution brick by brick. Every last cubano craved the limelight, but there simply wasn't enough room for eleven million stars. Just one.

———⟋⟍———

Star

I'm not beautiful, but I have what everyone wants: chispa. And talent. The ability to make you feel like you're the only person in the room. To the writers, I ask: Don't you have a little monologue for me? This isn't an act, though I'm an actress. I'm pushing forty, but I'm still in demand for the romantic roles. My body has the curves, but it's more than that. It's something that comes from inside, something that you can't fake. I'm lucky to be optimistic. You need optimism here. There's so much that crushes artists.

Years ago, I fell savagely in love with a Chilean poet and moved to Valparaíso. That's the prologue. Act One: He was very poor. Act Two: We had a daughter. Act Three: I returned home. I could've married a rich man but I fell in love. Why live if you can't follow your heart? Everyone in Havana gossips about me because I'm a single mother and successful. Women envy me; men want to sleep with me. Now and then I let myself go, but I choose carefully with whom. Ay, that evening I sang atop the piano at Simón and Naty's house was sublime! That sexy British actor was at the party. Gorgeous models orbited him, but it was me he wanted. And so we left together. The rest of the night—¡mi madre!—was beautiful.

—*Olga Lobaina, actress*

13.

The Swamp

Cienfuegos

Leave it to Fernando to suction all the fun out of a place. At the tiny Cienfuegos airport he strode up to the helicopter and made a show of stiffly embracing his brother. Then he whispered the lineup of interviews scheduled for the afternoon: *The New York Times,* Agence France-Presse, *El País, Der Spiegel,* CNN, Associated Press. The reporters had gone on a tour of Museo Girón, where key mementos of the Bay of Pigs—photos, film footage, weapons, tanks, even some airplane wreckage—were on display. Now they were eager to speak with the tyrant himself.

"No fucking way," El Comandante interrupted with a forced grin. "It's a press conference or nothing."

"Don't embarrass me, hermano. This took weeks to plan." Fernando glared at him but scurried off to arrange the press conference.

The heat was unbearable, three-dimensional. The tyrant stood alone on the scorching tarmac, accepting floral bouquets from one pretty schoolgirl after another, each reciting a well-rehearsed speech he ignored. All he wished was to go inside, where it was cool and he could have a drink. El Conejo appeared out of nowhere (a rabbit out of a hat, como siempre) and escorted his boss into the terminal. Soon he was seated comfortably at the evacuated bar with a scotch on the rocks. Nothing escaped his twisted little adviser's attention. In five minutes, El Conejo filled him in on everything he needed to know for the visit. He'd also dispatched an undercover agent to infiltrate the Bay of Pigs musical. The agent, a veteran of Angola, had been cast as a snapping turtle.

"A what?"

El Conejo assured him that nothing seemed amiss except for a certain extravagance of bad taste.

"Gracias, hombre." El Comandante chased his scotch with a swig of cough suppressant.

His adviser was rarely granted any direct expression of appreciation, and he flushed with pleasure. "A sus órdenes, Jefe," he whispered before vanishing as inexplicably as he'd appeared.

Fernando redirected the press to the Palacio de Valle, where the tyrant's birthday reception would be held later in the day. The palace was a garish mixture of Gothic, Venetian, and neo-Moorish architecture built by a local sugar baron in the early 1900s. Its sole redeeming feature was a stunning balcony overlooking the sea. El Comandante took one look at the place and decided to move the conference to the Castillo de Jagua instead. By the time Fernando and the sweaty, disheveled band of journalists found their way there, the mood was ugly.

El Comandante had been displeased with the international press coverage of him lately. This was his opportunity to remind these loser reporters who ruled around here. Last spring he'd stone-walled *Le Monde's* political correspondent after he'd referred to the

Revolution in a prominent Sunday feature as "an exercise in irrationality." It unhinged reporters to be denied access to power and made them lose credibility with their editors. The tyrant called on the irascible Associated Press correspondent first.

"Excuse me, but why the hell have we been moved here?"

El Comandante beheld the man for a moment before answering: "This castle was built nearly three hundred years ago to protect the bay from pirates. I thought it the most appropriate venue to host our friends in the press."

The room erupted with laughter, breaking the tension. The tyrant knew how much journalists hated leaders who took themselves too seriously. Essentially, the whole lot of them were cynics, relegated to the sidelines of history, never making news themselves unless they happened to be killed in the line of duty, after which they became footnotes to their own headlines. This inconsequentiality led to chronic bitterness and no small amount of Schadenfreude in their ranks.

"How many more birthdays do you plan on celebrating?" joked the sideburned correspondent from *Corriere della Sera*.

"Another three Popes' worth," El Comandante retorted to more laughter.

"It's said that despite your brother's official position as head of state, you continue to be in charge. Is that true?"

In the bright lights, the tyrant couldn't tell who'd asked the question. He spied the querulous Fernando standing against the far wall, balancing on the balls of his feet, hands clasped behind his back. Waiting, always waiting.

"I give him my full support as commander in chief, and I believe he's doing a good job on multiple fronts."

Fernando's grievous face brightened.

El Comandante then leaned mischievously into the microphone. "But I can still kick his ass."

"Tell us what we can expect at tonight's performance." This came from a Peruvian reporter, an old newshound whose few strands of hair were unattractively plastered to his forehead.

El Líder shrugged. "That, ladies and gentlemen of the press, will be my brother's surprise birthday gift to me."

"They say this citadel is haunted. What can you tell us about it?" asked the feisty bureau chief from Madrid's largest daily newspaper. Years ago El Comandante had tried, unsuccessfully, to bed her.

"Bueno, legend has it that a mysterious lady in blue—very much like yourself, Señorita Díaz"—an outburst of wolf whistles here—"roamed the rooms and corridors of the castle, frightening the security guards. One morning a guard was found at the edge of the moat in a state of shock, twisting a swatch of blue cloth and babbling nonsense." The tyrant rolled his eyes heavenward. "Ay, the torments of a beautiful woman . . ."

Laughter and hooting all around.

"Many say that the Cuban people are starving, that they are resorting to prostitution again to survive—"

The tyrant turned to his brother. "Who the hell is he?"

The reporter, a hulking redhead with a jutting chin, persisted. "The country's rations are lower than during the Special Period and they last for only six days out of—"

"You are misinformed!" El Comandante roared. "You should get your facts straight before embarrassing yourself and your publication. What is the name of your rag?"

"*Harper's*," he said, and the journalists tittered.

"Since the triumph of the Revolution, our people have never gone hungry," the tyrant boomed, jabbing the air with his forefinger. "Nor have they gone without medical attention, or a world-class education. These privileges cost your people untold billions every year and the quality is substandard. Starving? What rubbish! If anything, we need to go on a campaign to *lose* weight . . ."

Fernando approached the podium. The dictator rattled off a stream of facts: the caloric discrepancies between rich and developing nations, the nutritional value of yams, the unrivaled purity of island sugar. Once he got going, he could talk for four, eight, twelve hours, his hacking cough notwithstanding. For once, Fernando wished he could just tell his brother to shut the fuck up.

"Perdóname, Jefe, but we need to continue this conversation at another time." Fernando placed a hand on his brother's shoulder, then turned to the reporters. "We look forward to seeing you at tonight's performance of *Bay of Pigs: The Musical!*, and to your positive coverage of this historic event."

"Get your fucking hands off me," the tyrant growled, close enough to the microphone for everyone to hear. How dare Fernando humiliate him in front of these vermin? If he didn't control himself, decades of revolutionary history would boil down to this: a Shakespearean tragedy between two brothers. El Comandante looked out at the sea of scribbling hyenas. "If you thought that was good," he teased, "just wait until you see the play."

Bilingual Specials from the Best Paladar in the Capital

Croquetas de pescado / Fish croquettes

Frituras de malanga / Fried taro root

Cherna frita / Fried grouper

Arroz con frijoles / Rice with black beans

Plátanos maduros / Fried sweet plantains

Pastel de limón / Lemon pie

Shortly before dusk, the whole world was on the balcony of the Palacio de Valle. Waiters circulated with mojitos and tropical drinks, and the thirty-foot-long buffet offered up the island's finest: fresh grilled lobsters, calamari, garlic shrimp, deep-fried snapper, roasted pork, baked plantains, marinated hearts of palm salad, coconut flan . . . The despot was still incensed over the press conference. The insolence of those questions! As if he were ruling over a Haiti or a Sudan, not the most enduring revolution on the planet. Despite the food shortages, nobody went hungry in Cuba. Only the goddamn dissidents were starving—and that was by choice. Even those hard-core Damas de Blanco were a portly lot. In any case, why the hell should the Revolution supply food for thirty days a month when citizens stole enough for twenty? Furiously, he ferreted out pecans from a bowl of roasted nuts.

A conjunto from Santiago was playing a traditional *son*.* Its singer had won a nationwide Beny Moré impersonator contest last year. If the tyrant closed his eyes, he could imagine himself in a nightclub circa 1950, listening to the velvety crooner. The singer was a dead ringer for Beny, too: the same slicked-back hair and soulful eyes; the same smooth moves. El Comandante had known the real Beny but quickly discovered that the singer had been infinitely more interested in rum than in politics.

The aging president of Zimbabwe greeted El Líder with an

---

* "Una Noche con Tí" is our signature song. I picked up the maracas so I could spend more time with Feito, the lead singer. Mami taught me that all men are lying, cheating dogs like my father, who left for Miami when I was a baby. Feito wrote "Una Noche con Tí" after our first night together. I felt the pain before I felt the pleasure, but now I live for the pleasure. Our conjunto has swing, everybody says so. Feito promises me that we'll be famous someday and travel the world like the Buena Vista Social Club.

                                                    —*Eva Molina, maracas player*

entourage of stunning consorts. The two statesmen compared notes on folk remedies for insomnia and virility—*not that we would ever need it, ha!* The tyrant offered the Zimbabwean a Cohiba and promised him a tête-á-tête in the morning. The Nigerian leader joined them, and the talk turned to the superlative skills of their respective drug-busting airport dogs: Rottweilers in Lagos, heat-tolerant Chihuahuas on the island. If only they could sniff out their enemies as easily, they joked. "Most of my friends *are* my enemies," the Nigerian added, and everyone laughed.

Thunderclouds darkened the skies. The rumbling drowned out the conversation, and the first drops of rain drove the guests inside. Lightning struck a nearby royal palm, torching its fronds into a fiery headdress. "Changó is with us this evening," the Nigerian said with a nod. As the rain came down hard, the crowd fought its way into the ballroom, which grew insufferably close from the sudden body heat of a thousand guests. The waiters did their best to continue serving drinks, but the commotion impeded their efforts. The atmosphere grew anxious without the music and nerves-soothing rum. To make matters worse, the air-conditioning died with a deafening clank, replaced by the drone of mosquitoes carelessly let in by the stampede.

El Comandante held up an arm to quiet the crowd. "Distinguished guests," he began. "I am grateful that you've come to share in the triumph of our revolution this evening. No minor storm engineered by the CIA"—a surge of appreciative laughter—"will interfere with our celebrations." He signaled the reassembled musicians, who struck up "El Cuarto de Tula," a hit from the film that had traveled the world in the nineties.

The guests swarmed the dance floor, their heat and discomfort momentarily forgotten. Dancing to island music wasn't easy if you weren't born to it. In colder climes, people moved their hips like hinges—forward and back, or side to side with creaky imprecision.

But here, por Dios, hips swiveled, rotated, thrust, shimmied, lubricated by the humidity and the anticipation of the superior sex that awaited them. El Comandante chose to "dance" only in private, but he could tell everything about a person by the way he or she moved. For years he'd employed confiscated yachts for his most special assignations—unforgettable women from here and abroad—as armed frogmen protected the vessels anchored offshore.

The band transitioned into a salsa version of "Happy Birthday." The waiters rolled in a gigantic meringue cake with flaming candles. It looked like a forest fire glowing over a field of glittering snow. El Comandante approached the cake warily, as he might a land mine, searching for anyone who could help him extinguish the flames. This was either another plot by his enemies to burn him alive or an homage to his longevity. The guests joined him in a collective gasp, then blew as hard as they could. The chaotic crosscurrents of high-alcohol-content breaths fueled the flames to new heights, ultimately requiring the efforts of six bodyguards and a rusty fire extinguisher to put out. Nobody got so much as a soggy piece of cake.

The Teatro Tomás Terry, a splendid two-tiered theater with ornate balustrades, had been restored to its former colonial glory for El Comandante's birthday celebration. Both Enrico Caruso and Sarah Bernhardt had performed here in their primes, a source of great local pride. The tyrant was escorted to his seat in the third row center (no one was permitted to sit in front of him). The program cover featured a vintage photo of him looking quite dashing at the height of the Bay of Pigs invasion: a megaphone in one hand, a pistol in the other, the ubiquitous cigar in his mouth. The excitement in the theater was palpable.

At last, the overhead lights flickered off. A bespectacled narrator in a turtle's carapace stepped out from behind the curtain into a spotlight and began singing in a high tenor. *"Fever and madness consumed many men . . ."* El Comandante perused the program. The musical consisted of a single act divided into three scenes: Day One—Advance on Playa Larga; Day Two—Mercenaries on the Run; Day Three—Victory at Playa Girón. So who the fuck was this turtle? He squinted and checked the program again. Cojones, it was supposed to be Fernández, the hero who'd commanded the main column of Cuban forces during the invasion!

The curtains slowly opened to reveal a spectacular swamp scene populated by amphibians toting toy machine guns. They were determined to defend their swamp and swore allegiance to their bearded commander in chief, a frog in fatigues. "Fear not," Commander Frog croaked, simultaneously chewing on a cigar. "The tanks, antiaircraft guns, and other artillery are on their way!"

The creatures burst into jubilant song:

> *On their way, on their way*
> *The guns and artillery are on their way*
> *Our leader rules the island fearlessly*
> *In our hemisphere he has no peer . . .*

The audience laughed uproariously. "*Animal Farm* meets La Revolución," the British ambassador stage-whispered directly behind the despot. A cardboard cutout of a B-26 bomber—the silhouette of a pig in its cockpit—incited pandemonium. "Is that our plane?" squeaked a crab with blue eyestalks before the chorus kicked in again:

> *Bombs they will drop*
> *On our innocent folk*
> *Steal our dignity*
> *Make us drink Coke!*

Even these preposterous lyrics got wild applause. Had everyone gone stark raving mad? The audience seemed entranced by the animals, the sets, the songs. The whole farce was an incurable disease to which all had succumbed. The tyrant had half a mind to walk out, but doing so would only call more attention to this disaster. He felt like a condemned man. In the next scene Commander Frog set up headquarters at the Australia sugar mill, issuing orders in his bass baritone. He was unintentionally hilarious, woodenly reciting his lines with a slight lisp. (Where was that handsome militiaman the despot had handpicked to play him?) This was no homage but a grand mocking of him and his revolution. He'd have that faggot's head for this.

The spectacle trudged on as both sides suffered significant casualties. In spite of himself, the tyrant cheered the melodramatic deaths of the mercenary pigs. One of them performed a swoon worthy of *Swan Lake,* to much enthusiastic applause. At the height of the battle, Commander Frog ordered an artillery bombardment of Playa Girón, deafeningly rendered by the orchestra's percussion section. He followed this with a showstopping aria, "Victory Is in the Air":

> *Our victory will be sweeter than sugarcane*
> *Sweeter than sweet potatoes, sweeter than rain*
> *Our victory is righteous, it's preordained . . .*

Soon the swamp animals had the pigs on the run. U.S. Navy destroyers attempted to rescue the squealing swine to no avail. The audience gasped when one of the cardboard destroyers went up in flames (it'd gotten too close to a spotlight), believing it was part of the special effects. The pigs charged to put out the fire but were promptly taken prisoner. In the last scene, Commander Frog and his cronies launched into the grand finale, a reggaeton that had them hip-hop dancing under the erratic lighting.

The audience got in the swing, and a conga line broke out in the back row, snaking its way through the aisles, converging on the stage, shimmying and gyrating to the beat. The Danish ambassador swung a lacy black bra over the heads of her fellow dignitaries while the ordinarily reserved delegation from Japan let loose with hip bumping and high-fiving. El Comandante stayed put, smiling his lockjaw smile, mentally going down the list of people who would pay for this heresy.

14.

Fireflies

Nuevo Jersey

The dog's hot, humid panting was driving Goyo crazy. For the last
two hundred miles, Rudy had been the subject of Goyito's avid
conversation. The life expectancy of Great Danes was approxi-
mately seven years (Rudy was six and a half). The dogs suffered
from severe hip dysplasia (ditto Rudy). Many could not exercise
immediately after eating because of their torsion-prone stomachs,
the details of which Goyo didn't have the mental stamina to review
after his son's exhaustive tutorial. And according to Goyito, these
gentle behemoths were, by temperament, the biggest lapdogs ever.
On this last leg of their trip, Rudy had refused to sit alone in the
backseat (as evidenced by his vengeful assault on the upholstery)
and rested his massive, drooling head on Goyito's thighs.

Goyo checked the rearview mirror. Rudy grinned back, his
tongue lolling to one side. He'd just happily devoured a sack of

chicken strips. The stench of two semiwashed men and one colossal, flatulent dog—even in a vehicle as capacious as his Cadillac—was suffocating. It was a miracle they'd gotten as far as New Jersey without killing each other. So much had deteriorated in the state since Goyo had last passed through: abandoned factories; shuttered Main Streets; unsightly, sprawling malls. For years Goyo had regularly crossed the George Washington Bridge to practice at shooting ranges alongside other relatively normal gun owners—deer hunters and law enforcement types who enjoyed exercising their Second Amendment rights.

"Stop. Dad."

"What's the matter?"

"My legs are asleep." Goyito's chin bobbed to a rhythm only he could hear. "I have to sit up front."

"What about Rudy?"

"I spoke to him. He'll be okay."

Goyo pulled off at the next exit and into a gas station. His son sprang out the back door and into the convenience store, emerging moments later with several hot dogs smothered with condiments, a jumbo-size bag of spicy chips, and the biggest cherry Slushee this side of the Greenwich Meridian Line. Goyito slipped into the passenger seat, fed one of the hot dogs to the hypersalivating Rudy, then did the unthinkable: he removed his sneakers and put his bare, sore-infested diabetic feet on the dashboard.

Goyo tried to keep his eyes on the road, but his son's feet were mesmerizing—the thick, corrugated nails rising off the toes; the grilled-meat look of the flesh; the open, deeply crimson wounds. It was evident that poor Goyito was dying from the bottom up. His feet reminded Goyo of the photographs of lepers that had scared him senseless as a child. Without preamble, Goyito started to cry. The tears ran down his cheeks and neck, soaked into his junk food. His face shone with suffering.

"What is it?" Goyo asked. "Do you need me to stop again?"

His son carried despair like a set of car keys, losing and finding it almost at random. Goyo wasn't sure what to do. He'd already backtracked to North Carolina to pick Goyito up, losing a whole day's driving. Rudy barked in sympathy, his immense head canted toward the roof of the car. The barking felt like sledgehammer blows to Goyo's cranium. Soon the Great Dane lapsed into moaning arias that, combined with Goyito's wails, forged a mournful, synchronous duet. Still sniffling, Goyito reached into his pants pockets and pulled them inside out in a hobo's gesture of "broke."

"You're worried about money?" Goyo felt a tightening wreath of pain around his skull. The stress of driving with these two was taking its toll. They cruised past a run-down town fluttering with American flags. His daughter had once theorized that if three or more flags were flying on any given suburban street, Republicans were preponderant.

Both Goyito and Rudy scratched behind their ears. Please, God, Goyo prayed, don't let his Cadillac be infested with fleas. Or ticks.

"I'm, uh, uh, trying to remember," Goyito stammered.

Goyo understood this. Memory could be a plague sometimes, corroding one's soul with all that was lost and unforgotten. Who could have imagined their fates? At times Goyo felt madly in love with his loss, painful as it was. His lifelong devotion to Adelina was a testament to that. He didn't know a single Cuban of his generation who wasn't besotted with the past. But his son's regrets were of a different order altogether.

"I'm very sorry, hijo," Goyo said, anticipating a fresh volley of accusations: how he'd abandoned him as a boy; surrendered him to a cruel, mercurial mother. These were the recurring themes of his psychotherapy.

Dusk was falling, and the sun seemed no more powerful than

a lightbulb. The passing trees whistled the same B flat. Goyo felt the beauty of impending evening, something he hadn't noticed much before. He barely remembered the years he'd worked at the diner, recalled only a few of his extramarital affairs. (Where were all those gorgeous, soft-eyed, wet, breathy mistresses now?) Alina and Goyito both claimed he hadn't been around when they were kids except for their annual Easter Sunday expedition to Radio City Music Hall to see the Rockettes.

Goyito had a photographic memory of his childhood, especially the hurts and degradations of which he kept an interminable tally. Now he was tearfully refuting his mother's assertion that he'd never worked: he'd cleaned offices at night; worked as a hospital orderly, a job he loved because when anyone asked him what he did for a living he could retort: "I save lives"; selling men's clothing at a suburban Nordstrom, not far from here, in fact. When he disappeared from that job, his manager said that Goyito had been the best damn salesman they'd ever had. Later, when Goyo had to break down the door of his son's apartment in Brooklyn, he found a hundred dress shirts still in their plastic wrappers, a carton of Italian silk ties, and thousands of hours of videotaped pornography.

Goyito also had worked at the diner, against Luisa's will. It hadn't lasted long. Goyito made off with a freezer filled with hamburger meat. The next thing Goyo knew, his son had turned himself over to a chicken farm in the Florida panhandle run by missionaries who bragged success with men like him. Shoveling shit in the hot sun would leave him too tired, they promised, to want to use drugs. Goyito hadn't understood "hardscrabble" until then: the unyielding earth, the vicious pecking order of the South, the heat and bugs that nearly killed him.

Another crime spree landed him in a county jail with a new set of missionaries, who got him praising the Lord for a while. But his son's last "Hallelujah!" expired on his first day out.

"Dad, are you listening to me?" Goyito gave him a psychotic stare. His hands looked lumpy and mutilated.

For a moment, Goyo thought his son capable of strangling him to death, but he shook off the thought. This had been Luisa's fear, one she masked behind her unrelenting disdain.

"Díme, Goyito."

"Is it true that Mom refused to touch me when I was a baby?"

"We've been over this, hijo. There was no name for what she suffered then. No treatment. Now it is common for women to be depressed, to reject their children. Allow me to say this with deep love and empathy: you are not the only tragedy in the world."

"Did she ever touch my penis?"

"How should I know?" Goyo felt a jolt of disgust. He had his doubts about how useful such psychological delving was to anyone.

"Did you?"

Goyo looked over into the great pity of his son's eyes and tried to feel remorse. He wasn't sure he had any more to spare. What he really wanted to do was focus on killing the tyrant without further interference. He needed to check in with his friend, the Russian security guard, who always admitted him to the UN with barely a cursory inspection. Had the protocols changed? Could he sneak in his handgun? Might he trust Goyito enough to tell him his plans?

"She hated me even before I was me." Goyito looked forlornly out the window, then turned the dial on the radio, which whined like an espresso machine. "I . . . don't . . . like women."

Goyo snapped off the radio. He felt a certain expertise on the subject. If his son wanted to discuss women, Goyo was all ears.

"Remember that girl I was engaged to?" Goyito asked.

Goyo remembered her well. A good-looking redhead, big-boned, with a strained expression. Aileen something-or-other. She'd been studying to be a nurse and sometimes wore a black patch over one eye. His son had met her at an AA meeting. Everyone in her family was a drunk. Goyito had stolen the girl's credit card to buy her the diamond ring and pay for a trip to Miami to meet everyone at Christmas.

"She used to tie me up." His son extracted a handful of pills from his shirt pocket, popped them into his mouth, swallowed. One of them was the size of quail's egg.

Goyo didn't know which of his son's pills were legitimate— there were so goddamn many of them—and which were not. "Are you sure you want to—"

"Whipped me. Pissed on me. Stuck metal up my ass." Goyito coughed into the back of his hand and looked straight ahead.

Goyo was speechless. He reached over and patted his son's shoulder as if it were the edge of some vast mystery. He'd known about the woman in the projects who gave him blow jobs for a percentage of his disability check. But this?

"Ballbreakers. Bitches. That's what gets me off."

It had been excruciating for Goyo to picture his son homeless, or smoking crack, or more recently submitting to fourteen sessions of electroshock therapy in a Tallahassee mental hospital. But trussed up like a pig for a woman to abuse? This was more than he could stand. If someone had taken a hot poker to his brain, Goyo thought, it might feel something like what his son felt every day.

Goyito pushed a button in the passenger armrest and watched his window glide open. The wind filled the car with a disorderly sound and the smell of blood, summer wildness, and shit. Rudy barked maniacally in the backseat. Goyito pulled a hunter's knife from who knew where and held its glittering tip to the meaty pink of his outstretched tongue.

"Coño carajo!" Goyo saw a tawny flash and hit the brakes hard. The Cadillac twisted off the road with a sickening thud. They'd struck something big and heavy. His eyes ached, but he was relieved, at least, not to be dead.

His son dropped the knife and stuck his head out the window into the diminishing light. "Jesus Christ, you hit a deer! You hit a goddamn deer!" Goyito flung open his door and fell to the ground. He scrabbled up and, fumbling, opened the back door and let Rudy out. The whimpering dog shot off into the darkening woods, streaking through the keen grass. "A fucking deer, a fucking deer," Goyito muttered as he, too, disappeared into the woods.

It took twenty minutes for Goyo to find his son hunched over Rudy's dead body in a firefly-lit clearing. Goyo stood perfectly still, leaning on his cane and breathing hard. The fireflies seemed a dazzling frippery of nature, pointless and purposeful, like so many dancing lies. Or perhaps they were a manifestation of his son's twitching misery. Goyo traced the fireflies' paths, ribbons of hopelessly entangling light, crisscrossed now and then by the ropier trajectories of flycatchers and jays. The sky was immense, more immense now that Rudy was gone.

Goyo sighed. He was growing tired of these constant derailments to his plans. It'd taken him a lifetime to make up his mind to do the right thing. He needed to focus on getting ready, not waste time lamenting the death of a deer and a dog.

"Rudy shouldn't have run," Goyito choked out. "His stomach got b-b-locked."

His son wanted to blame him even for this, to have Goyo eat his heart out and cry right beside him. But what were their tears worth? Goyo wasn't made for such histrionics. He'd had to parcel out his grief judiciously, or he would've died from it long ago. A part of him wanted to be sympathetic, but a bigger part wanted to get as far away from this disaster as possible. It wasn't enough that in his worst dreams, he couldn't have pictured a crazy drug addict for a son. He gazed over at the sad bulk that was Goyito, filthy and on his knees, his tattered cummerbund coming undone. (Goyito never went anywhere without it, as if it magically kept cinched his top and bottom halves.)

"Come, hijo, we have work to do." Goyo led his son back to the Cadillac and popped open the trunk. They could use the tire iron to break the ground and maybe the base of the jack to scoop out the dirt for a shallow grave.

Goyo watched as his son dug, scraped, sweated, and cursed, all the while crying out to the luminous moon for pity. "Remember how he used to chase rabbits in his sleep?" Goyito's legs shook as he worked. The air was slippery hot, as if saturated with cooking oil. The bees, the birds, the ants did their day's last chores. It took Goyito an hour to dig the two-foot hole, disturbing the earth to bury his dog's giant, tender body. Goyo was overcome with a sense of futility as he and his son finally dragged the 150-pound beast to his resting place. His flanks were dank with flies, teeth still bared, as if in self-defense, the stubby tail inert and sad.

When they were done shoveling the earth over Rudy's stiffening corpse, the moon was high in the sky. A few drops of rain fell from a wayward cloud. Goyito stretched out on the grave and settled in for a nap. It was useless to argue with him. His pale face looked almost peaceful; the gray tufts of his hair stuck up in every direction. His breathing was normal and deep, and Goyo remembered the few times he'd gotten to tuck his son into bed when he was a boy; a beautiful boy he'd been, too, before the madness kicked in. Sí, Goyito had slept like a baby. The problems began when he woke up, restless for adventure. But to love what was lovable wasn't truly love, Goyo thought; only suffering made love worthy. By the time his son stirred from his nap, Goyo's joints were painfully stiff.

Goyito yawned and announced that he wanted to go to a motel to "grieve in private," but Goyo was nervous about dropping him off anywhere but a hospital. They were just seventy-five miles from New York City, and he wanted to get there without delay. As they cruised up I-95, Goyito began pounding on the passenger door to be let out. What choice did Goyo have? His son would be sixty years old in two months. There was nothing he could say to him that he hadn't said a million times before. If Goyito wanted to be dropped off at a motel in the middle of New Jersey, then Goyo was helpless to stop him.

The next exit had several choices of accommodations. Goyo handed his son the $220 in his pocket and wished him good luck. He noticed Goyito spying the bar on the frontage road with the blinking, half-lit neon martini. Diesel fumes from the passing trucks poisoned the air. Goyito seemed impatient for him to leave. If only he could kiss his son's eyes, wash his feet, take away his suffering, ease his inexhaustible heart. But Goyo knew none of it would do any good. Goyito had endured prison, watched men raped and shanked, and somehow managed to survive. Nobody had dared touch him, Goyo didn't know why. He held his son for a moment before letting him go. It was all too sadly familiar. Who knew? Maybe the best of Goyito was yet to be born.

The sun rose as Goyo crossed the last stretch of New Jersey, its foliage a blinding, end-of-summer green. In his heyday, this would've been a normal time for going home after a night of drinking and whoring with his brothers in Havana. Once in 1957, Goyo had spotted Senator Kennedy at the Palette Club cozily nuzzling Bobby de Milanés, the notorious drag queen. If only Goyo had had a camera, he might've changed the course of history, singlehandedly stopped that traitor from becoming president and sabotaging the Bay of Pigs.

He called Víctor Ticona, his employee of twenty-seven years, Ecuadorian and reliable as day. He spoke an amalgam of Spanish and Quechua that nobody but Goyo understood. Víctor had put nine children through high school in Cuenca, where he'd also built a palatial home. In New York he mopped hallways, changed lightbulbs, and took out the garbage, but back in Cuenca, Víctor Ticona was a king.

"Víctor!" Goyo shouted into his cell phone. "I'm arriving this morning."

"Bueno, Jefe. I'll have your apartment ready."

The early commuters were out in force, sensible men and women going to their sensible jobs in the suburbs—employees of banks and insurance firms, optics laboratories, the telephone company. How many other lives he might have led . . . rancher, chemist, singer, clarinetist. He'd wanted to marry Adelina Ponti, too, but that hadn't happened either. Goyo toyed with the idea of wooing back Carla Stracci, his sexy mistress from the United Nations. How might he impress her after all these years? It was for women like her that men went to war, behaved like fools.

The Holland Tunnel was a nightmare. Goyo sat in its rush-hour fumes for over an hour. He scanned the news stations again but turned the radio off in disgust. In an age of continual information, who really knew a goddamn thing? He concentrated on ignoring his bladder and his fear about what Goyito might do next. When he emerged onto Canal Street, Goyo ran smack into a circus parading up the West Side Highway. Elephants in feathered headdresses lumbered along the Hudson, as if this were their natural habitat. Goyo was careful to avoid the bicyclists and skateboarders, the homeless man trying to wipe his windshield with a filthy rag. A gigantic coffin rolled down the middle of the avenue, narrowly missing his Cadillac.

It was just another day heating up in New York.

Island Blogger 2

I want to bring your attention, Dear Readers, to an editorial in _The New York Times_ regarding the fate of Arab strongmen. The argument, applicable to our own situation, is that despots stay in power only when they can continue rewarding the loyalists entrusted with carrying out their regimes' repressive tactics. Decrepit, bankrupt leaders are particularly vulnerable to being overthrown. Why? Because their henchmen can't count on the bribes lasting indefinitely. Citizens, our resources have run dry. Cerraron la bolsa. The time has come for revolt . . .

SEPTEMBER 8-10

TROPICAL FORECAST: Skies mostly cloudy in the western and central regions, with showers, electrical rains, and storms. Maximum temperatures between 30 and 33 degrees Celsius, higher in the eastern south portion. Marine breezes in the afternoons with speeds up to 20 kilometers. Depressions, disturbances, and cyclones are still possible. We're in the dangerous season, compays, so stay tuned. Tu Capitán de Corbeta, el último meteorólogo en La Habana.

15.

Lilies

New York City

Eighty-six years old and he could still get it up good and hard when the occasion warranted—and without pharmaceutical help. But what occasion was this? Goyo closed his eyes and tried to coax back the dissipating dream. He flipped his pillow to the cooler side and pressed it against his forehead. No luck. He wanted to squeeze in another hour of sleep, but a panoply of bodily torments prevented it: raging hemorrhoids (a souvenir from his long drive north), a crippling pain in his neck, his aching lower back. Goyo threw off the pillow and sheets and opened his window shade onto the hallucinations of Second Avenue: the corner newsstand floating off the curb, squabbling pigeons swollen as overfed geese.

Today was his sixtieth wedding anniversary and the feast day of Cuba's patron saint—La Virgen de la Caridad del Cobre. Before her untimely death, Luisa had been planning another party, more

extravagant than their fiftieth. She'd even been toying with the idea
of hiring Enrique Chia to play at their bash. At least Goyo had
dodged that exorbitant bullet. He looked up at the ceiling, hands
positioned for prayer: *Perdóname, mi amor, I'm merely relieved, given
my many expenses, that* . . . Oh, never mind. He'd stuck his foot in
it and might not get out of this alive. The last thing he needed was
to take on the dead as well as the miserable living.

A chunk of plaster fell from the ceiling onto his bed in a puff of
dust. Goyo sighed. His work here was never done. The brownstone
might look sturdy from the outside—geraniums on the window-
sills, an unimpeachable air of permanence—but below the surface,
all was decay. Cockroaches and rats infested its deteriorating walls
and had overrun the basement, where Goyo kept his archives: letters his father had sent to him at boarding school; a photo of Adelina Ponti playing piano; his moldering clarinet music; the birth
certificates of relatives near and far; and, most important, the titles
to the Herrera properties in Cuba.

Twenty-three years ago, he and Luisa had sold their old apartment, a spacious three-bedroom in Turtle Bay, and crammed
the bulk of its contents into these thousand square feet of now-
collapsing building. His wife's devotion to the baroque was evident everywhere—in the gilded Florentine boxes and porcelain
figurines, in the crystal decanters half-filled with watered-down
scotch. Every overpriced knickknack and silk-upholstered chair,
every chandelier and lamp, down to the fringed one on the nightstand to which a spider had attached its web, murmured: "I am
Luisa Miyares de Herrera . . ."

A flock of sparrows rushed in a slanting mass toward the East
River. A jogger, probably from another time zone, pounded his
way north. Goyo reached for a tissue and trumpeted away the
night's accretion of mucus. How his younger self would've recoiled
at the hoary vision of him now, with his back brace and bifocals,

his bruised and bleeding gums, his lamentable sag of balls. His eyes felt sticky, too, as if they'd been smeared with honey. Sometimes he pictured himself growing wild in old age: his shoulders upholstered with mold, his lungs wheezing like a leaky bassoon. Only infirmity or impending death truly showed people what tedious organisms their bodies could be.

Goyo hoisted himself out of bed, steadied his cane, and hobbled past his wife's bric-a-brac to the bathroom. He kept a shelf of Marcus Aurelius and José Martí above the toilet paper dispenser. Goyo could always count on them to provide a modicum of solace. He'd memorized many of Aurelius's most famous quotations: "A man's worth is no greater than his ambition." "And thou wilt give thyself relief if thou does every act of thy life as if it were the last." "Despise not death, but welcome it, for nature wills it like all else." Aurelius had died at fifty-nine after ruling the Roman Empire for twenty years. Martí was even younger when he perished, saddling up in the name of Cuban independence and charging into his first—and only—battle at forty-two.

Twenty minutes later, the toughest part of Goyo's day was done. He took extra care with his morning ablutions, maneuvering his tongue to plump out his cheeks and upper lip while shaving his face to an impeccable sheen. He brushed his teeth—they were holding up better than the rest of him—and doused his solar plexus with cologne. What was left of his hair he smoothed back with a soft-bristle brush. Goyo was fond of his old mutt's face, no matter its devastations, particularly his chin with its still handsome, beckoning cleft. How the ladies had loved that cleft!

At 7:00 a.m. Víctor Ticona knocked on his door, regular as a rooster. He set out Goyo's breakfast in silence—sliced papaya, multigrain toast, café con leche. Goyo dictated the day's tasks, which included purchasing black support hose and spying on the Turks for any breaches of kitchen regulations (Goyo was compiling evidence to evict them). The taciturn Andean could be provoked to garrulousness only with regard to his hated in-laws, whom he blamed for turning his wife against him. Occasionally, Goyo joined in with complaints about Luisa's family, who'd chosen to remain in Cuba and had devoted their lives to fleecing him at every turn.

Goyo inspected the contents of his closet and chose his linen suit and two-toned shoes. Back in the day, his ensemble would've been regarded not as foppishness but as a stylish gentleman's summer wear. After checking his appearance in the foyer mirror, Goyo adjusted his Panama hat, then swung open the front door. The dust hung thick in the corridor. He extracted a handkerchief from his breast pocket and covered his mouth. Esposito had been charging Goyo triple his initial estimates, certain that he wouldn't risk switching contractors in midconstruction. Now the elevator was broken, too. With Víctor's help, Goyo gingerly descended the three flights of stairs.

"I'll be back by noon," Goyo said. "I'm counting on you, Víctor. We need to evict those Turks one way or another."

"A sus órdenes, Jefe."

Goyo hailed a cab (he rarely drove in New York anymore, keeping his Cadillac safely stored in a midtown garage) and asked the driver, a Haitian, judging by his name—Henri Jean-Baptiste Dorcelus—to take him to the Brooklyn shipyards in Red Hook. In Havana, he and his brothers had grown up with chauffeurs. When they got old enough to drive, they borrowed the family Cadillacs and cruised them up and down the seawall, flirting with the pretty girls. Back then piropos were high art, not like the coarse come-ons of today. The challenge was finding the perfect balance between worshipful and provocative. Too crude, and the ladies wouldn't give you the time of day. Too proper, and they stifled a yawn. The best flirtations were respectful but had a seductive edge. For example, if a woman had a florid backside and a tiny waist, one might say: Mujer de guitarrón es un viento de ciclón.

The taxi coasted across the Brooklyn Bridge. To the south gleamed the East River, emptying into the widening expanse of sea. What was the point of sending satellites into space, Goyo thought, when the greatest wilderness on the planet lurked at the edges of its shores? If he were young again, he might become an oceanographer like that French underwater explorer from the sixties who nobody remembered anymore. Goyo rapped on the glass partition dividing him from the taxi driver.

"Have you heard of Jacques Rosteau?" Goyo asked.

"Mais oui," Henri said, surprised. "He was my great-uncle on my mother's side."

"How's that?" Goyo leaned forward.

"He fell in love with Maman's youngest aunt. She was his companion for many years. In Paris, they lived. In a grand apartment on the Rue Bonaparte."

"Is she still alive?"

"She drowned herself in La Seine after Jacques died." Henri shook his head.

Goyo was convinced that the world's greatest love stories remained hidden behind scrims of propriety.

Henri swerved from the bridge onto Tillary Street, driving through downtown Brooklyn and its newly gentrified neighborhoods toward the abandoned shipyards. With Goyo's guidance, he pulled up to a chain-link fence that partially hid a building with a battered tin roof, exposed pipes, and tangles of rusted wiring. Once this had been the crown jewel in Papá's archipelago of offices throughout the Americas—Buenos Aires, São Paulo, Panama City, Veracruz. All this from a boy who'd herded sheep in the mountains of Galicia. Papá liked to recount the time he'd fattened one of his sick sheep with bloating grasses and sold it for top dollar at the farmers' market. His lesson: to strike a bargain with the Devil himself in pursuit of a profit.

Goyo recalled a visit to these Brooklyn offices when he was twelve and en route to the Jesuit boarding school in Canada. It was a September during World War II, and his father was nattily dressed, his gold pocket watch linked by a fine chain to his belt loop. Behind him, a rose-throated Cuban parrot preened its feathers in a bamboo cage. Papá's executive secretary was a dead ringer for the Italian starlet Assia Noris, with her perfect brows and lush, wavy hair. Goyo watched as the secretary touched his father's wrist, delicately, as if she were brushing away crumbs. Nothing was ever said, of course, but Goyo grew up to become, like Papá, a chronic philanderer.

In 1961, as panic over the Revolution skyrocketed, the Herrera ships were transporting people along with their usual cargo of sugar, tobacco, and coffee. The going rate for a spot on a northbound ship: three thousand dollars per man, woman, and child. Passengers accused Papá of extortion, but later, after his suicide, Goyo received dozens of letters from exiles claiming that Arturo Herrera had saved their lives. On that last voyage from Havana, Goyo was cheek by jowl with Cuba's elite like so many peasants on an immigrant ship. The socialites hid their jewels in unmentionable places, and their impudent children wore three and four outfits at once. These days, a reverse flow of goods trickled into the island via returning exiles bearing aspirin, tires, panty hose, and cheap Chinese sandals for their relatives.

Goyo wondered how many of those same exiles had taken their lives after the catastrophe of the Revolution. His father had lived for the promise of return but soon became a man with no country, a homeless man. He killed himself one Sunday afternoon when Goyo was due for supper. Papá had left a simple meal on the kitchen table: a Spanish omelet with a side of still-steaming white rice, a salad cooling in the refrigerator. Goyo imagined his father slipping his 1927 Detective Special, the one he'd had inlaid with a mother-of-pearl handle, into his mouth; imagined him, unflinching, as he pulled the trigger.

Across the river, the lower Manhattan skyline brooded. It'd never looked right to Goyo since 9/11. The towering twin ghosts still hovered there like gigantic phantom limbs. He'd been uptown when the planes hit, lingering, dry-mouthed, in the luscious Carla Stracci's bed after a night of drinking champagne and smoking pot (it was the one and only time he'd tried it) and nursing a splitting headache. None of his family was in town: Luisa was in Miami, Alina on a photo assignment in the Serengeti, and Goyito in a Jacksonville county jail for petty larceny—all safe, thank goodness.

The driver leaned against the hood of his taxi, smoking a cigarette. Goyo was inclined to join him with the cigar in his pocket but decided against it. Everything had its time, its place, its appropriate level of reverence. It was too early in the day for his puro. The traffic back to the city was bumper-to-bumper. Men and women bound for Wall Street trekked across the Brooklyn Bridge. Goyo was glad that he hadn't spent his life slaving away at a big corporation. He'd been a slave all right, but to the demands of his own business.

On an impulse, Goyo had the driver stop at a Korean fruit stand on Thirty-Seventh Street and bought a bouquet of lilies for Carla. Then he instructed the driver to drop him off at the United Nations, where his ex-lover still worked as secretary to the Italian delegation. Goyo was anxious to see her, longed to bury his head in her magnificent breasts. The Russian security guard, a hulking vestige from the Cold War, was on duty as usual at the north entrance for visitors. Poor Yuri's face looked like badly baked bread: lumpy cheeks, sagging chin, a crusty, split upper lip. Over the nearly three decades that they'd been friends, the Russian had proved an invaluable resource to Goyo, briefing him on potential paramours and arranging catering opportunities in exchange for roast-beef-and-horseradish sandwiches and multiple quarts of borscht.

Today, the Russian inspected the lilies with a conspiratorial smile. "You are inspiration to mankind, Comrade Herrera," he said, gargling his *r*'s. As usual, he waved Goyo into the United Nations without the security protocol required of visitors.

"Is she in today?" Goyo asked, bypassing the metal detector. At one time, he was probably better known at the UN than its transient secretaries-general. With a nod, he promised Yuri a care package that very afternoon.

The General Assembly building was undergoing renovations. All of New York, it seemed, was on the brink of collapse. Goyo circumvented the construction zones and found his way to the Italian offices. At the reception desk, in all her glorious curves, sat La Carla in a tight cashmere sweater. (Not even that bombshell Vilmita could hold a candle to her.) Coño, he would walk on coals for this woman! Goyo stopped in his tracks, seized by a nervous spasm of sneezing that made his ex-lover laugh out loud. Whatever awkwardness may have existed between them (the affair hadn't ended well, rife with recriminations and flying crockery) dissipated. Sheepishly, he handed her the flowers.

"Eh, you are allergic to the lilies," Carla purred, patting his cheek. She offered him a tissue and made him blow his nose like a schoolboy. Then she reached inside a cabinet for a crystal vase. An imposing diamond gleamed on her ring finger.

"You're married?" Goyo asked stupidly.

In response, she held up a silver-framed photograph of a disturbingly muscular man in a military uniform, one trouser leg pinned neatly to thigh level. The astonishment must've shown on Goyo's face because Carla put a hand on her hip and said, a touch defensively, "He's a war hero."

"From where?"

"Bosnia."

Goyo coughed into his fist. He struggled not to think of her husband's stump; like a blunt hand, he imagined, lacking articulation. "You are happy then?"

"Only animals are happy," Carla snapped, her voice dropping an octave.

Goyo recalled the night at boarding school when the first-floor boys had procured a hooker—one for nine of them—at the cut-rate price of ten dollars per customer. She, too, had been missing a leg.

Carla produced an espresso from the sleek cappuccino machine behind her desk. Goyo wanted to say that he missed her skin, her scent; that he'd often wondered in the days following 9/11 whether he'd made a mistake staying with his wife.

"Luisa is dead," he said.

"Yuri told me. My condolences."

Since when had that Russian become such a chatterbox? Goyo drank his espresso and watched Carla watching him before he dared take a peek at her cleavage. Her breasts were perfect, majestically situated on her torso. He should've come better prepared to win her back.

A group of men in guayaberas walked down the hall speaking Cuban-accented Spanish. Goyo looked quizzically at Carla. Every nerve in his body fired up.

"Tomorrow, at noon," Carla said.

"Damn it." Goyo wasn't expecting the tyrant until next week. There'd been nothing about this change of plans from those idiots at Hijodeputa.com.

"When he went to Harlem many years ago, i negri loved him," Carla said, but Goyo wasn't listening. "I negri . . . they loved him."

Goyo descended into his blackest soul, stirring up from its

bottom the residue of his scoured life, of the lives of thousands of his fellow exiles. His blood roiled anew at the thought of El Comandante extolling the virtues of his last-gasp regime at the UN.

"Querida, I need to ask you a favor," Goyo began, slipping his pistol from its holster and eyeing her spotless desk. He needed a safe place to keep the Glock until tomorrow. Security quadrupled when a controversial leader like El Comandante visited. Goyo couldn't risk not getting the weapon through security, even with his Russian friend on duty. He knew by the expression on Carla's face that she would comply. She would comply, Goyo knew, because despite her one-legged husband, she still loved him.

There was no time to waste. The tyrant was coming to his very door, to ridicule by his unrepentant presence everyone he'd so brutally driven away. Bueno, let the bastard come. Goyo was ready.

Gold

I lie awake at night worrying that they're going to screw me. This is my big shot and I don't want to blow it. Finally, I have something they want. "They" meaning the world beyond this fucking island, the golden goose—Hollywood itself. I'm just one writer, vulnerable against those sharks. Yes, I have an agent in Spain, but we're talking major cifra here, and when that's at stake I could be sold out with a sneeze. It's neocolonialism all over again. I haven't written a damn word from all the stress. Detective Harry Morales is my invention. If I play this right, he could become the next Sherlock Holmes, or James Bond; my family set up for generations. I need to hang tough, hold my ground. Nobody gives it to me up the ass. Nobody.

—*Manolo Goytisolo, detective novelist*

Havana

The older El Comandante got, the more he hated traveling. Even that day trip to Mexico two months ago had exhausted him to no end. The last thing he needed today was to get tricked out in his Armani suit and travel to New York City. It was too cold there no matter the season. The beds were uncomfortable and the unfamiliar noises jangled his nerves. The truth was that he no longer felt at home anywhere but on the red, clay-rich soil of his island. Long gone were the days when he'd cut a handsome figure in fatigues, inciting crowds the world over with his stirring speeches. Now he could count on one hand the places left where he remained a hero: Bolivia, South Africa, parts of Mexico, Vietnam, and— yes—Harlem.

Harlem's love affair with him had begun in 1960, after he and his men had been evicted from their midtown hotel under pressure from Washington. El Comandante suggested pitching tents in the United Nations gardens, but black politicos rallied to bring him uptown to the Hotel Marisa, famous thereafter as the place where he and Malcolm X had met. None of his subsequent visits to the UN—not in 1979, when he'd gotten a standing ovation for condemning apartheid; nor in 1995, when he'd memorably called the U.S. embargo a "noiseless atom bomb"—could replicate the thrill of his first, hours-long harangue of the General Assembly.

Another stifling September day dawned. The tyrant loathed early autumn, when the threat of hurricanes and the dropping barometric pressure pushed everyone to the breaking point. A muscle spasm cinched his waist. He drank the water left for him on the nightstand and stared out at the Caribbean Sea. The Focsa tower* jutted high above the city's dilapidated skyline. It'd been the last major building to go up before the Revolution. On the other side of town, the blanched dome of the Capitol seemed to mock his revolution. Carajo, he was responsible for this mess, for a society in which prostitutes were revered as "heroines" for keeping their families afloat during hard times.**

El Comandante pulled the Browning from his nightstand drawer and slipped the tip of the barrel into his mouth. His chapped lips clung to the steel. What else did he have left to prove? The real trial was crossing the chasm from dying to dead. Non est ad astra mollis e terris via. There is no easy way from the earth to the stars. Another Jesuit chestnut. The tyrant chambered a round and closed his eyes. Memories floated behind his eyelids: Mami napping in her hammock with a flock of baby chicks; the Jamaican cutter's girl kissing him under the tamarind tree, then pronouncing them married; the time he heard his parents fucking while Papá's legal wife and daughters sat in the parlor, pretending not to listen.

The phone rang, and he knew without looking that it was Fernando.

---

* I was a middleweight Olympic boxing champ. I could've defected and gone professional, but when my chance came, I choked. The state rewarded my loyalty with this plum job: head bartender at the rooftop bar of El Focsa. Views in every direction and tips enough to live better than most. Here in the skies, I mix drinks—forgive the pun—that pack a serious punch.

                                                           —*Romero Fino, bartender*

** So much history and what do the tourists want to know? Where they can get cheap cigars, the best mojitos, and where to find the women. Tell me, what has changed since 1959? What do these imbeciles care about the Grito de Yara, or the Treaty of Zanjón? My knowledge is wasted. And yet I know this much: the wheel of history will turn and our country will be free again.

                                                           —*Sebastiano Durán, tour guide*

"I had a terrible dream about you." His brother's voice swallowed the last syllable. "I thought you'd . . ."

"I'm fine," the tyrant said drily.

"Are you—"

"Pick me up in an hour."

In the early years of the Revolution, when their safety was continually in jeopardy, Fernando had wanted to hire body doubles for them. El Comandante had scoffed at the idea, not wanting anyone to take a bullet meant for him. Persistent, Fernando sent him one doppelgänger after another and selected a blacksmith as his own impostor. That lucky bastard enjoyed the good life well into his sixties—wining and dining minor dignitaries, cutting factory ribbons, bedding small-town beauty queens—until the day he feasted on a platter of cyanide-laced crabs at a mechanics' convention in Varadero. There was the awkward business of "Fernando's" resurrection after thirty-seven eyewitnesses had seen him drop dead. But the Revolution was adept, if it was adept at anything, at revising history.

El Comandante put away his pistol. His suicide would only serve as propaganda for his enemies. The best course of events would be for him to be killed in action, like José Martí. This would yield the optimum political capital, which the Revolution could then exploit for years to come like it'd done with Che and Camilo. The ultimate vindication, of course, would be to outlive every last one of his enemies. If only he could.

The tyrant grasped the bedpost. The day had barely begun and he felt wasted as chalk. He ran his tongue along the gluey roof of his mouth. How sick and tired he was of cooperating with his handlers like some sorry gelding. This was what old age demanded: reasonableness and a resignation to the obliterating sameness of meals, solitude, sickness. As he made his way to the toilet, a turkey buzzard momentarily landed on his balcony, then flew away. El Líder pried open the iron-grilled window. The air smelled rancid, like days-old shellfish. He'd come to resemble the view, sun-faded and devoid of grandeur.

Delia appeared at his door in a lavender nightgown, her hair in disarray. She, too, had dreamt about him. "You were wallowing in the swamp like an injured crane. You opened your beak to cry for help but no sound came." She nestled against her husband's chest, nearly toppling him.

"It's that fucking musical! I shouldn't have told you anything about it." He'd been having nightmares from that goddamn play— mostly of giant, imperialist crabs running amok in Havana.

The backfiring of a fifties Chevy in the street below startled them both.

"Don't go to New York, mi cielo. I beg you."

"Carajo," he muttered, then repeated it for good measure before disappearing into the bathroom.

16.

Turbulence

Goyo

Goyo scrabbled westward in his linen suit and Panama hat, his cane barely grazing the sidewalk. This was his chance, the grand opportunity offered to him by Fate, or God, or the Devil. He stopped to rest against the display window of a Madison Avenue jewelry store. A steam vent fogged up his glasses. The back of his suit was soaking wet, and he gave off a sharp ammonia smell. A security guard emerged from behind the gleaming watches and asked if he was all right. Goyo didn't have the breath to respond and waved him away. He reached for his inhaler and took a breath. Fear, courage, courage, fear; the two were inextricably bound.

He reminded himself to go about his usual business so that nobody would suspect his motives. Goyo agonized about leaving his affairs in such a disorganized state. His brownstone was practically in ruins. He hadn't heard a word from Goyito since dropping

him off in New Jersey. And Alina had been evicted from the Fair-
child botanic garden for swimming in its lagoon (photographing
endangered waterfowl, she claimed). Maybe his dream of dying a
hero was illusory—eight parts smoke, two parts vanity.

At his physical therapist's office, Goyo adjusted the torturous
quadriceps machine to the lowest possible weight. He set his jaw
and attempted to raise his shins. Nada.

"Lift, Mr. Herrera, lift," the therapist urged him. "This will
strengthen your thighs and the muscles around your knees."

Goyo put every ounce of energy he had into budging the ten-
pound bar. It rose half an inch, then clanked back into place. If his
legs wouldn't raise it, then his mind would. The Jesuits used to say
that the mind was the body's most powerful organ, after the heart.
Slowly, painfully, the bar rose until his thigh muscles quivered and
his legs were at a right angle to his body. This was his boot camp,
his antechamber to glory. He must be in the best possible shape to
complete his task. In less than a day, he would restore the tarnished
name of the Herrera clan. He'd lost much more than an island
paradise to that tyrant. He'd lost his brief season of youth.

"You're making progress," the therapist encouraged him. "At
this rate, you'll be dancing in no time."

That had to be a joke. Goyo was a pariah at dance parties,
inflictor in chief of bruises and swollen toes. At the Key Biscayne
Yacht Club Christmas parties, drunken bacchanalias where wife
swapping was occasionally still practiced, Luisa used to dance with
everyone but him.

On the culo machine, Goyo groaned like a straining rope as he
lifted another stack of bars.

"Tell me about your diet, Mr. Herrera," the therapist asked, his
pen poised over the clipboard.

"No diet," Goyo grunted, finishing his last set.

"I don't mean for you to lose weight but for your health."

"Cojones, what does it matter? I won't eat my vegetables." He pictured his insides looking like so much ground beef.

"What about fruit?"

"I eat fruit."

The therapist brightened, clicking his pen.

"Mangoes. Papayas. Piñas." Goyo disentangled his legs from the machine. When he was growing up, there were no such things as gyms or cardiovascular anything; only fun, and swimming, and sex. People ate whatever the hell they wanted. No one taught you how to take care of your body; your body took care of itself.

"What else do you—"

"I'm very busy today. Can we finish this next time?" Good move, Goyo thought. When the FBI interrogated the therapist, he would have to say that his client had come to his regular appointment and behaved normally; that is to say, crankily. No one would think him capable of committing such an act.

His daughter called and sounded uncharacteristically forlorn. "When are you coming home, Papi?"

"Pronto, mija. Muy pronto," Goyo said, and his voice broke.

He limped down West Forty-Sixth Street, tempted to stop in for a feijoada at Via Brasil, but he feared even a modest bowlful might knock him unconscious for days. He decided to head to Saint Patrick's Cathedral instead. It'd been a regular stop for him on his travels to boarding school in the 1940s. Goyo had filled an entire album with the photographs he'd taken of the magnificent bronze Atlas across the street. Atlas represented the sort of man the Jesuits admired, someone who not only inhabited the world but also literally shouldered its burdens.

Goyo hoisted himself up the front steps of the cathedral, tucking in behind a group of Korean tourists. The cool, Gothic interior reinforced the ideal Catholic view of the world as orderly, righteous, enlightened. Pain seared through his joints as he knelt down in a back pew. Mass was under way. Luminous white gladioli girded the altar. When he was a boy, the priests' sartorial splendor had appealed to Goyo's sense of style, and for one fervent week following a bout of post-tonsillectomy quinsy, he'd deluded himself into believing that he'd been called. The organ bellowed a hymn in G minor that echoed throughout the cathedral. Goyo tried to imagine the bells of Saint Patrick's and every last church from here to Tierra del Fuego pealing jubilantly with the news: *Murió el tirano!* The tyrant is dead!

If he were lucky enough to survive an assault on the bastard, he'd be hailed as Cuba's new liberator, take his place in history alongside José Martí. Goyo bent his head and recited an Our Father and two Hail Marys. He was seeking inspiration, a definitive direction, but no answer came. *So it is for your own glory that you contemplate this?* The voice was his, and not his, metallic and oddly feminine. *I want to redeem my life,* Goyo answered. *I want it to mean something.* He felt a sudden, unexpected tenderness for his broken body. How fragile it'd proved against life's slow river of ruin.

Goyo hailed a cab and headed to Central Park. The trees were in their last summer fullness, and a couple of softball teams in bank logo jerseys battled it out on the Great Lawn. Everywhere, old people with their polished-apple skin sat on benches with newspapers and books. In another month, the leaves would turn an ember red in the unforgiving chill of fall.

"Pull over here."

"We get ticket!" the driver protested.

"I'll pay, don't worry." Goyo flashed a wad of cash and stepped outside. He wanted to breathe in the world one last time, take notice of everything he usually ignored—the resinous air, the immaculate gray of the clouds. A turkey vulture peered down at him from the top of a pin oak. With a great flap of its wings, it rose high into the sky before wheeling away. Goyo got back in the cab and returned home.

The contractor was on the sidewalk, shouting into his cell phone. He flung out his arms in exasperation.

"Where's Víctor?" Goyo asked.

"Inside with his fucking feather duster. Listen, we got business to discuss."

Goyo's temples ached, and the pain was spreading to the back of his skull.

"Hey, you don't look so good."

"Son of a bitch," Goyo managed to gasp.

"Let's get you upstairs. I got the elevator fixed."

Johnny helped Goyo inside, then up to his apartment, where Víctor put him to bed. Goyo was sweating so profusely that his clothes left stains on the coverlet. It couldn't be another heart attack, he reassured himself, because his chest didn't hurt. He closed his eyes and tried to steady his breathing, to tamp down the anxiety he felt. Víctor propped Goyo's feet on a pillow and pressed a cool cloth to his forehead. A swirl of colored dots swam beneath his eyelids before he passed out.

When he awoke hours later, it was dark out and a mug of chamomile tea steamed on the nightstand. This meant that Víctor was nearby, probably watching reruns of *Gaucho Love* and wearing one of Luisa's old bathrobes. A votive candle flickered on the dresser. Goyo shook his head, trying to clear his thoughts and prepare himself for the day ahead.

Víctor entered quietly and handed Goyo an envelope addressed to him in an old-fashioned script. It was from Adelina's son, the tyrant's namesake, now nearing retirement as an ophthalmologist. He'd enclosed a letter from his mother, writing from another century, a suicide note, hidden from him for almost seventy years.

There were two things Adelina wanted Goyo to know: first, that she loved him (ay, his singing, aching heart!) and had been a fool to leave him; second, that the tyrant may have seduced her but she'd never cared for him, not for a second. Goyo pressed the letter to his chest. His grief strained every muscle in his back and groin. The tyrant had seduced Adelina, stolen his one great love, disgracing her for any other. And Goyo's own arrogance had prevented him from saving her. He folded and kissed the letter—a fragile, transparent blue—and slipped it into his wallet. Then he hobbled to the bathroom and began the day's ablutions.

Simón and Naty

NATY: We are the unofficial hosts for artists' parties in Havana. Everyone who's anyone comes to our rooftop.

SIMÓN: Bunch of freeloaders.

NATY: I think of our place as a Paris salon except we're in the tropics.

SIMÓN: Don't think it's easy playing host to these queens. They don't trust their own mothers. They never tell me what I need to know.

NATY: The other night, the singing and dancing got so out of control that our neighbors demanded to be let in! We ran out of ropa vieja!

SIMÓN: It's my job to keep tabs on these sons of bitches. Who's meeting whom, who's going abroad and why. They avoid my questions, drink our whiskey and rum, and then they—

NATY: We're living in a dream, a beautiful dream . . .

En Route to New York

There were sixty-three people in El Comandante's entourage, all on the same flight. Fernando had argued against this, fearing that a single act of sabotage could take out the island's top brass. But if he was going down, the tyrant retorted, then every last bastard was going down with him. He regarded his fellow travelers. Many of the faces were unfamiliar to him, a new generation of bureaucrats and ass lickers. Not a true warrior among them. He squinted at an enormous negrito four rows back. His face was a beefy blue, his chin a shelf of bone. The man returned El Líder's stare with a respectful nod. For all he knew, this giant could be anyone from the minister of health to the baritone chosen to sing Cuba's national anthem at the United Nations.

El Comandante desultorily thumbed through his speech. He hated reading from scripts. Nothing was more boring than knowing exactly what he was going to say next. It was only after Fernando had shown him a video of himself rambling incoherently at a recent rally that he'd agreed to consider a few talking points. What he needed now was a nap; just a short nap and he would wake up on the razor's edge again, his legendary memory intact.

The plane shuddered as it banked between stormy clouds. Even with the best mechanics on the planet, these old Russian planes held up poorly. They looked decent enough—spiffy with the island's flag freshly painted on their tails—but the engines coughed like consumptives and frequently stalled in midair, causing precipitous drops that had a man chewing his own ass. El Comandante bit his tongue as the plane dropped a thousand feet. He focused on his toes to keep from throwing up. They were pinched in fancy Italian shoes that sported brass buckles instead of laces. If he could, he'd trade them in for a solid pair of hooves.

El Conejo appeared at his side, his complexion tinged green. He hated flying, and suffered from motion sickness on even the shortest of flights.

"You look a mess, hombre."

"Thank you for your concern, Jefe." El Conejo pulled a perfumed handkerchief from his vest and dabbed at his perspiring hairline. "There are a few, eh, security matters I wish to discuss with you."

"Who's trying to kill me this time?"

"An old faction of Omega 7 is mobilizing for your visit."

"Pathetic bastards. They haven't done a goddamn thing since the seventies."

"They've taken on younger recruits, expert marksmen, veterans from the wars in Afghanistan and Iraq." The adviser, nostrils flaring, pressed the handkerchief to his cheek. He stared at his boss like a forlorn dog.

El Comandante was losing interest. "More security, right." He tilted his seat back, shorthand for *This conversation is over and bring it up again at your peril.*

The stewardess approached them in her snug carnelian uniform. She'd competed in the 2006 Miss Latin America pageant and came in second only to Miss Venezuela, who'd undergone head-to-toe plastic surgery. El Comandante wasn't averse to a pair of inflated tits, but he hated how artificial they felt. Years ago, he'd ruptured a Mexican soap opera star's rack during vigorous foreplay.

"Cafecitos, gentlemen?"

"You're too generous," the tyrant flirted.

The stewardess waited until he finished his espresso, then placed his cup on a silver tray. El Conejo's eyes bulged from the caffeine. Soon they'd be flying over Miami. El Líder was inclined to order the pilot to empty the latrines over his enemies' liver-spotted heads. He adjusted the ventilation fan, which emitted the faint, unmistakable scent of borscht. It stoked his appetite for the lunch that everyone but him was getting—lechón with rice, beans, and fried plantains. He got a goddamn salad topped with two shriveled strips of chicken.

The pilot announced that they were flying through an electrical storm and everyone, including the stewardesses, needed to take their seats. When Mamá visited the tyrant during thunderstorms, she mostly complained about her inability to track down Papá in the afterlife. "He's hiding from me," she would grumble, adjusting her slack, ghostly breasts. "Probably shacked up with some cual-quierita." The despot had hated hearing about his parents' marital problems when they were alive, much less so posthumously.

El Comandante plucked a loose thread from his sleeve. His uniform drooped on his shrinking frame. He'd had the waist taken in to the measurements of his youth, but he'd refused to have his pant legs recuffed, and so they dragged along the floor collecting dust. Fernando even had the nerve to suggest that his brother wear the same ridiculous elevator shoes that he sported. The tyrant still regretted allowing his tailor of thirty-six years to emigrate. After his departure, dozens of other tailors vied for the job, but none had a fraction of the talent of Amado Cantún.

A pinkish crane flew by his window. El Comandante followed its flight path until it vanished south. He wrenched his neck trying to see if anyone else had spotted the spindly bird. But everyone was in a postprandial stupor, with the exception of a sole workaholic hunched over his laptop. The tyrant racked his brain for any omens he may have received concerning cranes, but none came to mind.

A wise man in the Niger had once predicted for him "a fiery death in the skies." Could this be the time? What none of the many auguries had foreseen was the brutal truth: his rage at a canicular old age.

In New York, the skies were drizzling and gray. El Comandante descended the ramp of the Soviet plane and was met by a sea of black umbrellas. He had the disconcerting feeling that he'd landed in the wrong city, in the former Eastern Bloc, perhaps, on a typically dreary day. Not until he had both feet on the tarmac did he smell the danger, unmistakable as carrion.

"Fernando!" he bleated like a lost boy.

"Aquí, hermano." His brother raised his arm and waved him forward.

With a prearranged signal, four bodyguards in bulletproof vests surrounded El Líder and lifted him toward the terminal. A Caribbean steel drum band was in full swing. Die-hard leftists from around the region erupted into applause as he entered. The dashing revolutionary they'd all hoped to see was a decrepit viejito, but they were pleased to welcome him nonetheless. The tyrant inched forward, his mind empty of everything but the suspense of surviving another attempt on his life. This was the last real power left to him: to thwart his enemies to the bitter end.

As the crowd clamored for their hero, a hail of bullets shattered the huge terminal window. People shrieked, scattering and falling to the floor. Fernando's men wrestled the assassin to the ground—some buzz-cut punk with crippled Spanish insulting El Líder at the top of his lungs. How the boy freed himself nobody knew, but he managed to jam a handgun into his mouth and blow out his brains. The tyrant took a deep breath and turned his attention outside. A flock of cormorants had gathered in the skies like a jumble of ideograms, endlessly diving and lamenting in their old women's voices. Then as if on cue, the birds screeched out to sea, toward the equator, to a distance measurable only by light.

17.

The Works

El Comandante

The tyrant was unfazed by the attack, a lamentable occupational hazard. It might've meant something for someone to have killed him in his prime, but to knock him off when he was already at death's door? What triumph could there be in that? Fernando was extremely agitated by the disruption. He never kept his cool in a crisis. The only time he ever felt in control was pointing a gun at the head of a bound and blindfolded man.

"Let's walk up Fifth Avenue," El Comandante suggested.

"That's imp-p-possible," his brother sputtered.

"It's your job to make it possible." He wanted to show these lily-livered leftists how a real leader behaved under fire.

On their procession uptown, someone procured a wheelchair for him, but the tyrant refused to occupy it, finding the strength to walk on his own. The brush with death had invigorated him, recharged him to life's purpose. As they made their way past astonished shoppers, not everyone recognized El Comandante. Had he changed so drastically? Some idiot shouted that Qaddafi's ghost had come back to haunt Manhattan. Another brayed in a nasally accent: "What, that bastard's still alive?" To which the despot contested: "Yes, and there is no greater victory."

El Comandante stopped on the northeast corner of Forty-Ninth Street and ordered a hot dog with the works. Onlookers cheered when he took a bite dripping with sauerkraut, relish, onions, mustard, and ketchup. New Yorkers loved anyone who loved their hot dogs. Never mind the gastric repercussions, he couldn't buy this kind of publicity. The image of the oldest living dictator eating a hot dog went viral and ended up on the front page of the next day's *New York Post* with the headline TYRANT WANTS THE WORKS!!!

Next he demanded to be taken to the planetarium. A prickly Fernando and El Conejo flanked him in the backseat of the limousine. These two detested each other from way back. Neither uttered a word, but El Comandante sensed their displeasure with his impromptu street diplomacy. "Sic semper tyrannis," he joked in between coughing fits. At the planetarium, he watched with great interest a film on the life cycle of stars. The tyrant sympathized with the supernovas, which, upon expiring, took entire galaxies with them. He was distraught to learn that the sun would burn out in five billion years. He, too, felt the life ebbing from him, as if it were trickling from some unknown hole. Why struggle so hard to have it all end in eternal nothingness?

After the movie, El Comandante paid a visit to the dinosaur hall. By then a motley group of municipal officials was trailing him, chatting inanely about baseball and hurricanes, as if these were Cuba's only exports. He examined the remains of an *Apatosaurus* and an impressive skeletal reproduction of a *Tyrannosaurus rex*. Behind the beast hovered that Vásquez fellow, a wispy crown of smoke over his head. The tyrant's knees buckled as he reached for his pistol. Around them, everything froze.

"You're not going to try that again, are you, Jefe?" Vásquez cleared his throat. "I'm disappointed. I thought we'd ended our last visit as friends." He produced a bowl of guavas from behind his back, peeled ones that looked like wobbling, bloodshot eyes. "Have one," Vásquez offered. "I brought them for you."

El Comandante picked up a slippery fruit and popped it into his mouth. The sweetness coated his tongue, shot through his veins. He ate another one, then another. Bits of pink pulp trickled down his beard. As he slurped up the last one, a saluting Vásquez slipped through a porthole in the exhibit's west wall and ascended into the tempestuous skies.

On 125th Street, thousands of people came out to welcome El Comandante. There were Mexican and Central American faces in the crowd along with blacks and a notable contingent of whites. He felt less a prodigal son than a prodigal grandfather to this younger generation of admirers. Former president Clinton waved to him from the top step of a brownstone, his face fat and ruddy as a Russian barmaid's. *Make way, brothers, make way!* The crowd parted and the two leaders embraced like old friends.

Clinton tried out his twangy Spanish, to the amusement of the native speakers, and El Comandante dragged out his beggar's English—"Good to see you, mister!"

"You old warrior, you!" Clinton thumped him on the back. If he was shocked by the tyrant's deterioration, he didn't show it.

El Líder fake-punched the ex-president's gut, to the delight of onlookers. Clinton wore jeans and a checkered shirt. With a straw hat, he could pass for a guajiro.

"Tell me, hombre, how do you stay in such good shape?" Clinton bellowed.

The tyrant was down to 146 pounds—the least he'd weighed since his high school basketball days.

"The embargo, mi amigo," he answered slyly, patting his stomach. Clinton's eyes turned to flint. Fuck him, El Comandante thought. He needed nothing more from this impostor.

He pushed eastward toward the Hotel Marisa. Fernando had arranged a fund-raiser in the hotel ballroom for longtime supporters. Why did his brother insist on such stultifying gatherings? More and more, his old comrades had died off, and the younger activists, stupid from TV and computer games, had no real clue about Cuba's history. El Comandante looked around at the four hundred strangers, then peered down at his plate of fried chicken. At the head of the table, a bespectacled man was linking civil rights to the Revolution. "We are indebted to you, Comandante," he said with genuine feeling, "for lighting the way during the darkest days of our struggle."

El Líder waved back noncommittally. He felt ill at ease, exhausted. Another fit of coughing took hold. With some effort, he stood up and excused himself. Fernando caught up to him at the exit.

"I don't give a damn!" the tyrant exploded before his brother could say a word. "Tell them whatever the hell you want. I've had enough."

El Comandante went to his suite and lay down on the lumpy bed. Gas cramped his belly. He felt weak, wasted by insomnia and an excess of grease. The air conditioner pumped freezing gusts into his room. He hated air-conditioning, considered it a waste of valuable energy, but he let it blast to help drain—symbolically, at least—the Yankees' bottomless resources. In the alley below, a chorus of dogs howled. It was the last sound the tyrant heard before falling asleep.

Goyo

Tyrant . . . son of a bitch . . . descarado . . . assassin . . . atheist . . . thief . . . Goyo spat out the list of insults as he methodically scoured himself with a brick of yellow deodorant soap. And seducer. Adelina's seducer. He attacked one underarm then the other, his neck, the crack of his ass. After rinsing off, he dried himself with a monogrammed towel and reached for his bathrobe, also monogrammed. He wiped a circle of fog from the bathroom mirror and examined his face, pulling at the corners of his mouth to inspect his gums. Fans of wrinkles and delicate, purplish pouches padded his eyes. His cratered nose had been scraped of carcinomas more than once. He clipped the errant hairs from his nostrils, twirled cotton swabs in both ears, then snapped a mental picture of himself.

"Adiós, cabrón," Goyo saluted himself. "La historia te llama."

Víctor brought him a cortadito, perfectly made. He'd already pressed Goyo's white linen suit, polished his shoes, and reshaped his Panama hat, as if he understood the significance of the day. He'd set out a pale blue shirt, also freshly ironed, a matching handkerchief, and a silk tie from his Miami haberdasher. What was civility, Goyo thought, if not endless ritual? He didn't bother checking his blood sugar. What for? He reminded himself to call his children and his brother, Rufino; transfer gratitude money to his mistress Vilma's account; leave a sizable check for the saintly Víctor, who'd spent another sleepless night watching over him. And for Carla? What could he do to repay her?

The midmorning news was banal: a topless woman protesting who-knew-what at the Supreme Court, more politico peccadilloes followed by a rehash of yesterday's assassination attempt against the tyrant. *What?*

"Did you know about this?" Goyo demanded.

Víctor twisted the kitchen rag in his hands. "Sí, Jefe."

"Then why the hell didn't you wake me up?"

The Andean hung his head.

"Speak up!" Goyo lost his temper.

"You n-needed to sleep," Víctor stammered.

"I'll be sleeping for eternity!" Goyo pushed himself to standing but fell back, crab-like, onto the sofa. "Help me up, goddamnit!"

Víctor ran to right his boss, who was trembling violently.

"What time is it?" Goyo barked.

Víctor pointed to the clock on the far wall. It was nearly ten in the morning. Goyo rushed to his desk and turned on the computer: fifty-two messages, including several all-points bulletins from Hijodeputa.com. So it was true then. Somebody had tried to kill El Comandante again, and failed. Now every exile group on the planet would be taking credit for the dubious heroics. Carajo. After nearly sixty years, it was time to get it right. Goyo envisioned the act precisely. It must be executed in a clean, controlled manner. If all went well, it would be over in six seconds. Six seconds, and the world would finally know his name.

_____ᘒ

Word

Nobody talks to me anymore. From one day to the next, I've become persona non grata. I look back over what I've written. Nothing egregious. My fair share of praise for the Revolution and whatnot. I'm not one to go around throwing rocks at glass houses. I come to every writers' union reception dressed in my one good jacket. Yet everyone finds an excuse to leave me con la palabra en la boca. At least there's plenty of rum. That's how they keep us in line here, try to force the illusion that we're free men, not the kowtowing scum we've become. ¡Salud!

—Francisco Sotomayor, poet

18.

Exeunt

Sic transit gloria mundi

The chapel around the corner from the United Nations was open twenty-four hours a day to accommodate the faithful from every time zone. The interior was modern with abstract stained-glass windows and Stations of the Cross that merely hinted at the blood and suffering. The signs were in English, Russian, French, and Chinese, the languages of the five veto-wielding members of the Security Council. Goyo searched for a confessional and ducked inside. A handwritten note was tacked under a buzzer: PRESS HERE TO SUMMON PRIEST. His legs felt shaky, out of fear or tiredness he wasn't sure.

The loud clap of the wooden slat announced the arrival of the priest. "What brings you seeking the Lord this morning, my son?"

Goyo's eyes watered at the phrase "my son." It'd been so long since his own father had called him mijo. He remembered their last afternoon together in Papá's sparse apartment in Brooklyn Heights. He'd served Goyo a fried hamburger and sliced tomatoes with olive oil. Papá was in his late sixties then, but he'd looked much older. The Revolution had aged him, had taken his youngest son, driven him to penury and despair. "Don't worry about me. I've had a good life, mijo," Papá said as he sent Goyo on his way. A few days later, he shot himself in the head.

Goyo got right to the point. "Can murder ever be sanctioned, Father?"

"There are exceptions to everything," the priest said. His voice clacked like river stones. "Are you a believer?"

Goyo hesitated. "Most days, I guess."

"And on the days you're not?"

"I think of all the evil that goes unpunished."

"It is for God to decide who are the sinners—"

"Then why do we have courts?"

"Such judgments are preliminary. The last and final judge is Our Lord." The priest seemed to weigh each word as he spoke. "No Christian ought to die in any other state than that of a penitent."

"What else can you offer me, Father?" Goyo struggled to keep the irritation out of his voice. His entire history felt diminished, wilted. He wanted to die the way he should've lived, like a blow to the head.

"Hope."

"And to the hopeless? And to hopeless situations?" Goyo's voice rose. He reached for a caramel in his pocket and noisily unwrapped it.

"More hope," the priest said with finality.

"In my homeland children don't have milk, Father. How can you say to one child, You will grow, and to another, You will not?"

"You must rely on the Lord, on the power of prayer."

Goyo grasped the ledge of the confessional booth and pushed

himself to standing, tonguing the caramel to one cheek. A back molar felt loose and he feared uprooting it. He'd hoped to take Communion, but he didn't want to risk sacrilege on top of murder.

"Go in peace, my son."

The United Nations loomed on the banks of the East River, its flags snapping in the wind. It was supposed to be a bulwark against rogues and anarchists. Why, then, did it permit criminals to give speeches? Goyo remembered something his history teacher used to say, quoting Shakespeare: "No king, be his cause never so spotless . . . can try it out with all unspotted soldiers."

The Russian guard was expecting Goyo at the visitors' entrance, smacking his thick lips. The smoked salmon and caviar delivered to him yesterday afternoon had had the desired effect. "Good to see you again, Comrade Herrera!" Yuri thundered, enveloping him in a fishy embrace. Goyo was relieved that Yuri, as usual, didn't ask him to empty his pockets or walk through the metal detector. No matter that the Glock was safely locked inside Carla's desk. Magnanimously, the Russian ushered him past the security station without a second glance. Goyo stopped by Carla's office but, as prearranged, she wasn't in. It was just as well. He feared that one look at her might make him abandon his plans. But he'd come too far to forget the past. The gold key to the bottom drawer of her desk was in his pocket. Goyo's knees creaked as he bent to unlock the drawer and remove the pistol.

El Comandante was dressed in full military uniform for his speech. The damn thing weighed a ton, but he was aware that this might be his very last public appearance. Why not look his best? If he could make just one woman swoon—he'd try for that new delegate from Swaziland—and a convocation of diplomats rise to their feet in adulation, he would consider it a day well spent. Fernando strode alongside him, whispering furiously. The tyrant paid him no mind. His speech was in his jacket pocket, but he wasn't inclined to play by the rules today. He was feeling good, energetic. Perhaps he would replicate his first visit to the General Assembly and shoot off another two-hour harangue. Everyone—delegates, newsmen, pundits, los gusanos themselves—would have to acknowledge that nothing at all had changed; El Comandante was still the same handsome, fiery devil the world had fallen in love with nearly six decades ago.

El Comandante and Goyo proceeded, almost simultaneously, into the gilded chambers of the General Assembly. It was the first day of its fall session, when even the laggardly diplomats appeared in their dazzling national costumes, eager to swap the summer's gossip. The tyrant moved through the crowd with ease as Goyo took a seat behind the Trinidadian delegation. Its ambassador, corpulent and jet-black in a wide-lapel suit, turned and smiled at him. Goyo recognized the ambassador—he used to order the cottage cheese in a half pineapple special—and this made him uneasy, as if el negro could read his mind, or X-ray the pistol tucked inside his jacket. Nonsense; Goyo tried to calm down. He reminded himself that he looked like any other distinguished emissary from the tropics. Even those who'd known him as a purveyor of fine sandwiches probably couldn't have identified him out of context.

Goyo's nerves fired furiously as he watched his nemesis make a show of walking to the podium without assistance. The Turkish foreign minister, with his movie-star mustache, rose to his feet, and the rest of the delegates followed suit, giving El Comandante a standing ovation. Hadn't the Jesuits warned everyone about demonolatry? Goyo looked around and spied Fernando in his executioner's uniform to the right of the platform. Soon he, too, would know Goyo Herrera's name. This wasn't pity, the tyrant reassured himself, but an outpouring of gratitude for a lifetime of heroism. The applause was pure music, a balm, redemption itself. Goyo couldn't endure the welcome the bastard was getting. He refused to stand, though he knew he was calling attention to himself. There he was, the monster himself, waving like the fucking Queen of England. Even with the best doctors that stolen money could buy, the son of a bitch looked a wreck, if a defiant one. Goyo thought himself to be in much better shape, and this flooded him with unreasonable pride.

El Comandante couldn't get enough of the hero worship. Reluctantly, he lifted both arms to call for silence, but the diplomats were in no hurry to end the flattery. He felt a rising frenzy to talk, to dazzle them one last time. A part of him was tempted to cause a scandal and drop his pants, show his detractors that he was still the man they feared. Goyo was sickened by the farce, by the tyrant's fatal deceptions. He recalled Adelina's delicate wrists as she played Schubert's piano sonata in A major; imagined her looping the deadly rope through her parents' chandelier. El Comandante began with an old joke, saying that reports of his death had been highly exaggerated. The delegates clapped and screeched like monkeys. Impostor. Creator of ruins. The bastard had turned their island paradise into a fucking cemetery. How dare he perfume the weeds?

Goyo reached into his jacket pocket. The metal was already warm from his body heat. Six seconds. Six seconds was all it would take. El Comandante thanked his many supporters and allies. The list was long, the names and places mellifluous. That fiend could sneeze and lie at the same time. Goyo gripped his pistol and in one fluid motion took aim. A riptide of pain surged through his chest, numbing his arms. Carajo, his heart was giving out again, the blood bursting its chambers, but he managed to pull the trigger. El Comandante collapsed onstage, cracking his head against the marble floor. His breath escaped as if from a vacuum. His body rolled slightly to the left. Whoever the hell had shot at him had missed. Instead the bullet hit the pillar behind him and bounced who knew where. If he hadn't turned at that exact moment to salute the Canadian delegation, he might've welcomed the bullet straight to his heart. He tried to get a glimpse of the gunman. From the corner of his eye, he spied a Panama hat, a linen suit, the stubby physique of what had to be a no-account gusano. Infamy would be his for all of an hour.

The tyrant fumbled for his gun, but it skittered a million miles away. Voices floated around him in a dozen languages, a chorus of dissonant bells. "Don't leave us!" "Have courage, Jefe!" But the tyrant kept on dying. He wandered through a vast palace, the furnishings covered with sheets, the dust inches thick, a lonely view of clouds through the windows. Ash blew on the wind. It was over. He'd done it. He, Goyo Herrera, had shot the son of a bitch dead. Let his heart stop, let the heavens fall down on his head, but he'd accomplished his mission. He'd come face-to-face with his destiny and pulled the trigger. Soon his countrymen would be chanting his name in the streets. There would be trumpets and merrymaking, congueros banging their drums round the clock. And his beloved Adelina, arms outstretched, would greet him in heaven with wild, white lilies. Goyo slumped over a row of empty seats, his face as radiant as his agony. He heard the commotion, but none of it mattered. Death, insistent, touched his brow. An ellipse of darkness engulfed him. Beyond it were vague shapes, a fading chaos. A hero. Sí, he would die a hero . . .

Where the hell was Fernando? The pain in his chest was unbearable. A knife thrust to his heart. Damn it, he should've taken the fucking bullet. He'd wanted to die in battle, on horseback, like the great Martí. Or like Caesar, looking his killers in the eye, the blood between them the last word. Too many years of surviving hadn't prepared him to die opportunely. It infuriated him to succumb to something as mundane as a heart attack, or whatever the fuck was happening to him. He refused to surrender, to accept this as the story of his death. With a last surge of energy, El Comandante lifted his head and called for his brother. His inner voice diminished to the faintest of breaths. A slow roar surged inside him, but it, too, faded away. A dirigible floated on the horizon, its flesh-toned snout tilted toward the sun. An inexplicable joy overcame him. The tyrant imagined flying high over the Sierra Maestra, over Pico Turquino, which he'd scaled as a young man. Then he felt himself rapidly sinking, a leaky dinghy, deep into the Caribbean Sea without the prerogatives due him at death. Cojones, not like this!

Around him, loved ones began to gather: Mamá, her apron filled with silky rose petals; Miriam, beckoning to him in her wedding gown; his naked father, prodigious balls quivering, shouting: "Get up! Get up!"

"You're very brave, mijo," his mother whispered. "You are my bold boy."

"Sí, Mami, lo soy," the tyrant sang back, and then he, too, was gone.

Acknowledgments

Many thanks to my dear friends, near and far, who generously read this novel and made excellent suggestions, especially Alfredo Franco (gracias, hermanito), Scott Brown, Evelina Galang, and Dean Rader. Special thanks to my daughter, Pilar García-Brown, and to Elizabeth Frietsch for their editorial assistance; to La Madonna di Cosimo and Jill Patterson for extraordinary kindness; to my incomparable agent, Ellen Levine; to Alexis Gargagliano, editor extraordinaire; and to Walter Kiechel for his fount of humor and title ideas. My deep gratitude to Tom Grimes and the English Department at Texas State University–San Marcos for generous support and the gift of time. Finally, mil gracias to Las Dos Brujas family—Denise Chávez, Chris Abani, Katie Blackburn, Kimiko Hahn, Juan Felipe Herrera, and all our participants—for extraordinary community.

About the Author

Cristina García is the author of six novels, including the National Book Award finalist *Dreaming in Cuban;* children's books; anthologies; and poetry. Her work has been translated into fourteen languages, and she is the recipient of a Guggenheim Fellowship and a Whiting Writers' Award, among other honors. She is currently University Chair in Creative Writing at Texas State University–San Marcos.

A Conversation with Cristina García

King of Cuba takes place partially in Cuba and partially in the United States (primarily Florida and New York). Tell us a little about your personal connection to these two places.
Although I grew up in New York City, both Cuba and Florida loomed large in my imagination because they were home to family on either side of the political divide. My maternal grandmother was a diehard Communist while her daughter—my mother—was as capitalist as they come. As an adult, I traveled extensively to both places and saw firsthand how radically similar the people and places were in spite of their dramatic, tragic rifts. I became fascinated with what I considered the common bedrock to their wildly divergent surfaces and set out to explore them.

Your character El Comandante is clearly based on Fidel Castro. What kind of research did you have to do to write his character?
I went on a Fidel Castro immersion program, bizarre as that sounds. I read everything I could get my hands on, saw lots of old footage, listened to his speeches, watched documentaries. It was important for me to get his gestures right, the way he caressed a microphone when he paused during his signature tirades, for example. I also read a lot of great fiction about Latin American strongmen by such

masters as García Márquez, Vargas Llosa, and Miguel Ángel Asturias. In the end, I shelved all the facts about Castro and tried to create as fully fledged and human a tyrant as I could.

Footnotes featuring the voices of a diverse cast of Cuban characters are woven throughout this novel. What inspired you to include this chorus?

These voices came to me late during the writing. For a long time, I was alternating exclusively between the perspectives of El Comandante and his exile nemesis, Goyo Herrera. However, I felt that I wanted to open up the narrative to include other viewpoints and assessments of the current situation in Cuba. This chorus of voices, then, serves to contest, skewer, even ridicule the "official" and often rigid histories that these two men represent. As a novelist, I'm devoted to writing about Cubans and Cuban Americans in all their complexity, not simply repeating the same old black-and-white bromides.

Cuba itself becomes almost a third main character in the book. When was the last time you went to Cuba? What do you love about the country?

I was last in Cuba in the spring of 2011 for a couple of weeks after a ten-year absence. It was invaluable for me to hear Cuban voices again—their complaints and expressions and their stories, stories, stories. Most of the chorus emerged from people I met in Havana, Trinidad, and Matanzas. Their voices went hand-in-hand with my own impressions and the daily barrage of sensory details. So much changes in Cuba from year to year and yet so much remains the same. To me, it is endlessly fascinating.

El Comandante and Goyo Herrera share a surprising number of similarities despite their stark political differences. Do you consider them to be alike even as enemies?

The parallelism between Goyo and El Comandante—their synchronicity, narcissism, and attitudes toward women—was something I wanted to underscore, though not too heavy-handedly. What I was hoping to show, ultimately, is the false dichotomy between the two, their deep, incestuous, codependence. To my mind, they are flip sides of the same Cuban coin.

What does authenticity mean to you in the context of this story? Do you consider *King of Cuba* to be historical fiction?
Yes and no. I consider the novel authentic in that it captures, I hope, a kind of emotional and spiritual essence of the postrevolutionary Cuban condition, as portrayed through these problematic, priapic men. But it is in no way a biography of the real El Comandante nor of any particular octogenarian in the Miami Cuban exile community. They are specific fictional distortions that purport to shed light on aspects of both Cubas.

Questions of mortality and legacy plague both men throughout the novel. Is this a product of their age? Their obsession with Cuba? How do their concerns mirror your own?
Their obsessions became my obsessions during the years I was writing *King of Cuba,* and even to this day. I consider it a gift and a privilege to have inhabited characters who, at the end of their lives, are taking stock, assessing their triumphs and despairs, and trying to rectify through action, delusion, or revisionism their remaining days on earth. The process of writing them radicalized my own sense of fully embracing every day. I don't want to get to my own end and wallow in regrets.

For all the tragedy that has transpired in both your characters' lives, the novel remains a dark comedy, a satire even, of a divided Cuba. Why did you take this humorous approach?

Humor is the saving grace of Cubans on both sides of the Straits of Florida, and beyond. It is what has helped us survive the travails we've suffered. It enables us to laugh at ourselves and at others, to keep moving forward. For me, humor is a nonnegotiable. Sometimes I force absurdity onto the bleakest of subjects and watch what results. The juxtapositions can salvage even the most untenable of situations.

You've written a lot about Cuban women in your past work. Yet the women in both El Comandante and Goyo's lives are relatively marginalized, as they are in the book overall. Why?
It was not my intention to marginalize Cuban women but El Comandante and Goyo just sucked up all the oxygen in the room. Remember, we're dealing with men of another generation, who grew up in a culture of sexism—and a certain chivalry as well—so ingrained that they never deeply questioned it, even when their own daughters rebelled against them or criticized their actions. That's not to say that sexism isn't alive and well in Havana and Miami, only that these two characters are definitely a dying breed.

Without giving it away, the ending came as such a surprise. How did you go about constructing the ending? Or did it happen organically?
I must have written and rewritten the ending a hundred times, no exaggeration. For me, the novel's end had to reflect the Aristotelian ideal of being both "surprising yet inevitable." This is much easier said than done. Surprising isn't that hard, and inevitable is boring. But to create something that not only surprises readers but makes them feel as though no other conclusion could work as well—now, that's a killer ending.